OUR MOTHERLAND

by the same author

JUSTICE IN MOSCOW
MESSAGE FROM MOSCOW
THE GIRL FROM PETROVKA
SOLZHENITSYN (*with David Burg*)

Our Motherland

AND OTHER VENTURES
IN RUSSIAN REPORTAGE

by

GEORGE FEIFER

The Viking Press
New York

Part of this material has appeared, in somewhat different form, in the
*Daily Telegraph Magazine, Dance News, Oui, Reader's Digest, Reporter
Magazine,* and the *Sunday Times Magazine.*

Contents

OUR MOTHERLAND

1. *Reporting in Russia*

Once again, a book about Russia begins with an apology. Happier stories wait to be told, but when I sit down to start, thoughts of my limitations nag me into a familiar unease. Why didn't I interview *x*, visit *y*, investigate ж, as any competent reporter should have? I want to explain – and hope that my personal experience will also raise some broader issues. A sketch of the difficulties posed by the country's singular rules and prohibitions – in particular, the obstacles to practising investigative journalism – can serve as an introduction to the 'story' itself of the national way of life.

For many years, I aspired to live in Moscow, unattached to the foreign colony if that were feasible, and to earn my living at freelance journalism. I saw myself roaming the city to report on a wide variety of subjects: film and sports stars, cultural developments and *causes célèbres*, social fads, fashion trends and interesting personalities ... as far as possible, I wanted to examine what a journalist in any major capital would. Of course I knew that political personages and processes would have to be excluded, but it was everyday social activity – 'slice of life' stories with no direct political overtones – that interested me rather than Kremlin secrets. In one sense, Moscow promised a reverse advantage in this, for most accounts set there, from the gas-meter murder case to the Black Sea pastimes of the cultural elite, held the special interest attaching to the country of riddles and enigmas.

I acquired my relish for reporting the Russian scene in 1962, when, as a student at Moscow University, much of my time went to exploring the back streets. I wandered at all hours through the city's least known districts, where log cabins, kerchiefed grandmothers and occasional drunks resting in the snow kept alive the spirit of pre-revolutionary, even pre-industrial, Russia. In the courtyards of out-of-the-way apartment blocks – the political atmosphere was such that to enter such prosaic places seemed an

exploit – children made mudpies, their mothers gossiped about
their neighbours and teenagers giggled over sexual discoveries. As
with most Russian buildings, the interiors of these residential ones
were distinctly humbler than their sometimes grandiose façades:
two steps through the back entrance (called 'back' in Russian,
in distinction to the 'parade' or 'show' entrance, which for some
reason is almost always locked in contemporary Moscow) took me
from apparent solidity to sad dilapidation. But the courtyards were
far less intimidating, too, for in them daily Russian life was lived,
with no pretensions or future-of-mankind theories to mask the
smell of boiled cabbage and sight of patched underwear on a line.

In dingy workers' cafeterias, I ate mealy frankfurters garnished
with potatoes fried in stale grease; in little-known beer-halls,
tough truck drivers sometimes invited me, on the strength of my
unstylish overcoat and acquaintance with Moscow slang, to join
the traditional 'three-way split': three strangers sharing an under-
the-coat half-litre of vodka. Notices on walls and in shabby rooms
forbiddingly named 'Agitation Centres' directed me to lectures by
professional political orators in parks and factory auditoriums.

I was rarely stopped during these wanderings, and for the guards
demanding passes at the entrances to 'closed' harangues and
Young Communist meetings, the vigorous nod and purposeful
stride of an important participant occasionally sufficed. It seemed
wonderfully easy to poke about in obscure, semi-secret places: a
push on a door, a seat on a bench amidst the heavy smell of bodies
and old wool, and I was genuinely inside Russia, observing how
Russians really talked and Soviet institutions actually worked. So
many eccentricities and bizarre personal histories; so much to
write about! I decided that after my student year, I would return to
collect material. Certain that I could, I took no notes – a mistake I
still regret. In the next decade, I did return on a dozen extended
visits, but my notion that freelance journalism could be an exten-
sion of these early discoveries steadily faded. 'No one is young
twice,' as the Russian proverb says. No foreigner is nearly as free
as an exchange student.

*

For the next few years, I nurtured my ambition. It was sustained by the hope of contributing to an understanding of aspects of Russian society not covered in political dispatches, and by a knowledge that editors were liberal with space for copy casting any light on what daily life was actually like. In this sense, Russia seemed to me the virgin land of reportage, and I still hoped to reap the first harvest.

The attractions were more than professional. I had spent not only a student year in Moscow but a long summer in 1959, when Russia's emotional spell caught me immediately. The poverty of matrial things, then very dire, did not drain, in some ways only enhanced the riches of friendship and of uninhibited emotions. Russia was, as it had always appeared in its literature, a place of heightened feelings. Despite the government's steady pulverization of thought and expression into its own ritualistic slogans, despite even victims' pitiful tales of inhuman treatment, like so many Western residents before me I became enamoured of the atmosphere of the country's 'inner', sitting-room life. Perhaps it is enough to say that my future wife and best friend were both Muscovites.

Even after the excitement of passing as Soviet in public places and immersing myself in ordinary activities had abated, there was a constant sense of discovery. The tumble of daily life so little accorded with textbook impressions of Soviet uniformity. Russians' inherent disorder, unpredictability and impulsiveness – qualities lying just below, and partly responsible for, the crust of callous authoritarianism – made the country as fascinating for 'going native' as it is dreary to visit on Intourist's guided routes. Together with the multiplicity of sanctions to avoid – a dead weight of rules, regulations and proscriptions promulgated in the persistent hope of combating latent Russian anarchy – the chasm between the supply and demand of goods and services inevitably brought some degree of plotting, wheeling and dealing to the procurement of food and clothing, all of which provided daily adventures. One afternoon, I was sneaking past hospital guards with a friend to visit his impetuous lover; the next day, hunting for a carburettor for someone's car or bribing a minor official to lay aside some provisions for a forthcoming party; and on the following morning, helping a secretary in an important Ministry invent an excuse for skipping work.

Although the external atmosphere of oppression and hard times helped sharpen reflexes and generate a sense of adventure, this alone did not account for the dramatic flavour of Russian life. Many Russians *did* behave like fictional characters, partly because in their private affairs they are less conformist and regimented than their Western counterparts. Beneath the priggish Soviet surface, young Muscovites in particular enjoy more authentic hedonism – many more weekly hours devoted purely to eating, drinking, love-making and forgetting – than young Westerners. And for all its bureaucratic frustrations, and despite the overriding drabness and sadness, Moscow occasionally offered the haunting, almost visionary, truths, the beauty of despair and paradox, revealed in the best of Russian letters – qualities enhanced by the loyalty of deep friendships in the face of external pressures and delight in such small change of life as a kilo of bananas unexpectedly procured and gleefully consumed on the spot.

I tried to introduce these perceptions into my first articles about Russia, based on trips in 1959 and the early 1960s. Selecting subjects which avoided the harsher aspects of Soviet society and the dictatorship's methods, I wrote about daily life and the national character – above all, about Russians as people. Of course, I knew the odds against my winning permission to live in Moscow, and knew the government's morbid dread of unchaperoned journalists exploring even such institutions as circuses and football teams. But press officials considered my articles tolerable, and I felt that if anyone had a chance to open at least a few doors, it was I. Their pleas for 'mutual understanding' founded on a firmer Western acquaintance with Soviet life surely had some sincerity. Somehow I would overcome the obstacles, convince the authorities that I was not hostile, and settle myself in the city for many busy years.

This hope no doubt sprang partly from my youth; certainly it reflected a naïveté about Soviet methods which, for all my lengthy trips, I was slow to lose. In any case, the notion of a freelance foreign journalist renting a room in Moscow without high official sanction was quixotic. In the late 1960s, I abandoned my plan.

The alternative was to take a job with one of the Western news services permitted to maintain Moscow bureaux. This would have put me in the city, of course, but, because of the systematic exclusion of accredited foreign correspondents from ordinary Soviet life, as far as ever from the journalism I wanted to pursue. Western reporters have distinctive identifying numbers on their cars, live in special blocks of flats visited only by daredevil Russians, and are surrounded by household servants, translators and office help who must report to the K.G.B. Conditioned over decades by a diet of articles about the perfidy of foreign correspondents, well aware of the consequences of co-operation with 'the ideological enemy', the population at large shrinks from all but casual contact with them.

Isolated in the island known as the diplomatic colony or 'ghetto', followed by concealed and conspicuous secret policemen, spied on by informers and electronic equipment ('living-room, dining-room, bedroom and bathroom walls and even automobiles are bugged,' an expelled correspondent wrote recently), fearful for themselves and for their Russian friends if they have them, accredited correspondents are often informed about major developments in Russia by cables from their home offices in Washington and London. And since the secret police are convinced that journalists are spies, they are often more restricted professionally than casual visitors: a Scottish clerk on his brief Russian holiday may well secure an interview with a city administrator more easily than the bureau chief of *The Times*. The Soviet law that a resident reporter must obtain prior Foreign Ministry permission for any contact whatever with any Soviet citizen is often ignored in the case of friends and strangers met in buses or cafés, but cannot be circumvented in approaching Soviet officials, a category including almost everyone in a position to supply facts and figures, from museum curators to grocery warehouse superintendents. The handful of Western correspondents who in the face of all this manage to establish a circle of Russian friends, and (with their invaluable help) file informative and/or skilfully analytical dispatches, face expulsion, the probability of which increases in close correlation with their reportorial achievements. For those who remain, threats of reprisals are a significant factor in their every important story.

Almost any expelled journalist's descriptions can serve to convey the conditions in which his colleagues work. As it happens, a former *Newsweek* bureau chief is more restrained than average. He arrived sceptical of old hands' tales of interference, and optimistic that by being consistently reasonable he would find a way to practise his profession. But like his predecessors, he ended by learning more about the Western colony's isolation than about most other aspects of Soviet life.

A cordon sanitaire of surveillance, crippling travel restrictions, tapped telephones, bugged apartment walls, bureaucratic obstacle courses, life in special foreigners' compounds, secrecy and the deliberate withholding of even the most elementary information – all this surrounds diplomats and correspondents in the Soviet capital. It shuts them off from direct knowledge of the U.S.S.R. and prevents Soviet citizens from gaining access to, or learning too much about, the foreigners in their midst ...

The conditions of secrecy, distrust and isolation under which diplomats and newsmen must work in Moscow force the majority of them to spend most of their time reading the official Soviet press and interviewing each other in the hope of eliciting information which neither group has. For correspondents, it is next to impossible to gain access to officials in order to discuss Soviet Government policies ...

As a result, most foreigners are compelled to search for hidden meanings in the party and government press, to sift truth from fiction out of the myriad rumors that make up the gossip of the daily cocktail circuit and to evaluate the leaks planted by 'semi-official' sources whose veracity and identity no one can check. It is generally assumed that these shadowy tipsters are agents of the infamous 'Department of

Misinformation' of the K.G.B., the secret police. Thus, the best any foreigner in Moscow can say with certainty is what he does *not* know.

In addition to physical restraints psychological pressures are used whenever possible; and sheer relentlessness of application in those isolated conditions can make them effective despite their want of subtlety. Expelled in 1972, the correspondent of *The Times* outlined the procedures.

One last word about intimidation. The first technique, used against most new correspondents, is to attempt to involve them with provocateurs, so that they will either compromise themselves or ever afterwards be afraid to have contacts with any Russians at all. The second technique (because the first one usually fails) is to try and involve them in illegal transactions, pseudo-espionage and relations with Soviet women.

Later, there are instances of physical violence, not usually too extreme, but unpleasant enough. The violence is used sometimes against the correspondents, sometimes against their Soviet friends. There are attempts to subvert the Soviet friends, and turn them into informers or provocateurs. Then there are cases of blackmail, and the spreading of malicious rumours. The correspondent is attacked psychologically by being constantly told he is a liar, merely because he is trying to tell the truth. There are libellous attacks in the Soviet press, referring both to a correspondent's writings and to his personal life. For these, a correspondent in the West could obtain large sums in damages; but he cannot possibly sue in Russia, because the results of all political court cases are decided on the basis of secret instructions to the judge from the K.G.B. or the Party ... When a correspondent is attacked in the press for his writings, it is done on the basis of quotations taken grossly out of context, distorted, and even actually fabricated. (The case against me in the *Literary Gazette* was based to a great extent on fabricated quotations.) When all this fails, there is an expulsion.

I regret the solemn note I'm sounding here, but anything lighter or less persistent would be untrue to this aspect of Moscow's atmosphere. Comic relief must be self-supplied – by sending a letter to yourself, for example, and having a laugh over the envelope resealed with thick censors' glue. One diplomat instructed a former secretary returning to Latin America to send him a passionate letter without the love-token lock she was to say was enclosed. The letter arrived with a snip of blond hair; the secretary was a brunette.

Paradoxically, the panoply of restrictions can make the Moscow assignment one of the world's softest. The very impediments to journalists' work, together with the distance to their home offices and sympathy for their plight, can disguise lassitude and slipping talent. One of the funniest, most endearing ghetto men I knew put himself in this category. 'It's crazy,' he used to say in puzzled delight. 'I earn a small fortune here, more than I could anywhere. My stuff couldn't possibly cut the mustard in London or Paris – but how can the old editors check on things *in Moscow*? When they get impatient, I answer with the magic words "prohibition", "surveillance" and "K.G.B.". My own standards sink lower and lower. How Russian it all is. And me too: have another drink.'

Despite his keen sense of how ordinary Russians behave, this man had given up even trying to write stories about, say, the life of an Olympic gymnast. Clearly, I could not pursue my kind of journalism as an accredited correspondent.

The compromise I eventually reached relieved me, as something of an exception to the procedural rules, of at least some of the more onerous restrictions. Freelance journalism being impossible and the price of accreditation too dear, I travelled to Moscow frequently for specific articles commissioned by magazines and approved in principle by Soviet officials. The critical task was to find subjects of interest to the West which could also be covered honestly and win Moscow's sanction. One can only write so many times about the Bolshoi Ballet – and important elements even of this story, such as the morale of the corps de ballet, are considered 'slanderous'. Foreign journalists not trusted to confirm the overall superiority of the Soviet system and way of life are kept from all stories considered capable of 'misinterpretation' or 'manipulation' so that they cannot paint Russia differently from its official image.

In my case, permission was not often denied because I took great pains to avoid suggesting subjects which invited denial – and the accompanying hardening of the official attitude towards me. Knowledge of Soviet attitudes was helpful here: a newcomer would know the obvious prohibited subjects which were better left unmentioned – profiles of cosmonauts, Party leaders and prominent scientists, for example, and investigations of such problems as the generation gap and drug addiction – but only experience could warn that sharp antagonism would greet a request to write about Lenin's living relatives.

As a result, one of the countries richest in the raw material of journalism was oddly devoid of usable subjects – for at least some of the same reasons that the country richest in mineral wealth is also incongruously poor in serviceable consumer goods. Weeks with editors trying to conceive workable ideas were followed by months preparing for each trip, negotiating with Soviet representatives in the West, waiting for replies from their Moscow superiors, writing and re-writing prospectuses of my proposed articles to 'clarify' my intentions and, at last, awaiting my visa – which sometimes came and sometimes didn't. Once admitted to the general area of my subjects, I could hope that experience, observation and, occasionally, the help of my interviewees themselves would provide material for stories usable in the West, rather than the quasi-propagandistic pieces outlined in my 'plan'. However, I could not publish my articles in their entirety and hope to return; it was only shortly before writing this that I was able to tell the 'full' story. My own expulsion from the country removed the need for much self-limitation.

*

The officials who approved my subjects* (or obtained approval from the K.G.B. and other state agencies) were employees of the Novosti Press Agency, a relatively young organization whose services complement those of TASS. Novosti describes itself as an 'independent', 'non-governmental' institution, a weak bluff in a country where not so much as a hiking club is free of Communist Party supervision. Media organizations are among the most assiduously instructed and controlled, but there is no way of knowing how many Novosti employees also work for the K.G.B. As they have relatively frequent dealings with foreigners and dispatch some of their own material abroad, the complement of secret police informers – voluntary or paid, as a primary or supplementary duty – is presumably very high, especially among its representatives in Western capitals and in the Moscow departments which 'collaborate' with visiting journalists. The men who dealt with me confirmed this universal assumption beyond reasonable doubt.

But association with the K.G.B. is hardly the final word about a Russian's character. Though one or two of the nastiest men I have met were full-time agents, several of my most intelligent and amusing acquaintances occasionally 'informed' about something innocuous and already known, in exchange for freedom to receive foreign books without undue hindrance, to keep company with foreigners and to pursue in relative peace an avocation – cubist painting, a study of Freud, collecting English limericks – in ill repute. My Novosti associates too ranged from rigid bureaucratic chauvinists, as socially disagreeable as politically narrow-minded, to members of Moscow's meagre 'modern' intelligentsia: bright, responsive and cheerful men, who, although they had never been to the West, managed a considerable worldliness and political sophistication through their acquaintance with foreign newspapers. All Novosti men were eager to keep my articles clean: censorship

* The reports on Maya Plisetskaya, the Hotel Rossiya and the collective farm called 'Our Motherland' were compiled with Novosti's partial help. The material for the account of a trial for speculation in a People's Court and the description of prostitution in Moscow was gathered independently during trips for 'official' stories.

by leading me to 'positive' achievements and keeping me from
'negative' shortcomings. But since the 'new' men were struggling
to widen their own professional freedom within the confines of
Soviet journalism, their censorship of me, largely in the interests
of keeping their own jobs, was performed with an occasional quip
and embarrassed smile. This was in contrast to the suspicious, self-
righteous hostility, not to mention the outright lies, of neo-
Stalinists who opposed them within the Agency and the Soviet
government at large. Obviously, it was pleasanter to work with
the former type, even if closed doors remained closed.

My dealings with Novosti consisted of checking in with them
upon arrival in Moscow, reviewing my plans for their approval,
requesting interviews through them, and taking along one of
their number on most of the interviews and other outings which
were arranged. My chaperon would come in the guise of a guide,
ostensibly to smooth my path, find the proper offices and make
introductions; in general, Novosti called itself 'host, helper and
friendly colleague of visiting journalists'. In fact, they did help as
well as hinder. The inhibiting effect of a 'guide's' presence at most
interviews can·be imagined, but in any case, most of my interviewees were accompanied by their own 'colleagues', presumably
assigned by the Party or K.G.B. organization within their establishments to monitor the conversation.

In a Western country, no self-respecting journalist would tolerate such 'help'; in Russia I would have obtained hardly any formal
interviews without it. It was Novosti who obtained most permissions for me, taking the responsibility for the outcome upon themselves. My escorts squirmed or smiled in proportion to how favour-
ably my material seemed to reflect on the Soviet Union. More than
once, they made considerable efforts to get me access to harmless
material, failing only because of the low prestige of even native
journalism in the Soviet Union. Occasionally they themselves
resorted to elaborate duplicity. But I could not free myself of them,
any more than a tourist to Russia can escape Intourist.

Although Novosti's intermediacy gave me certain advantages
for non-political reportage – principally easier access to people in

the ordinary run of cultural, economic and social life, and lifting of the 'representative-of-the-bourgeois-monopolistic-press' stigma – I was hardly free to research stories on my own initiative. The difficulties of dealing with Russian officials, widely known since Gogol, have vastly increased over the intervening century: while the ranks of Tsarist functionaries were swollen enough, virtually every office in the land, every butcher, baker and candlestick maker, is now an integral part of the state's leviathan bureaucracy – and this makes for more rules, and much greater apprehension of infringing them. Once I attempted an article about motoring in Russia. After ten days of bidding, plying and dunning, I was received by the manager of Moscow's sole spare-parts outlet for private consumers, and I asked the price of a new headlight.'I'll have to check whether I can tell you that,' the manager replied. 'Personally, of course, I've nothing against it – but it's state information and I'm a state employee. Call me next week.' I called him throughout the next month, without results.

A question about pencils too – or peanuts – is literally a matter of state. Early in 1972, to take one of ten thousand examples, special measures to start the manufacture of wider neckties were ordered (years late, as is customary with changing fashions). But although the new models were to be double the width of the old, factories were assigned the same production quotas with no increased allocation of cloth. Eight organs of government, including the Ministry of Light Industry and State Planning Commission, tackled the crisis.

Although among the more streamlined of Soviet offices, Novosti is a division of the larger bureaucracy, and the first problems on every story were with my monumentally disorganized 'colleagues and helpers'. Novosti always asked me to make the outlines submitted in application for my visa as detailed as possible in accordance with the Soviet practice (which extends to professors' quotas of published pages) of each citizen working to his own miniature Five Year Plan. But I would arrive in Moscow to blank shrugs, and the suggestion that I draw up yet another set of blueprints, as if they were the first. To arrange a meeting with one of the officials who wanted to review the re-drafted plans sometimes took days.

'Call me tomorrow at ten o'clock,' I would cheerfully be told.

'Tomorrow at ten o'clock,' I'd repeat with the emphasis of experience.

'Perhaps just before ten.'

But the next day, calls from nine to six would establish only that the official was not at his desk, and no one knew whether he was in the building or even in Moscow. Many days were devoted to trying to contact someone with whom I'd had a precise agreement about when to do it; and others to 'calling tomorrow', the harvest of my conversation after finally getting through.

In part, Novosti's leisurely approach can be attributed to elements of the Russian national character: vagueness; indolence except when inspired by some private crusade or strong personal interest; procrastination corresponding in size to that of the Russian land and to the tasks imposed by geographic conditions and backwardness; unwillingness to submit to the dictates of a commercial, not to speak of mechanical or technological, age. These are the same qualities which, in phrases such as 'want of organization', 'disorder' and 'waste of time' (to quote the 1914 Russian Baedeker), observant Westerners have been describing for centuries, and which the Communist Party is continually combating with commands, pleas and slogans about increasing work discipline and establishing businesslike procedures. Despite many (if often overdrawn) similarities to Americans, Russians are their near opposites in the drive for achievement and to keep busy; in place of the American urge to 'get the job done' is the celebrated Russian *nichevo*: 'it doesn't matter' or 'nothing much can be done about it'. But everything considered, I was the gainer from this enduring Russian haphazardness. While waiting, I enjoyed the joy of Russian fellowship; my friends took me walking in the snow, and we indulged in languid days with meals to daunt the Western appetite.

For the very attitudes that make the conduct of business extremely frustrating at any but the most exalted levels – the primacy of whim, friends and one's individual inclination over the

impersonal obligations of one's job – infuse social intercourse in
Russia with great charm. In this psychologically most northern of
countries as in Latin ones, *mañana* is a guide to life; in the motherland of socialism, as in many underdeveloped lands, it is a case of the
public be damned – with conscious vengeance, in the case of the
Soviet office caste – while private interests are zestfully pursued.
This determined indifference, even positive antagonism, to anonymous clients, petitioners and consumers is one reason why almost
every transaction as a member of the public in Russia is unpleasant.
Offices and, especially, shops are hostile free-for-alls, full of queues,
elbows, salesgirls' insults and exasperating delays. But the inner
world of companions and private pursuits is completely different.
Where in the West will your friends drop everything without a
moment's thought, not to speak of guilt (or telephone calls to
cancel their business appointments), to treat you to a day of
spontaneous and unselfconscious pleasure in the countryside?
Despite the political despotism – or perhaps partly because of it –
Russians are comparatively free of the tyranny of conformism and
social compulsions.

But in my case in particular, Novosti's sluggishness was not due
to *nichevo* alone. Part of the time, its seemingly vanished officials
were in fact trying to obtain preliminary permissions for my
requested interviews and visits, to inform me of what was possible
and what I must abandon. And here they encountered heavy
sledding caused by much more than the Russian national character.

Since the people I wanted to see were inevitably employed by
state institutions, Novosti letters establishing the purpose of my
inquiries had to be drafted in the proper form with the necessary
countersignatures and seals. But before resorting to this, the agency
would attempt to expedite matters through unofficial, verbal
contacts. It was this outwardly simple endeavour that incidentally
revealed some of the Soviet economy's greatest problems, which
no study of facts and figures, nothing but personal observation, can
demonstrate.

The difficulty lay in the general area of Soviet etiquette and
business practices, seemingly intended to *prevent* communication

between people not personally acquainted. For example the telephone is virtually useless as a medium for reaching the simplest agreements, and officials must often leave their desks, travel across town, and present themselves in person to state their cases. With luck – and an untypical sense of urgency – a man can be back at work in an hour or two, but the better part of many days is spent accomplishing what would seem to require minutes.

Apart from the vagaries of the telephone system,* lack of trust is a major cause of this colossal waste of time. Although Soviet journalists writing about Western countries are extremely guarded in introducing 'positive' aspects (never mentioning, amidst dutiful descriptions of strikes and imminent disaster, the wages which workers are demanding), many do single out for praise the practice of concluding important business by a gentleman's word – even over the telephone, without so much as a handshake, let alone a long exchange of documents in quadruplicate. But it is hard to see how this potentially glorious liberation of the Soviet economy can be achieved in a system where every handful of paper clips is state property, to be signed and accounted for, and where no system of payment by cheque exists (all consumer transactions, from the payment of a three-ruble gas bill to a 10,000-ruble royalty settlement, are carried out in cash, after travelling to the appropriate office and waiting in the necessary queue). Although most Russians trust their close friends with loans and 'sensitive' information more readily than their Western counterparts, in their public capacities

---

* Decrying the malfunctions of the local telephone network has become a cliché of residents abroad, and I shall not add my comments about Moscow's system except to say that in mechanical failures and unreliability alone, it is second to none, even when one is speaking from an untapped telephone. Dialling the first numeral of the city's seven-figure numbers can produce an engaged signal for a full quarter of an hour, and even when one has the good luck to complete the number in a city where forty lawyers share two telephones, the delays caused by waiting for a clear line can be imagined. (God help you if you don't have the proper number: Directory Inquiries, if you can ever get them, puts a violent sting in your ear.) The tales of woe I have heard about Paris, Tangier and Palermo only made me envious. In Moscow even with unusual patience a morning can be wasted in making a few calls, by which time your men may well have left for the day, and less patient callers often give up until tomorrow. *Nichevo.*

they take each other's word for almost nothing – and have every reason not to, since even seemingly trivial actions and decisions involve them with state responsibilities and possible punishments defined by the criminal code. Reluctance to commit oneself to anything by telephone to a stranger is partly a reflection of this general condition. Most officials and office staff decline even to provide innocuous general information, and the few callers who against the odds try to save themselves a trip usually are told, irately, to 'come in and find out for yourself'.

The rudeness of office staff, too, does much to diminish the telephone's usefulness. Why are so many Russians ill-mannered when at their desks or behind their counters? Some of my friends attributed it to general irritability caused by low wages, slim chances of promotion and long hours of queuing; others claimed that decades of struggling with bureaucracies in their private lives have produced a calloused 'official skin' which protects them against the faceless masses competing for answers in offices, permissions in Ministries and provisions in food shops. ('The whole country's on permanent strike,' said one sarcastic friend.) Almost everyone mentioned Russians' striving to be left in peace, a desire which has become unusually intense in the face of the multiplicity of state and 'communal' agencies poised to inspect Soviet citizens' personal and professional affairs. The protective cocoon is also important as insulation from the steady drone of propaganda and exhortation; intrusions from outside the private world are assumed to be additional burdens of bad news.

For these reasons, among others, the 'official' bark has become all but instinctive, and it is usually sharpest when the personal element in the exchange is lowest: when the intruder-supplicator is no more than a telephone voice. Unsolicited calls normally prompt a show of temper, and the equivalent of a company vice-president can be bewilderingly hard to find if not at his desk.

'What do you want?'

'May I speak to Evgeny Pavlovich, please?'

'He's *not here*.'

The receiver is slammed down instantly, and it takes many

minutes to overcome mechanical troubles and switchboard congestion and get through again.

'Yes?'

'Do you know where Evgeny Pavlovich is? When he might return?'

'*Nyet.*'

Again, the receiver crashes to its cradle before anything useful can be elicited, and a third call must be made to blurt out the quick plea, 'I'm very sorry to trouble you, but please don't ring off, I'm a foreigner and don't quite understand' – which holds out the best chance of persuading someone to leave a message. But at certain times of day, even this cannot be relied upon. After two dozen rings, the receiver will leap up for a wrathful shout of 'I'M BUSY!' or 'LUNCH!' before hurtling down again. (Somehow this increased my own appetite for a large, long Russian meal.)

It is to protect influential foreign visitors from such treatment, as well as to keep close watch on them, that they are assigned guides-interpreters-fixers-adjutants to insulate them as far as possible from ordinary transactions. From incoming to outgoing flight, a trail is blazed for them through every encounter and appointment, just as Intourist smooths the way for less celebrated visitors with their less individual service. Occasionally guides can be overheard whispering the magic 'it's for a foreigner' urgently into a telephone. Unsung heroes of socialist labour, they cut their way through the dense bureaucratic jungle of papers and permissions with its undergrowth of negativism and antagonism to the public.

With some exceptions, the delays and difficulties encountered by Novosti are experienced by any official approaching any other. Additional problems arise for journalists. Quite apart from Soviet citizens' resistance to the potential dangers of being written about in the Western press, they are instinctively reluctant to involve themselves even with reliable Soviet reporters. A visit from the press is almost universally regarded as a tiresome waste of time or nasty intrusion into cherished privacy.

This attitude (shared by artists, performers, scientists, scholars and virtually all others most wanted for interviews) reflects and enhances Russians' social charm. Raised on a heavy diet of publicity, most Westerners naturally want some of the 'nourishment' for themselves, and will make time for interviews during their busiest days. In my own experience, few decline, even when they suspect that the copy will reflect unfavourably on them. By contrast, very few Russians can be bothered, even when the story is certain to be flattering. They are engagingly indifferent to seeing their photographs on magazine covers and their judgments recorded inside.

Russian film stars provide the most vivid illustration of this, since they would presumably benefit most from publicity. Years of effort provided me with material for a total of two or three paragraphs. Once, when representing a popular English magazine, I managed to arrange a series of interviews with an actress of a certain age whose newest film would soon be released in Britain. Despite the urging of her director-husband (who had travelled to the West and knew some of its ways) that the article would be a priceless plug for her and her work, the carefully coiffed lady herself was so aloof that I could not have written a page about her for a teenage audience. 'How did you become an actress?' I asked, after more imaginative efforts to pique her interest had fizzled. 'That's not interesting for outsiders,' she answered, opening a novel she'd brought to our first meeting. All later ones were cancelled.

Although flatness of personality was a contributing factor in this case, the general indifference to the press reflects some of the most important elements of Russian life. Russians generally have so full a sense of themselves, and are so absorbed in their inner world of family and close friends, that they feel little need of recognition from newspaper readers and television watchers – outsiders with whom they have no personal relationship. An adoring, highly supportive upbringing within a close, relaxed family unit with important roles for grandparents, unselfconscious attitudes to physical contact, and loving self-assured guidance has sufficiently nourished the ego to protect it against the twentieth-century anxieties about identity, status and success. Recent studies by

Western psychologists and sociologists explain in detail why so many Russian children are remarkably contented, but my favourite description is an older one by Wright Miller, an English journalist with deep insight into the Russian character.

> The Russian, I suggest, growing up in self-confidence without much childhood discipline, a member of a secure, ancient, but loose community, not conditioned before his schooldays to any large number of habits, rituals or taboos, displays that naturalness which has so often enchanted foreigners ... The average Russian can be plunged for long periods into either pessimism or optimism, either apathy or concentrated effort, and under the stimulus of persons around him, he can also change his moods rapidly and show that they are changed, yet he cannot be called volatile or superficial. The root self-confidence and the security in his community are always underneath ... So that though it may be true, as I suggested, that it is the infant upbringing and the looseness of the Russian community which allows the individual to behave so freely, it is also to some extent true that the spontaneous and natural behaviour of individuals is what makes the loose and at the same time secure Russian community. The 'sincerity' and the community feeling seem to make an integrated system, in which each is an effect and each a cause.*

Of course, this rule has many exceptions, but its general validity can be illustrated by comparing parties in New York and Moscow where most of the guests are meeting for the first time. At the Moscow gathering, as in Russian society generally, people will be far less concerned to impress others with who they are and who they know, how much they earn and what triumphs they are currently planning – all ploys designed to camouflage an underlying unease. A single Sunday in Moscow, observing children strolling serenely with their caressing parents, is enough to indicate why.

* Wright Miller, *Russians as People* (London: Phoenix House, 1960; New York: E. P. Dutton, 1961).

But again, more than national character accounts for Russians' disinclination to be interviewed. Another major cause is their aversion to journalism specifically, which they consider among the least useful and admirable of professions. Many members of the intelligentsia think so little of it that they avoid newspapers for weeks at a time, as if allergic to them. Because the broad masses are inclined to believe what they read – that the Soviet Union is the best country in the world and they are the most virtuous and best rewarded people – their suspicions of the press are milder. But among intellectuals, 'newspaper' is used as a pejorative in such phrases as 'newspaper speech' and 'newspaper talk' – euphemisms for expediency and distortion, drivel and puerile philosophizing. The steady production of (rather unfunny) jokes about the shortage of toilet paper and the use of *Pravda* as a substitute gives some indication of their attitude.

A thorough reading of one day's national papers will probably explain their scorn. Apart from occasional informative articles, most of the daily press is as readable as a machine-tool catalogue. Interpreting world events to fit the current version of an over-simplified Marxism-Leninism, exhorting readers to produce more at their lathes and to strengthen their political faith, the papers drearily cleave to Lenin's guiding maxim: 'A newspaper is not only a collective propagandist and collective agitator, but also a collective organizer.' The result is a stream of cliché-ridden copy – about potato production and Central Committee theses – which, like yesterday's and last year's, repeats the same 'newspaper messages' Russians have heard a million times since childhood. The Party has made journalism largely an advertisement for itself, aimed at the intellectual level of its own political thought.

Although I knew this in abstract, the full implications of my metier's low esteem struck me only after a quarrel with my best friend, the Muscovite mentioned earlier. It grew out of my failure to complete a profile of another actress, this time one of the handful with a name in the West. A long campaign in London and Moscow had secured me an evening with her, during which she became so incoherently drunk that the interview was unusable: she had remained sober too briefly to glean enough material, and to describe her extraordinary abandon after gulping nearly a half-litre of vodka would have constituted a grave violation of the 'Kremlin Code' of decency, which is far stricter than its Hollywood predecessor. Months of preparation and many hundreds of dollars were lost, together with my almost-realized hope of at last portraying a Russian star.

To help make it appear a social occasion (the importance of which I shall discuss directly) my friend accompanied me during the early part of the evening. But although he had witnessed the celebrated actress's vulgar insults and bizarre promiscuity, and vigorously agreed that such things must not be mentioned, he understood neither my disappointment nor dilemma.

'Right, she's a nympho, as everybody says. Clean off her head. But what's all the fuss about? Write what you have to, it can't take more than an hour or two.'

'What does that mean – writing "what I have to"?'

'You know what she looks like now. Dash off something that'll fill the bill for the overseas public without getting the dander up of our prudes over here. You're an experienced journalist, after all.'

'Which means I don't spin yarns. I may leave things out, but I don't *invent* them. Do you know what journalism means?'

'Who are you kidding? I know that journalism is a hell of a lot worse and a hell of a lot uglier than what I'm suggesting. Of course you mustn't write anything that will hurt anybody. Just make it easy for yourself, for hot-pants, for your editor, for everybody.'

'And who will take care of the truth?'

'Are you serious? You're in the wrong racket.'

'You've known me ten years. Do you really think I've been inventing things on all these trips? Do you believe that all journalism is like the Soviet stuff? Forget virtue, but why be a reporter if you add to the lies and confusion? There's such a thing as honesty, self-respect ... '

'Pass the coffee and calm down. I do know one thing: journalism is whoring. If that upsets you, change your profession. But who the hell cares? What's it between *us*?'

The squabble raged throughout the following morning. Nothing I said in defence of my profession or its different standing in the West convinced my friend, who kept urging me to sit down and produce something appropriate about hot-pants, so that we could sweat out our alcohol in his favourite *banya* and have a big dinner to 'disrecollect the world's absurd cares'. Despite our friendship, for which he had taken real risks over the years, he continued to regard journalism *per se* as an easy way to turn a penny with copy worked to fit one or another socio-political formula. He conceded that in the Western formula, sensationalism was probably more important than ideological imperatives; but to create obstacles for myself in the name of truth only increased his suspicions that I was hiding some other, personal reason from him for not writing about the actress.

In short, Russians serious about their work have little time for reading journalism and less to give interviews to the correspondents who produce it. For these reasons, Novosti appeared to be near the nadir among Soviet agencies in terms of its ability to induce co-operation, and it hardly exercised any open-sesame powers over my potential subjects. Their first instinct was avoidance. The same factors made protracted, slippery and sometimes futile my attempts to actually see the people who finally succumbed to Novosti's adjurations; and many who agreed in principle managed to keep themselves unavailable for the duration of my trip. Thus, more waiting for calls that never came, trying to locate officials who had promised, *this time without fail*, to see me ten days ago, and biding my time for final permissions. What might be the objection, after all the prior agreements, to seeing someone so apparently 'safe' as an architect? But without this bumbling, tedious, comic, wearying, infuriating process Russia would hardly be Russian, and I'd have had much less time for 'escaping everything' with my friends.

Once one actually meets one's subjects, other characteristic conditions obtain. For example, a tape recorder should ordinarily not be brought to an interview – not only because the sight of one can set in motion a chain of unfortunate associations, but also because the cardinal rule of journalism in Russia is to make your interest appear personal. Just as the key to what sustains Russian life is private interests and relationships, the journalist's *sine qua non* is somehow to make contact with his interviewee as a person. To Russians, an interview as such represents only an official intrusion, of which they are so weary and wary. A reporter must get beneath the level on which he represents one organization (his magazine) and his subject another (his institute or hospital; even his art) so that the latter feels he is conversing *po dusham*, literally 'soul to soul'. Because of the requirements of the Soviet press, even Russians of considerable achievement rarely know what it is to give an interview in the Western sense, and are likely to provide a stiff, distracted mouthing of platitudes, the more quickly and painlessly to free themselves. But as ordinary people they are their usual artless selves, so long as they feel contact with a kindred spirit. Far more than the West, the material is 'produced' in reaction to the journalist's personality, rather than simply gathered.

For this reason, a candid outpouring about my own hardships in getting the story always seemed far less inappropriate and correspondingly more effective than in the West. Cold as my subject had been to the official request for the interview, he could be warm to the victim of circumstances seated before him. In Russia, compassion for specific personal adversity exists side by side, often in the same people, with great rudeness to strangers. And laying bare my problems never made me ashamed; in the Russian community there is rarely any embarrassment about giving way to emotion.

Soviet journalists too are taught to approach their subjects on a personal rather than a professional level. In his lectures to Moscow University's department of journalism, a well-known Russian correspondent's first rule for interviewing is, 'whether your man be the chairman of a collective farm or the Chairman of the U.S.S.R. Council of Ministers, *never* carry a pencil or notebook where it can be seen. Always *talk* to him as intimately as possible, as

you would to your friends. If possible, *drink** with him; you all
know how this can help to make contact with a stranger, if he's
Russian. Because it's making contact with the man's thoughts and
being, making him feel that you are "one of the family", that will
get you your story. Without this, all the journalistic credentials in
the world will leave him unimpressed, and you without material.'

These tactics often bring more than usable copy. The official
skin once penetrated, the celebrated Russian characteristics of good
humour and outgoing generosity, simplicity and sincerity – all that
is known as the 'wide' Russian nature – exert their spell to make the
interview an enchanting experience. I often remembered Wright
Miller's impressions of his first encounter with Russians.

> I found myself in a scene where costumes and *decor*, so to
> speak, were vague and of small account, except on a few very
> formal occasions; almost everything significant seemed to be
> concentrated in the *dramatis personae*. I found myself received
> into a milieu where personal relationships and personal
> expression had an importance, a development, a naturalness
> and 'sincerity', as I called it, such as I had never imagined.

The striking difference between the candour, tolerance and
compassion of many Russians in their private lives and the rigidity
of their official bearing may help account for the often-observed
contrast between Russians and their government. It is frequently
commented that the likeable Russian people – warm, artless,
unaggressive and even instinctively democratic – are oppressed by
intolerable rulers. But a likelier explanation is that, appealing as they
are in personal relations, Russians are incompetent in dealing with
public ones. Not only do they tolerate bad management and
government, but individuals who are charming in private can be
insensitive and sometimes brutal when at their desks. On average,

---

* The drinking implied here is not a social sipping of cocktails, but the swallowing
of quantities of vodka in the Russian manner, until the point of considerable inebri-
ation and sentimentality is reached, in which one's drinking partner seems a shining,
profoundly perceptive and compassionate soul who fully understands the world's
hardships and potential beauty.

even the newspaper officials who daily throttle and distort the truth are distinctly more relaxed and engaging company than their Western counterparts. Living amidst Russia's isolation and propaganda, one appreciates Western editors' political maturity and fairness as never before; but to social enjoyment – an evening of eating, drinking, story-telling and joking, an atmosphere of warmth and intimacy – the Russians give much more.

But whatever a reporter's facility for 'reaching' Russians, his principal obstacles lie neither in the national character nor in the Russian tradition of discretion about public figures' private lives, but in the regime, which uses its absolute authority to suppress real and imagined objections to its rules for viewing mankind. The demand for praise is proportionate to the political power, and journalism is regarded as a more sophisticated adjunct to the ubiquitous signs erected to the supervisors themselves: 'GLORY TO THE COMMUNIST PARTY!' 'GLORY TO THE SOVIET GOVERNMENT!'

Severe feelings of inferiority and the accompanying defensive suspicion thrive on their own, even when wholly 'innocent' subjects are involved and when there is no cause for embarrassment in comparison to the West. On one occasion, after overcoming the usual obstacles and waiting out the customary delays, I travelled to an educational institution of which Soviet officials were justifiably proud. At the last minute, without explanation, I was told I could not enter the building. Desperate to save something of a story, I began photographing some children playing in the snow near the entrance. Bundled in scarves and furs, this chubby, happy group, like Russian children generally, would have enchanted even W. C. Fields. But an angry institute official, probably the Party Secretary, stepped from the building and ordered me to stop. 'What are you trying to prove to the Americans?' he challenged. 'That Soviet children are forced to play outdoors because we lack proper kindergartens?'

Xenophobia, the isolation of Westerners and relentless surveillance have lengthy traditions in Russian history, and one can amuse oneself – or reinforce one's pessimism about the country's eventual political maturation – by thumbing through the books of early visitors. Some four hundred years ago, for example, *Description of Moscow and Muscovy, 1557* recorded the author's long wait for a visa, exasperating delays in securing interviews with officials and constant snooping by security men who explained that they were only protecting him from harm. Since that bestseller of its day, dozens of travellers have described aspects of the quarantine of foreigners which have remarkable parallels with contemporary Russia.

But Soviet intolerance of independent reporting is not merely a continuation of pre-revolutionary policy. Much progress had been made, especially in the second half of the nineteenth century, from the worst of Russia's dark past; in the decades immediately preceding the revolution, the country was far more open than now to tourists and journalists and, with occasional regressions, this trend continued until the outbreak of the First World War. Soviet attitudes are atavistic, bearing greater resemblance to medieval than to late Tsarist times.

The regime's effectiveness in suppression derives from its use of a rapidly developing technology of surveillance and its control of the country's every social, political, economic and cultural organization. But the zeal to suppress cannot be understood without reference to ideology: the canon that the Soviet Union is something wholly new on earth, infinitely better in every substantive way than what it replaced, and that under the Party's revelational leadership, the Soviet people are uniquely free and happy. The reality of life in this 'new era of mankind' strengthens the determination to prevent first-hand reporting. As a character in Russian fiction (by Andrei Platonov, an author himself long suppressed) put it, 'The truth may also be a class enemy.'

But sociological factors are equally important. Most of the old Russian intelligentsia and commercial elite, those who had been most active in pulling pre-revolutionary Russia towards European ideas and standards, fled after the revolution, were killed in the

Civil War or shot by Stalin. Their place was taken largely by the loyal, almost wholly uneducated (in the broad sense) muzhiks whom Stalin recruited into the Party and who still control its *apparat*. Russia is ruled – more: all its norms, standards and tastes are established – by men given to village narrow-mindedness, obstinacy and resentment of their 'betters'. This mentality, which drives the dictatorship, has little to do with Marxism or any other social theory. The bullies would feel temperamentally at home in the office of a Mississippi sheriff, boisterously upholding local myths of their own superiority. Their extreme patriotism is no less primitive for its expression through socialist slogans. Only their power to crush what they dislike is modern.

Reports are leaking out of how these men react when they feel challenged. Political dissidents are exiled from Moscow, sentenced to periods in labour camps and, at worst, confined to mental hospitals and given mind-destroying drugs. But although more common, the punishments for lesser offences, many related to behaving incautiously with Western reporters, are not so well known. Recently, a Moscow official summoned a talented young chemist to his office. 'You snivelling traitor,' the former stormed, 'I'll teach you some respect.' He produced a photograph of the scientist taken by a Western correspondent in Moscow and published inconspicuously abroad: in the background a beaker of acid appeared directly beneath Lenin's portrait on the laboratory wall. To the official, this was a calculated insult to The Leader, and the chemist's long-sought trip to a conference abroad was cancelled. The scientist (who was to have delivered an important paper at the conference) was unsurprised. 'This is what our leaders busy themselves with,' he explained. 'A Vice-Minister of one of the country's largest Ministries is genuinely outraged by a beaker of acid somewhere; he'd lost face in the West.'

'Surely it can't continue in this way,' say Western visitors hearing such stories. 'It's so unfair, so wasteful – and it's *not normal*.'

'It's been going strong for fifty years,' my Russian friends reply, 'during most of which Westerners have assured themselves that "it can't continue in this way". *Why* can't it? ... The restrictions are as inane and rigid as ever, even if a few brave souls are willing to defy them.'

The few brave souls are indeed an encouraging development. In 1959, a kind of apartheid prevailed between natives and the few Westerners in Moscow. To venture alone into an apartment house courtyard was an achievement. Each tip-toeing, heart-pounding climb up a dark staircase and into a communal flat was an act of defiance, exposing oneself, and still more one's Russian host, to grave risks. I cannot forget the sight of middle-aged men, lips parched with excitement and fear, talking to me, their first foreigner. Now, by contrast, an American Congressman can find himself in a dissenter's flat days after arriving in the capital. And although he will be expelled from the country after a characteristic-ally coarse K.G.B. raid and statement, the fear of fraternization is gone, seemingly permanently, for small groups on both sides.

It was in 1966, when a current of open protest was generated in reaction to the trials of Andrei Sinyavsky and Yuli Daniel, that a small band of determined Russians established contact with foreign newsmen, and news of political persecution began flowing abroad. But the arrest, sentencing, exile and commitment to mental asylums of this defiant handful – often specifically for passing information to Western journalists – has again severely muffled the dissent. The K.G.B. is determined to close this channel to the outside press. Since then other developments have restricted even further the opportunities for 'slice-of-life' stories. While writers and protesters were being persecuted in the retreat from Nikita Khrushchev's tentative liberalization to hard-line orthodoxy, Western correspondents were being excluded ever more thoroughly from Soviet institutions and personalities. By early 1973, interviews and permissions were virtually unobtainable, and foreigners kept even from the public defence of scholarly dis-sertations, one of the last opportunities for a glance behind the scenes of institutional life. As if to symbolize the attitude towards the foreign compound, an eight-foot wall of grey concrete was built around the larger blocks of flats to reinforce wire fences, police kiosks and constant K.G.B. patrols. As part of the crusade to intensify vigilance against 'invidious bourgeois influences, hostile to Marxism-Leninism', a stream of articles warned citizens to be even more guarded with foreigners.

Why bother with journalism at all under these conditions? Because, I think, the game is still worth the candle. Despite her afflictions – or partly because of them – Russia's raw, puzzling greatness remains fascinating. We were all emotionally involved in it through the Russian literature on which we were raised and the great socialist experiment which still feeds our political passions. It is not accidental, as Marxists like to say, that other countries no less inaccessible, harsh and 'inscrutable' intrigue the West far less. It was specifically Russia, where European ideas bubbled like acid in the waters of Orthodox spirituality and peasant superstition, that gave the West so much of its post-industrial artistic and political stimulation: so much hope and disillusionment. Somehow, this land's hardship contributes to sublime illusions and creativity.

Beyond this, Russia's 'there-but-for-the-grace-of-God' relationship to the West makes our curiosity more personal than academic. China and India, Persia and Turkey are exotic but essentially alien; without Tolstoy and Chekhov, we cannot easily put ourselves there. And it was precisely Russia's thoughts which rang true to us in the great writers' works. Russians are we ourselves with some of our civilized comforts – and pretences – stripped away, the easier to see ourselves in a realm of spontaneity and sorrow, exalted dreams and cosmic despair.

Besides, the restrictions to journalism were an intriguing challenge in themselves. Sometimes the solution was simple: when the parts depot manager declined to reveal the price of a headlight, I asked a friend who owned a car. During the weeks when Novosti was searching for a 'typical' secretary or divorce case, a dozen girls told me their unrehearsed stories, and there were ten divorces a day to watch in each of the People's Courts. A librarian not forewarned once spent a full day assembling clippings on a certain residential construction project about which I'd been told no background information existed; and a friend of a friend easily tracked down a scholar supposedly on leave to a Bulgarian university.

It was always my friends, and sometimes my subjects themselves, who helped me, and this poses problems of conscience common to closed societies: how to balance professional honesty with their safety? The closer one's confidants, the more one learns about the reality of the country; but it is precisely information about the details of episodes which can provoke reprisals. As a veteran Danish correspondent put it, 'the unofficial things are always the dangerous ones, and you've learnt them from a Russian who trusts you and whom you must protect.'

Even attractive aspects of Russian life can make trouble. To describe any individual as hedonistic and scornful of self-discipline and Marxist-Leninist liturgies – as so many of the haute intelligentsia are – would be to invite retribution upon him. The promiscuous actress, for example, had better remain un-named. The regime wants the stereotype of the hardworking, politically active citizen confirmed, even though this evokes images of regimented personality which make the country appear far drearier than it is.

In these circumstances, it is virtually obligatory to camouflage one's sources by name-changing, mis-identifying and minor mis-representations in time and place. More substantive dishonesty is sometimes requested by one's subjects themselves. Recently, a young woman with a considerable reputation abroad was interviewed by an Italian journalist. She earned eighty rubles a month, the price of half a dozen pairs of tights. 'But you can't write that,' she whispered. 'It would infuriate the Ministry. They'd accuse me of "slandering Soviet reality" – it's happened before.' Asked for guidance, the young woman suggested that 250 rubles a month would sound respectable, and this figure appeared in the article.

I believe that omission is better than conscious distortion, but there is no satisfying solution to the Italian's dilemma. If they are not to lie, journalists in Russia must repress – at the stage of gathering information as well as citing it. A whole range of questions can scarcely be asked, let alone answered. The reporters I most admired gracefully stifled queries that could only cause their subjects anger, embarrassment or pain. On the grounds that progress is yet further retarded when Westerners as well as Russians submit to the blackmail of potential reprisals, more and more Moscow liberals – although their number is still tiny – disapprove of total safety. But the conflict between risk and potential benefit is eternal and unresolvable, even at second hand.

In their own encounters with their consciences and with censors, Russians range the spectrum from zealous servility, composing cynically dishonest work for money or position, to writing only 'for the desk drawer' and submitting nothing to avoid being tainted by the compromises inherent in publication. But most writers fall somewhere between: enduring the tampering with one article in the hope of winning a point in the next; tolerating severe cuts and the consequent distortions for the sake of what survives; writing ritual opening paragraphs in praise of Marxism-Leninism or the Motherland as 'locomotives' to pull later passages past the censor; abandoning hope of writing the whole truth in order to make a step in that direction, if only by hints and implications. Few are rich or heroic enough simply to ignore censorship and self-censorship; nor do they feel that defiance or withdrawal is best, even for those who can afford those luxuries. They see their duty as steady persistence from within, combining a realistic recognition of what is possible with a determination to stretch it at opportune moments. A writer's honour is considered whole if he preserves *elements* of an important truth, encouraging artistic and historical awakening in his own small ways.

No foreigner who participates in Russian life can avoid these moral impasses. ('Dictatorships are dirty,' a Russian friend once told me. 'You can't have any dealings at all with them and pretend to come away with clean hands.') Writing about the country without visiting it is one solution, but only by conceding the use of one's own eyes and ears. My own decisions about what to publish have been made in this context. I am not certain of wrong or right, only that every journalist in Russia makes his own choices: another cause of heightened feelings there. And that Russian conditions impose a responsibility upon the reader too: to read between the lines as Russians do, alert for clues and hints.

2. Maya Plisetskaya

In Plisetskaya, dance, musicianship and a sense of theatre are fused by a temperament burning with passion and spirituality. There seems to be no height to which she cannot rise with gossamer lightness, no distance she cannot soar in fiery trajectory, no speed at which she cannot spin or change gears with unbroken ease, no time limit for a frozen arabesque, no line of plastic body and limbs that is not sheer sculptured feminine grace. – *Newsweek*, 1959.

Plisetskaya talking always has overtones of Plisetskaya dancing – of the unique ballerina who always adds the delight of improvisation to the canons of academic ballet. Of that Maya Plisetskaya who can stun audiences, provoke arguments, and assert her own unmistakable 'I' in all the varied personalities of her heroines.– *Izvestiya*, 1969.

The first offstage meeting with Maya Plisetskaya is an immediate confirmation of the talk about her in Moscow. One has heard, from fellow members of the haute intelligentsia not given to star worship or petty gossip, that she is innately theatrical but despises cheap theatricalism – no *darlings* or precious kisses. That she has strong, sometimes gaudy tastes and an independent judgment. That both personally and (so far as this is possible in Russia) professionally she is highly individualistic and *temperamentnaya*: a woman of instincts, moods and irrepressible enthusiasms and annoyances, all expressed with extreme and sometimes cutting frankness. That she is opinionated, brusque, volatile and wilful, but will do or say nothing for attention or flattery; she is wholly herself at all times, and lacks even the temptation to pose. That she is a restlessly creative and dynamic woman who would have achieved renown even had she been born lame or otherwise unfit for the dance. That, above all, she is a creature of passion in all its aspects, which makes her personal life as fascinating as her performing is inspired.

It is a Sunday morning in February, so cold that fingers ache through thick sheepskin gloves. Inside the Directors' Entrance of the Bolshoi Theatre, a buxom uniformed attendant is wiping from the marble floor the pools of dirty slush from visitors' boots. 'Mayechka will be along in a minute,' she wheezes with a proprietory smile. 'Our Mayechka. Don't worry, she'll be here soon. But she has so much to do.'

But Mayechka (or Maya Mikhailovna, as Plisetskaya is known to all but charladies and intimate friends) does not appear in a minute. Or five minutes, or ten. Later she will explain, not without a trace of self-satisfaction, that she is always late, invariably rushing. One of the qualities for which she adores America is its punishing pace.

I have almost thawed out when she emerges above me on the staircase. There is an impression of nervous energy and taut skin; a woman who looks not more or less than her forty-five years; an expression simultaneously brittle and frail. Her being likened to Greta Garbo by news magazines seems trite; at first glance I think of Bette Davis playing herself. One quality makes itself felt above all others: she is excessively highly-strung.

'You're the fellow from England? Hello, come up.'

I do go up, wondering why I am suddenly full of misgivings after my success in actually meeting her. Am I intimidated because in person this idol – called 'the most exciting dancer of our day' by the usually restrained John Martin – is smaller and more womanly than I had expected? No deep insight is needed to sense that her brashness conceals what she feels to be vulnerability in dealings with men. Her thick hair is rinsed red; her face seems bony, as if nerves had consumed all spare flesh. Seen on a Manhattan street, she would be taken for a native New Yorker – a ballet-lover, but not a ballerina, and of Central European rather than Russian descent.

Somehow I feel that an accurate physical description of Plisetskaya would tell much of my story. She is wearing an ochre jersey dress, elegant by Moscow standards but smacking of Broadway, especially in contrast with her showy tights and boots. Her eyes are greenish and oblong; her smile was accurately described by a Soviet magazine as 'slightly predatory, faintly wanton, but extraordinarily magnetic'. The collection of jewellery seems weighty on her slender chest: a Léger pin and a heavy, handsome Finnish necklace. It is impossible not to ask her about her perfume; the scent would have been remarkable even had she chosen to use an ordinary amount.

'Bandit,' she declares emphatically. 'Always Bandit and only Bandit. Not easy to find anywhere except in Paris itself. But it's the only perfume that suits me – the name, the style as well as the scent. That's me: *bandit*.'*

She invites me into the Director-General's salon, the epitome of a Director-General's salon, glittering with gilt and walls of crimson silk. Louis XIV chairs are covered with canvas dust-protectors to complete the film-set effect. When we've settled ourselves, Plisetskaya scrutinizes me openly, trying neither to make me feel uneasy nor to put me at my ease. She lacks all trace of the condescending or patronizing air many celebrities adopt at the start of an interview. But neither is there a smile of welcome.

What do I want from her? she asks brusquely. How can she help? I explain that I want to write about her as a person, not a ballerina – aspects of her life which never appear in the Soviet press. She agrees in principle – 'suit yourself' – but doubts it can be done well. She is, I should understand, as excitable as changeable. A woman of moods, an extremely difficult person to capture. 'But capture what you will, ask whatever you want.'

We exchange information about ourselves and mutual friends. What is my nationality? Plisetskaya asks. Who will photograph her for my article? Avedon has taken some splendid portraits of her in New York, she says, but in Moscow, there's not a soul to recommend: Russian photographers are as bad as Russian film. Not a single Russian photographer can be entrusted with her portrait – which is what plagues her everywhere in life. 'The triteness and standardization of everything,' she says disgustedly. 'The lack of

* In Russian, too, the word carries a somewhat flattering implication of impetuous devilry.

creativity everywhere and the dreadful lack of *taste* !'

I have no answer. Many of my friends among Moscow's intelligentsia feel the same way about the country, but this is the first person I've interviewed who dared talk about Russia so outspokenly, without requesting that the comments remain unpublished. In the first five minutes Plisetskaya has given me more quotable copy than I have gained in three previous years of interviewing in Russia. But I am faintly bewildered: did she devise her costume this morning and bedeck herself with jewellery to demonstrate the hated 'lack of taste'?

'If you want to know the main thing in my life,' she continues vehemently, 'it is *taste*. Taste in all things, all periods, all styles; taste as *the* criterion of good and evil: creative taste. Avedon's photography is taste. Horowitz at the piano is taste. And of course taste means France. The French live it, love it, feel it in their bones. How can you even mention the English in the same breath? ... '

Suddenly she has launched into an angry discourse. It begins as a monologue, rises to a declamation, swells into a fierce harangue. It is laced with uncompromising opinions expressed in uncompromising terms, and another first for me in an interview: the ripest of four-letter words. I do not know what has provoked it, besides the fact that I live in England and write for English magazines. The subject is the worthlessness – the empty egotism, perfidy and viciousness – of critics in general and English critics in particular.

Critics are fools. Margot Fonteyn told me that she never reads any critics, English above all. Critics are people who can't do creative work themselves. 'If you can't make it yourself, teach others' – that's their motto. Write that down, I want you to quote my exact words on that. Critics are stupid, arrogant, egotistical bastards.

Any fool with enough ambition and spite can become a critic. They always attack anything genuinely creative. A hundred years ago they said Wagner was worthless. They said the same about Rembrandt – when he was at work on his most brilliant, inspired canvases. Why must this be tolerated? They demand that we have talent – that we not stoop and stumble on stage. Why should critics who have nothing to offer but arrogance and complacency be permitted to publish their trash?

I've been in England three times. By now I understand: whatever is cheap, empty, phoney, sloppy, tasteless, ponderous, grey the English adore. They love Posnikova but not Richter. They fawn over Struchkova – and, in general, all Russian so-called artists who are empty, and whom we Russians ourselves avoid. Whatever's in mothballs or full of lice, whatever's Victorian, petty bourgeois, cheap and vulgar, whatever's worthless – that's what the English love. They are a dreary people. A dead grey mass, at least in their art.

Critics are miserable little bastards. They become critics in their misery over not being able to create – then try to spread their misery to people who can. And English critics are the worst of all, of course. Lumps of you-know-what. Everything that's fresh and strong and creative and alive – everything that deserves the name of genuine art – the English critic hates.

How to interpret this outburst? It is said that Plisetskaya responds to countries as they to her; it is known that English critics have been less than ecstatic in their praise of her, especially in a ballet called 'Carmen-Suite', which seldom leaves her thoughts. This interpretation appears to be supported by other points in our conversation: between waves of hostility towards London, Plisetskaya speaks fondly of Helsinki and New York, which have praised her extravagantly. ('In terms of the qualifications of its critics,' she says, 'Helsinki is second only to Paris.') And she is rhapsodic about Paris, just as Paris is rhapsodic about her.

'Paris is the world. Paris is beauty. Paris is *taste*. Why do I love it? Why does a woman love her favourite man? – these things musn't be reduced to words. Paris is grace, is elegance, is the centre of *art*. They send me all over the world, but I only really want to go to Paris. Unfortunately, I've been there less than two months altogether ...'

Nothing in her conversation contradicts Moscow talk about Plisetskaya: that she loves Paris because Paris loves her. But surely there is something more to her loathing of England.

The English are a cold people. An anti-musical people. They love cold music, cold art, cold everything. A people without soul. Frankly, I'm an objective person, I see things as they are. Throughout history, there's

*never been a single important English composer, not one of any depth.
I don't know why, it's just a fact. It's a fact that they're drab and anti-
musical – and maybe their miserable stunted critics have something to do
with it.*

Finally, she has spent herself. She moves back in her seat,
scrutinizes me again and smiles. She does not apologize for her outburst, but explains that she cannot hide her feelings; if we are to get
on, she must be free to express herself. She smiles again and presses
my hand. By the time I leave, she is calmly describing her working
schedule and catholic literary tastes. And she promises to help me
see her as often as she can.

There is indeed something more to her Anglophobia, which will
show itself through her devotion to 'Carmen-Suite'. But it is
essentially a reflection of her personality. Plisetskaya is ceaselessly
temperamentnaya – which, of course, is what makes her dancing
unique.

Maya Mikhailovna has invited me to watch her in class the following morning – a gracious gesture without hope of fulfilment. Not
she, not even the Bolshoi management, may issue me a pass for its
own stage door; warrant must come from the *proper authorities*.
My case is sent to the Ministry of Culture, giving me another
glimpse, from another aspect, of the edifice of Soviet bureaucracy –
which does not fail to include the Bolshoi.

While I wait, I find out what I can from friends about the life and
times of my subject. Although the facts are extraordinary, the full
story cannot now be told, for the reason that most interesting
personal stories in Russia cannot: they would provoke the wrath
and retribution of a government that insists on presenting its
people, in contrast to the misery of the capitalist West, as wholly
secure, orderly and *happy* under socialism. Plisetskaya herself has
done nothing 'wrong', but to write of certain actions perpetrated
on her would be considered slander. If and when an honest biography of her is written, it will win her great sympathy and affection. Even in outline the story is moving.

She was born in Moscow in November 1925, and quickly demonstrated her potential. 'Her gift for ballet was obvious when she was three years old,' an uncle reminisced. 'She was already copying roles – with difficult steps – she'd seen on stage. She'd seat the family on a sofa and run through entire scenes for them. Maya Mikhailovna was a performer as soon as she was able to hear music and move her limbs.'

In the context of Plisetskaya's family history, this is not quite as remarkable as it seems. The uncle I have quoted is Asaf Mikhailovich Messerer, the Bolshoi's leading male dancer in the early Soviet period. Dazzling virtuoso, matchless teacher (of Ulanova, Lepeshinskaya and Preobrazhenskaya among others), fertile and inspired choreographer, Asaf Mikhailovich has been called the father of Soviet ballet.

He was one of many Messerers who exerted an artistic influence on the child Maya. When she was taken to the ballet, it was often by – or to watch – Sulamif Messerer, her aunt and Asaf's sister. A leading Bolshoi soloist in the 1920s and 1930s, Sulamif now teaches in the celebrated Moscow Choreographic Academy, source of virtually all Bolshoi dancers. Asaf's wife, Irina Tikhomirnovna Messerer, also a pre-war Bolshoi soloist, is now director of a new Soviet company, the so-called 'Young Ballet', under the general supervision of Igor Moiseyev. Plisetskaya's mother, Ra Messerer, starred in the early silent Soviet cinema, and another brother was an illustrious actor of the Moscow Art Theatre. Another sister, Elizaveta, was a distinguished character actress in a neighbouring theatre.

The younger generation of Messerers are marginally less famous but no less theatrical. Plisetskaya's two younger brothers are both dancers: Alexander in minor solo roles at the Bolshoi, the better known Azari in Cuba, where he partners Alicia Alonso. Asaf's sons, too, Plisetskaya's cousins, are involved with ballet. Boris Messerer is a renowned theatrical designer who works for the Bolshoi and Leningrad's Kirov, among other theatres. An adopted son dances with the Bolshoi.

The sire of this remarkable all-star brood – Asaf's father and

Plisetskaya's grandfather – was Mikhail Borisovich Messerer, a Jewish dental surgeon of extraordinary intelligence and sensitivity. A highly erudite yet modest family man, he knew eight languages. It was his and his wife's love of music and theatre that stimulated and nourished their children's interest, although he himself did not participate directly in any of the arts.

Plisetskaya's father was also a man of considerable accomplishment and standing. An engineer by profession, Mikhail Plisetsky became the director of the vast Soviet coal-mining concession on the Norwegian island of Spitsbergen, where he also served as the Soviet Consul. Maya herself spent a year on Spitsbergen when she was seven; otherwise she grew up in the Moscow flat of grandfather Messerer, where she was born.

The Messerers' rooms resounded constantly with music, and Mayechka could not sit still in its presence. When she heard it in the street, she danced in the street, attracting her first crowds and applause. When she saw 'Little Red Riding Hood' at the age of four – with aunt Sulamif Messerer in the title role – she returned home exultant and danced all the parts, including the wolf and grandmother. 'Her sense of timing and stage presence was acute before most children actually recognize music as such,' explains Asaf.

Growing up among luminaries of Moscow theatre and dance, it seemed only natural to Maya that she would take her place on the stage. A headstrong, undisciplined child, her attention easily wandered. Only music and the stage held her interest. 'It was all much simpler than people like to imagine,' says Plisetskaya about her choice of career. 'The "secret" is that I always loved music and loved the dance. My family took me to concerts and the theatre and ballet. I saw my mother in films. All this dazzled me. Nothing else did. Somehow it was clear to everyone that Maya was going to dance.'

At the age of eight, Plisetskaya was accepted by the Moscow Choreographic Academy (known as the Bolshoi School), where it quickly became clear she was going to become not merely a dancer, but an outstanding ballerina. 'She attracted attention from the first day of school,' says Asaf Messerer. 'Beyond everything the

family and her background had given her, she had unique advantages for ballet. Extraordinary precision and grace of movement.
Superb musicality. And an artistic disposition: the Plisetskaya
creativity and temperament were there from the start. Among all
the other talent, she was an extremely promising pupil.'

Plisetskaya was so good so quickly that her teachers, of whom
Elizaveta Gerdt was the most important, started her on advanced
exercises well ahead of her class. This might also have been in the
hope of channelling her energy towards constructive activities. For
as she puts it – again proudly – she was a 'wild little hooligan'
during her school years. Still, her talent eclipsed everything else;
within two years, Plisetskaya was on stage, dancing important roles
in school performances.

This is the fairy-tale part of the story; the nightmare was soon
to follow. For Plisetskaya's early blossoming years in dancing
school were the years of Stalin's most murderous purges, from
which few families of the distinction of the Messerers and
Plisetskys escaped. Her father was shot in 1937, the bloodiest year.
Plisetskaya was eleven. She was not told; her father, her family
explained, had made another trip to Spitsbergen. Soon her mother
was arrested, to spend six months in jail with Plisetskaya's younger
brother Azari, a nursing infant. Plisetskaya did not see him again
for years. She herself was withdrawn from ballet school and cared
for largely by Sulamif. As usual when someone like Plisetskaya's
father was murdered – a man not only totally innocent, but also of
distinguished character and service – the family too was punished.

'Her mother rotted in jail because of her father,' said a family
friend. 'And her father? – he was destroyed for nothing.

'Plisetskaya adored him, of course. In 1956, her mother was told
it was all an unfortunate mistake, her husband had been suppressed
"without grounds", they were terribly sorry. They bestowed a
pension on her: fifty rubles a month. A pair of shoes.'

Needless to say, the tragedy is nowhere mentioned in any of the
numerous Soviet biographies of Plisetskaya, which offer her as an
example of the achievements of Soviet culture and Soviet rule.
Moreover, she herself categorically, even angrily, refuses to talk

about her father. For one thing, his fate obviously still pains her. For another, the authorities would consider it 'anti-Soviet' to discuss such matters with a foreigner. Fear of severe discipline, which might easily include interference with her career, restrains Plisetskaya from saying anything about her father.

Because of Plisetskaya's silence, I do not know the details of her re-admission to the Bolshoi School. But she did return, and in the late 1930s was attracting attention as the school's most promising pupil. The next interruption to her studies came with Russia's next national tragedy – more destructive than the purges, but with the comfort that the destroyer was foreign and therefore could be fought.

The Germans invaded in June 1941. As they struck quickly towards Moscow, many of the capital's cultural institutions were evacuated out of range. Together with half the Bolshoi School, the personnel of the Bolshoi Theatre were hurriedly dispatched to the Volga city of Kuibyshev. Released from prison, Ra Messerer took Maya and her two brothers a thousand miles east, to Sverdlovsk in the Urals. Maya remained there a year, after which she made her way back to Moscow alone. It was a feat of great enterprise, cunning and determination in the impossibly difficult travelling conditions of war-time Russia. Plisetskaya talks of the journey's last hurdle with mischievous sparkle.

In those days (and until well after the war), entrance to Moscow was closed except for citizens with military authorization – which sixteen-year-old Maya could not hope to obtain. Contemplating the heavily guarded, seemingly impassable check-point, she despaired. Then she spied a grizzled peasant, and her 'creative imagination', as she puts it, 'clicked for the first time in my life'. Sidling up to the man as if she were his daughter, she chatted gaily as the guards waved her through. 'No one asked anything,' she says, still delighted. 'No one dreamed a skinny little kid like that could have such cheek.'

It was, of course, in order to dance that Plisetskaya went to these lengths. 'It would have been torture to stay in Sverdlovsk and not work another year,' she says passionately. 'But don't try to make me a hero and all that bullshit. The truth is, Sverdlovsk was incredibly *boring*. Instead of theatre we had the great joy of all-night queues for bread. I needed some *life*.'

Once again she returned to the Bolshoi School, and, despite the missed year, was graduated with her original class in 1943. Then the war, as war perversely can, gave her career an early boost. Throughout the evacuation, a small contingent of the Bolshoi Company remained in Moscow and continued to perform in a less exposed, less expensive theatre. Together with the handful of graduates from the much depleted Bolshoi School, Plisetskaya was snatched up by the management to make a quick, highly successful debut. By the end of the war, at the age of nineteen, she had mastered a large repertoire of solo roles that otherwise would have been awarded her more slowly. She perfected her art as a soloist on the stage rather than in rehearsal studios, and in two years, rather than ten.

From the war's end, Plisetskaya's ascent to stardom is thoroughly documented by Soviet biographies: in the context of socialist cultural opportunities and under the supervision of the superb Bolshoi training system, role follows role and brilliant triumph succeeds dazzling achievement on the Bolshoi's stage, then in Eastern Europe and finally in the West. Again Plisetskaya's life reads like a fairy tale – but only in Soviet texts, for in fact the triumphs required much more than Plisetskaya's artistic gifts and her seething ambition to be at the top of her profession. To travel to the West, even to stay on the Bolshoi stage, demanded struggles with the cultural bureaucracy and resistance to – and compromise with – crude and fearsome political pressures. For all her outspokenness, Plisetskaya does no more than hint that a lack of 'Party-mindedness' in her behaviour and attitudes gravely threatened her career at several junctures. Her friends are willing to explain more, but the full story cannot now be told ...

A week passes while the Ministry of Culture decides whether I can accept Plisetskaya's invitation to watch her in class. During this time, she does not answer my telephone calls: a puzzling as well as upsetting frostiness, until it reaches me by a circuitous route that she has been instructed never to see me again under any circumstances. The order has been transmitted by a middle-level official of the very Novosti which had secured permission for my article after long negotiation through their London office, and, upon my arrival in Moscow, had assured me that everything was happily arranged. That Plisetskaya is not mistress of her own time and company is by now entirely plain; but Novosti's secret reversal is confusing. Are they angered by the fact that I have my own 'unauthorized' channel to Plisetskaya through mutual friends? Or has someone higher up only now been apprised of the project, and halted it to take the entire question yet again under review? In any case, Plisetskaya follows her orders, understandably unwilling to court trouble for the sake of a journalist she hardly knows.

Several days later, however, she herself telephones me, and I learn by the same circuitous route that the official who had ordered her not to see me has now given permission for her to go ahead.

Soon after this, authorization comes too to accept Plisetskaya's invitation. The final frustration is at the Bolshoi's stage door: despite a special trip there the day before to ensure all is in order, the guards have misplaced the Ministry's authorization and will admit no one without proper documents. But telephone calls are made and at last I am ushered to Plisetskaya's class. Today it is in a large overheated studio on an upper floor of the famous building.

The teacher is Asaf Messerer, a diminutive elderly gentleman in an imported ivory shirt with sleeve bands and a slightly soiled Italian tie. There are thirty dancers at the bar; twenty-nine men, the Bolshoi's leading soloists, and Maya Plisetskaya. She is wearing a striking black practice dress, cream mohair leggings and a full kit of make-up. When the after-bar drills begin, she takes her place stage centre, surrounded by handsome, virile and obviously heterosexual young men. After the round of exercises, she moves to an inch from the mirror and stares at herself, with the same penetration and lack of affectation as she stares at others. This dazzling narcissism, her total absorption with herself, goes beyond egotism to an honest levelling with herself – the perception of Plisetskaya as an object which is essential to her approach to art.

Plisetskaya alone in a men's class: more confirmation of her image? For although Moscow's haute intelligentsia wastes few words on the every-day trivia of love affairs, no one suggests that passionate, impetuous Plisetskaya is impervious to the appeal of what Russians call 'interesting' young men. From the first moment with her, one is aware that *she* is aware, always, of herself as a woman, a circumstance that enhances her Carmen-like attraction.

The attraction is innate and irrepressible, even here in class; a current of sexual awareness seems to flow to and from Plisetskaya and several of the twenty-nine splendid specimens. But as much as this may please her, it is to satisfy a stronger and rarer drive – her obsession with professional excellence – that she trains in this class rather than any other. Men's classes, she explains, demand far more sheer physical output and stamina than women's. Asaf Messerer's class in particular is known as the Bolshoi's most difficult as well as its best, an exhausting trial for a woman. Plisetskaya must strive for the highest possible level – and she arranges for other women to be excluded from the class so that its level is not lowered.

At the moment, she is training cautiously: she tore a ligament in an ankle two months ago and hasn't performed since. Even with this disability, however, her technique is incomparable; and during the course of a brilliantly controlled series of turns, one is struck by the banal but easily forgotten thought that whatever Plisetskaya's preferences in men, countries and perfumes, her virtuosity is her most outstanding characteristic, together with the intense energy, concentration and self-control required to sustain it. Between her *enchaînements*, she smiles and gossips with her dashing young men – it is hard not to think 'flirt'. But when her turn comes, she is taut again: a superb artist, extending herself to her limit, without which exertion and struggle she could not have become one of the two or three best in the world. Sweat pours from her face. She wipes it away with a pastel towel, smiles coquettishly, studies herself in the mirror, and runs through a pattern of leaps that few women anywhere, even Bolshoi primas, would care to attempt. Even when the exercise is less arduous, her hands are the focal point of the studio. Brash, quick, spritely, alive, original, uniquely expressive – they reveal everything about Plisetskaya and her impetuous art.

After class, the studio empties quickly except for the pianist and two or three dancers who want to continue on their own. Plisetskaya stays on for an extra hour, working independently and with Vladimir Vasiliyev, a leading soloist who is choreographing 'Icarus', his first ballet. Still pushing herself to her limit, Plisetskaya displays her own nimble choreographic creativeness while devising new patterns with her partner. When they leave, even young Greek-god Vasiliyev is exhausted.

The pianist collects her things: an enormously fat woman with white hair and a black moustache. She used to work at the Bolshoi School, where she has known Plisetskaya since her first year as an eight-year-old. In those thirty-six years, she says, she has never met anyone with greater musicality. 'Maya Mikhailovna *feels* music more – more deeply, more precisely, more *personally* – than any-one in the entire Bolshoi, including conductors and some composers. Music is in her bones. For this alone, she's a delight to work with. She teaches us all.'

Asaf Messerer's daily-except-Monday class serves as the only fixed hour in Plisetskaya's otherwise elastic day. 'I have no routine,' she says. 'I dread the *thought* of schedules. But missing a class would be inexcusable – a sign of dilettantism, of smart-aleck indifference. I want to be an artist. Which means whatever else I do with myself, there must be a time to study and think and *work*.'

Barring rehearsals, other members of the class attend regularly too. After my fourth or fifth visit, some of the male dancers recog-nized me in other parts of the building and were willing to talk about Plisetskaya's professional temperament.

I had assumed she might be difficult to work with. Moscow wags have it that Plisetskaya likes two things in Russia: ice-cream and ballet. To which the reply is: 'not ice-cream but vanilla, not ballet but Plisetskaya.' Moreover, stories are rife about her rivalry with Raiisa Struchkova, the Bolshoi's second 'elder' ballerina. Plisetskaya is known to hold her colleague's dancing and hoi polloi taste in contempt, which she expresses in devastating references, literal and symbolic, to Struchkova's low-slung 'Russian' rump. According to gossip, Struchkova tries to reply in kind, but falls frustratingly short of Plisetskaya's acid disparagement. The two are said to maintain a stream of spiteful comments through their costumiers, for they themselves can barely speak to one another. The wrangling between these primas, the Bolshoi's only two 'People's Artists of the U.S.S.R.', has elements of high comedy. But if it is true that Plisetskaya has a strong competitive streak – and that she chafed for years at being second to Galina Ulanova as the Bolshoi's leading prima – this apparently does not extend to dancers with whom she works in class and on stage. On the contrary, her professional disposition is admired only less than her talent.

Several members of the class took great pains to assure me they were sincere when they said Plisetskaya is always extremely friendly and co-operative. Young dancers appreciate her help; older ones her professionalism. 'I've known her fifteen years,' said a well-known soloist. 'She has never, not once, put on airs about being a star. On the contrary, she tries to cover that up. She's probably the easiest person in the company to work with. A tower of strength, a constant source of help, a pleasure in every way. In short, a "regular guy".'

Not least of Plisetskaya's respected qualities is her legendary frankness. 'She herself likes to boast that she always tells the truth,' said another well-known soloist. 'She'll quote you a (Bolshoi) school saying: "If you want to know the truth about yourself, ask Maya." Usually, of course, the kind of person who talks that way about himself is in fact a calculating hypocrite. But not in Maya Mikhailovna's case. She can be impulsive. She can talk too much and too loudly – about herself as well as others. But she can't be phoney: she doesn't know how.'

*

On a late-February weekday, Plisetskaya finishes class shortly after noon and is driven across town to Public School No. 397. She is wearing a dark fur coat and hat with a lavender knitted scarf and matching mittens; in Moscow, an exciting and extremely luxurious outfit. Public School No. 397 is an ordinary, decaying primary school with an enterprising young music teacher who enjoys treating his children to personal appearances by cultural celebrities. By pursuing Plisetskaya for months, he has got her to attend a showing of a documentary film entitled 'Maya Plisetskaya' and to answer questions from the pupils. Plisetskaya, who dislikes speaking, has agreed to do this, and nothing more.

'But surely you'll give the children a little talk,' chides the school's matronly head-mistress upon meeting Plisetskaya in her office.

'Speeches aren't my profession, I'm afraid. I'll answer questions, as I promised, but sorry – no presentation.'

'Just a brief talk. Surely ... '

Plisetskaya instantly darkens, pivots on her heel and quits the room. 'I can't stand arguments,' she mutters. 'I *hate* people trying to pressure me ... ' Faced with her temper, the head-mistress quickly agrees that the ballerina will limit herself, as agreed, to answering questions.

The questions are childishly-charmingly straightforward, and Plisetskaya answers without any trace of condescension. The exchange takes place in the school auditorium, where an immense plaster statue of Lenin and a red banner above the stage – THE PRESENT GENERATION OF SOVIET PEOPLE WILL LIVE UNDER COMMUNISM! – stand out against a background of peeling green walls.

A LITTLE BOY. Why did you become a ballerina?
PLISETSKAYA. When I was a little girl, I always loved to dance. I danced whenever I could. It started like that.
LITTLE GIRL. Who's the greatest ballerina in the world?
PLISETSKAYA. Living or dead?
LITTLE GIRL. Living. I mean dancing.

PLISETSKAYA. I've seen two great ballerinas in my life. Neither is still dancing. No one dancing now seems to me great.

SECOND LITTLE GIRL. What would you have done if you hadn't become a ballerina?

PLISETSKAYA. I don't know exactly. Perhaps tried to become an actress.

OLDER BOY. What are your favourite countries?

PLISETSKAYA. All countries are great and beautiful in one way or another. My personal favourites are America and France. (*Pause.*) And Finland and Japan.

OLDER GIRL. What's your favourite role?

PLISETSKAYA. Carmen.

A TEACHER. After 'Carmen-Suite', what will be the future development of our ballet – in which style and direction?

PLISETSKAYA. I can't answer that. Ask the ballet-masters and choreographers. Unfortunately, dancers don't dance what they want, but what they're given. What they're told.

LITTLE GIRL. If you had another life, would you become a ballerina again?

PLISETSKAYA. YES!

How candid are Plisetskaya's answers – even, under the circumstances, somewhat curt. And how strange the ring in this auditorium – and society – of 'America' named a favourite country, without an instant's hesitation, a word of qualification or apology, even a ritualistic mention of the 'brotherly socialist camp'. Several teachers exchange quick glances.

The film, made in 1964, is primarily a collage of dramatic moments from Plisetskaya's Bolshoi performances – a bad print worsened by the school's sputtering projector and faded screen. But Plisetskaya, who has seen the movie a hundred times with better equipment, watches with rapt attention. And is irked when I, busy taking notes, fail to give the flickering images equal attention.

'Stop scribbling and *watch*,' she orders in an acid whisper loud enough to divert half the auditorium.

What disturbs her more, however, is a slight lag in the sound synchronization. None of the teachers, let alone the school-children, notice the split-second discrepancy, but it drives Plisetskaya to distraction. 'Good God, I'm not dancing to the music – *not to the music,*' she moans, and insists the lights go on and the operator re-wind the film. Even in this shabby school auditorium, even on an old film, the 'failure' in her musicality causes her to tremble with anger.

There is a danger of misinterpreting Plisetskaya's absorption with herself. Perhaps vanity plays a part in it, but a smaller one than a tyrannical professional superego: Plisetskaya must be perfect. And, as her coaches agree, the standards of perfection are her own, for she has long been her own best teacher. In this, she is served by qualities almost as important as her hands and limbs: a talent for self-instruction and a critical eye which turns ruthless when focused on herself.

'I'm my own best critic, meaning my harshest, because I see my own shortcomings better than anyone else. The point is, I'm not in love with myself. Which means I'm able to learn. And what I learn comes from inside *me*, not from class or teachers. I've always judged Plisetskaya from a distance – and believe me, I see her faults.'

The self-satisfaction ring of this pronouncement is belied by the set of her face as she watches the film. Every minute and movement of her own performances, even performances of a decade ago, are studied with a cold detachment – more: with a grim determination not to be fooled. Plisetskaya loves Plisetskaya? Perhaps – but only when Plisetskaya is beyond reproach.

She studies the old collage with especial interest, for film plays a critical role in her system of self-training. For almost a quarter of a century, she has danced at the Bolshoi's gala performances for Kremlin leaders and visiting heads of state. The two minutes of these performances which are *de rigueur* in Soviet newsreels have provided her with a unique chance of realizing the dream of all serious dancers: the opportunity to study and learn from action pictures of herself. But not only the two minutes. Plisetskaya usually manages to acquire the rushes – and, because the regular cameraman for the state occasions is a good friend, she even arranges for extra reels to be shot for her personal use. The teacher-critic is also a shrewd operator and consummate fixer.

Class convenes regularly at eleven or noon. Plisetskaya stretches diligently, sweats profusely, and by the end of the hour, when many dancers have left, has begun to improvise her spectacular *pas*. Asaf Messerer watches calmly, never raising his voice, never even criticizing directly. He is a gracious, gentle man whose authority is based on affection and respect.

Of Plisetskaya, he says she is unique primarily because she is indefatigably creative. 'Her physical gifts are phenomenal, of course. Her range of steps and movements is unparalleled. She learns new steps in half the time other dancers need. And there is that perfect musicality. But attitude is what really makes her: her singular approach to art.

'She takes a role she already performs brilliantly and rehearses it like a beginner. Because she's always searching for something new, the one little tilt of the head that says something deeper or more expressive. No two performances are ever the same – always new touches, new lines, new inflections. She's never satisfied with herself. I've never known anyone who makes quite her demands on herself, or with her creativity in re-interpreting old roles. Which, of course, is the living art of ballet.

'And something else: the depth of her characterizations. She thinks about her roles. First *feels*, then thinks. Her virtuosity is matched by a dramatic, emotional revelation on stage. She is a very serious person about her art.'

She was married in 1958 (at the age of thirty-three) to Rodion Shchedrin, a successful young composer who, in addition to his creative work, is saddled with administrative duties in the Composers' Union. Both belonged to the small circle of Moscow's

musical elite and had lived together for years before marriage.
Mutual interests, attitudes and friends still bind them firmly.

'I adore Robik. How could I not? He's an immense source of
support. He's steady as a rock – sensible, unlike me. He dedicates
all his music to me, beautiful things like "The Little Humpbacked
Horse". And of course he did "Carmen-Suite" for me. My
"Carmen-Suite", the best thing that's happened in my life.'

It is a rare day that Plisetskaya does not erupt in exaltation of
'Carmen-Suite', her child, her passion, her obsession. She will suffer
no criticism of it, by friends any more than loyal, admiring foreign
critics. If you are unimpressed by the gaudy spectacle, say acquaintances, break the rule of candour and keep your reservations to
yourself.

'You can tell Maya anything in the world,' said a girl-friend who
shares some secrets of her amatory life with her. 'You can tell her
that a certain young admirer doesn't admire her as much as he
should. But if you say that you don't care for "Carmen-Suite",
even if you hint that you're less than enthusiastic, you can forget
about your friendship with her. She's nuts about the subject.'

How to account for Plisetskaya's intolerance – and, as many of
her fondest fans feel, the lapse of taste? It is a reflection of her ego
and obstinacy, of course, and perhaps of the limitations of her
aesthetic standards. But there is a story to Plisetskaya and 'Carmen-
Suite', and the parts of it which may be discussed provide some
insight not only into her character but also into the ordinary
closed question of political controls of Soviet art.

The story is complex, but to simplify it would be to distort the
interplay of politics and personality in this 'case study' of artistic
ambition versus state interdiction. First, there is the family-affair
aspect of the long controversy. Rodion Shchedrin adapted the
'Carmen-Suite' music from the opera; the choreography is Alberto
Alonso's – the brother-in-law of Alicia, who is partnered in Cuba
by Azari Plisetsky, Plisetskaya's youngest brother. The result was a
'modern' work with a score suitable for a Technicolor film, and –
the nub of the controversy – a slight but distinct departure from
classical ballet movements. The ardent Carmen, after all, could

hardly float like an ethereal Giselle. The première at the Bolshoi in April 1967, with Plisetskaya dancing the title role, was the consummation of a fervent dream: she believed that off stage as well as on it, her personality uniquely reflected the tempestuous Carmen's. Moreover, it was, and still is, the only ballet written specifically for her.* It is said that she waited for the honour for some twenty years, increasingly hurt that the predominance of Ulanova and her Bolshoi champions kept her in the shadows.

Although Soviet newspapers rarely highlight artists' personal predilections, Plisetskaya's intolerance of the faintest criticism of 'Carmen-Suite' found its way into an *Izvestiya* interview. 'You can accuse me of bias,' she was quoted, 'but the fact that I'm personally involved with this ballet is irrelevant. Quite aside from this "biographical detail", I developed an aversion to people who didn't like "Carmen" or didn't understand Alberto Alonso's achievement. In this rejection of "Carmen", I see a failure of taste – the expression of a conservative, severely limited conception of art. I'm so convinced of the talent and creative originality of this work that no force on earth can change my mind.'

If anything, Plisetskaya has become more uncompromising since that interview. With me, she discussed the subject in hisses, as if I were 'Carmen's' sworn enemy. 'It's the only ballet ever written for me in my whole life. Which *means* something to a person, doesn't it? Besides, I've dreamt of that Carmen, I adore that Carmen more than any heroine I've danced – more than any I've seen. Because she's my kind of woman – Carmen is *me*.'

Or what Plisetskaya longs to be. More than the factory girl's hot blood moves the prima ballerina; the deeper attractions are the spirit of freedom and independence that the character personifies. As the 'Carmen-Suite' affair itself would reveal, Plisetskaya feels close to Carmen because the latter has the courage, and takes the risks, to break traditions and defy prohibitions.

Plisetskaya had never been fond of England, but it was the cool reaction of leading London critics to 'Carmen-Suite' that crowned

---

* Alicia Alonso is the only other major Carmen, and Plisetskaya's dislike for her has intensified her jealous fixation on the ballet.

her contempt for the English as a 'soulless' people who love only the tasteless and the dead. 'Those little fools. I don't care about my dancing – but they didn't even appreciate *the music*. Frigid English know-nothings. Maybe I should feel sorry for them – but as Pushkin said, ignorance is a sad excuse. And, incidentally, Shchedrin did a fantastic job adapting "Carmen-Suite". His being my husband is not going to keep me from recognizing the truth.'

But this is only the surface of the story. Political factors about which she hinted to *Izvestiya* ('a conservative, severely limited conception of art') also play a part in her fixation.

Plisetskaya's work on new roles is regarded with a certain awe, even by fellow soloists. Every movement is subject to experiments in a dozen variants; every choreographer and ballet-master knows her as an active participant in the creative process, giving as much as she takes in imagination and the secrets of characterization. But her labours on Carmen confounded even close colleagues: night after night, scene after scene, she re-thought and re-touched Carmen's every gesture, working herself and others to exhaustion. She was motivated not only by her image of herself as the passionate Carmen, nor by an extreme manifestation of her usual perfectionism. Above all, she had vowed to herself that she, single-handedly if necessary, would put the ballet on to the stage. At various junctures, powerful opposition seemed to doom the project.

The condemnation came from the proprietors of Soviet culture: high Party officials displeased by the ballet's faintly modernist flavour and angered by Carmen's 'wanton behaviour'. Come-hither pelvic gestures and front kicks held to the forehead, suggestions of smouldering emotion and Latin sexual appetites ... these new movements, danced with Plisetskaya's usual technical brilliance, made Carmen a believable *woman* – and stiffened opposition to the very idea of such a ballet, as well as an urge to slap Plisetskaya back into line.

In Soviet doctrine and practice, an inviolable conviction that all artistic creation must serve the Party's political ends is combined with an unshakeable Philistine conservatism; and although not five seconds of a scene may appear on any stage in the country without

Party approval, the Bolshoi's role as the showplace of Soviet arts makes it especially sacrosanct. Plisetskaya's 'challenge' was taken seriously, bringing threats not only to 'Carmen-Suite' but to her very career. Pressure on her to abandon the project took many forms, including personal abuse. She was summoned to Ministry offices, where Party officials accused her of plotting 'the subversion of Soviet ballet and its traditions of Russian classicism'. Her motives in campaigning for such disgusting decadence were questioned, and one powerful cultural official accused her of 'trying to make a whore out of a Spanish national heroine'. Another said ominously that Plisetskaya's motives had to be judged in terms of her attempt to 'put a whore on the stage of our national treasure, the Bolshoi – the platform from which Lenin addressed our people'.

In this context, the ballet's significance to Plisetskaya is more understandable. She was fighting not only her own battle, but that of all Bolshoi liberals. Suffocating in the stultifying atmosphere of political orthodoxy, many of the Bolshoi's more worldly dancers are gasping for a breath of fresh creative air. Above all, they long for new works in a repertoire of weary classics. To them as well as Plisetskaya, 'Carmen-Suite' represented a crack in the deadening mould of reaction and ideological purity, and carried with it, therefore, all the pent-up hopes of a crusade. Fellow dancers say that only Plisetskaya's reputation, fierce determination and arrogance made the ballet's production at all possible.

Beyond hinting at her craving for something new, Plisetskaya herself will make no comment about this to a foreign journalist. 'Art lives on contrasts,' she says. 'Unless new forms are found, the old ones will stagnate and die.' A leading male dancer in Asaf Messerer's class was less guarded. 'When she did Carmen,' he said bitterly, 'she was accused at the top of being a wrecker who wanted to destroy everything great in Soviet ballet. Of course the opposite is true: the Bolshoi is five minutes short of becoming a museum, and can only be revived by new forms. Maya Mikhailovna understands this perfectly. If she had her way with new ballets, we might become a living company again. I'm not crazy about "Carmen" – nor about Maya herself, except for the way she says what's on her mind. But how she worked on that role! What abuse she took from men whose only interest in ballet is clubbing down "deviationists" together with everybody else. No outsider can fully understand what she was fighting against. What we have to live with every day – to listen to, to bow to.'

'Carmen-Suite' illuminates many aspects of Plisetskaya's character. Her strong attraction to contemporary design, even if brash and in questionable taste. Her love of America, the country to which she not only feels temperamentally attuned, but which offers the exhilaration of unfettered artistic creation (and the country of her 'discovery', for it was not until she captivated New York on her first appearance there in 1959 that she emerged from Ulanova's shadow as an international star). Her restlessness, ambition and what a New York critic called 'fire and ardour', not contrived for her stage performances, but tapped from inner, sometimes painful turbulence. And, above all, the political pressures extraneous to her notion of art, which she must strive against every day, or succumb to.

The aesthetic tragedy of Plisetskaya and 'Carmen-Suite' is that Soviet cultural dogma has made her blindly devoted to a cause that is admirable in Russia, but lacks substance abroad. What is avant-garde choreography and daring dancing in Moscow is outdated by decades, and therefore faintly trite, in the West. Western critics cannot understand her fanatic enthusiasm for what is often more imaginatively done on Broadway, nor comprehend how tirelessly defiant she has been to produce this slightly stale and stilted adaptation. Plisetskaya has fought too hard to understand that only these considerations make 'Carmen-Suite' an achievement.

On Saturday February 28th, Plisetskaya prepares to perform for the first time in almost three months: 'The Dying Swan' is to be presented as part of a matinée review at the Palace of Congresses. The brief performance will not tax her still-weak ankle inordinately. Soon after her usual morning class with Asaf Messerer, she is showered, dressed, made-up (heavily), scented (pungently) and ready for the quarter-mile trip from the theatre to the palace.

Riding in the government car assigned to the theatre, her conversation with the driver is unforced and unpatronizing: an exchange of equals that reflects the instinctive Russian democracy frequently encountered at a personal level. But when the car has been waved into the Kremlin by armed policemen and towards the palace by armed soldiers, the guards at the gate demand Plisetskaya's pass. They recognize her, of course, but will not admit her to her own performance without the necessary *dokument*: an example of the instinctive Russian rigidity in all things official.

The matinée review is by a section of Bolshoi singers and dancers: a timeworn aria here, a *pas de deux* there – ninety minutes of cultural music hall. Of the six thousand spectators, nine-tenths are visiting Moscow from their native villages and provincial towns. Plisetskaya warms up for her number in a backstage corridor, unattended and unexcited: she has danced 'The Dying Swan' literally hundreds of times, and the longing of most Bolshoi stars to *try something new* seems stamped on her face. She stretches her limbs carefully and unobtrusively in a corner, watched only by a shy, Adonis-like Bolshoi dancer named Mikhail Tsibin. At twenty, Tsibin is already so promising in minor solo roles that Asaf Messerer smiles at the sight of him in class. He has come to watch Maya Mikhailovna today because they are good friends, and he is concerned about her ankle. Over the past months she has given the young dancer special help in class and he has painted her in oils – an engaging mutual affection.

As starched aria follows pasty duet on the stage, the huge provincial audience grows perceptibly listless. Then Plisetskaya is announced: ' ... danced', exclaims the compère, 'by People's Artist of the U.S.S.R., Lenin Prize Laureate, MAYA PLISETSKAYA!' The vast hall resounds to a stadium-like cheer. The spotlight finds Plisetskaya, and as she dances the often hackneyed 'Dying Swan' the restless, coughing audience falls silent. Despite her weariness with the old *divertissement*, even for this provincial matinée audience Plisetskaya produces an emotionally profound performance. The worldly-wise woman's occasional cynicism never shows on stage. When the curtain falls, there is a deafening uproar, laced with bravos. Plisetskaya reappears for nine curtain calls, working carefully on each deep curtsey.

'Do you understand now?' she says, striding to her dressing-room. 'It's not a question of whether I personally like "The Dying Swan". I dance for *them*, not myself; to give *them* aesthetic pleasure. Of course I like ballet, but I could live without it, *I* get no dazzling joy from it. But the public expects something from me, and I have no right to let them down.'

Later, she returns to this point more than once. 'I like to think factually. And why be coy? the fact is that six thousand people came today, paid their good money, to see *me*. It's a very real, very serious responsibility. This is what makes me work. I'm lazy by nature. Unbelievably, phenomenally lazy. I could easily lie in bed all morning. But how can I forget that *people expect something beautiful* from me?'

The adoration for her is indeed rare – and surprising, in view of her personality. One would expect the less intellectual, less subtle Struchkova to be more popular. But Plisetskaya is the favourite of the masses.

She will soon be forty-five. Asaf Messerer says he notices no significant diminution of her physical powers; her superb technique is still near its peak and may remain there for years, providing she maintains her devotional attitude towards training. But others in Moscow wonder how long she will continue to dance, and the question obviously suggests itself to Plisetskaya herself. 'I want to dance,' she declares in a hard whisper. 'It is my life. I want to keep travelling abroad. If I don't dance, I don't travel. The thought of being cut off again ... ' At this point in a career, a torn ligament is not trivial, and Plisetskaya's obviously concerns her.

And when the career has ended? Plisetskaya has not thought carefully about this, but suspects she may try theatre. Acting, after all, is not the least of her talents as a ballerina, and the stage is in the family's blood; if she had not gone to ballet school as a child, she would almost certainly have studied drama. Even after her graduation from the Bolshoi School, the director of a highly respected theatre offered her a job, and she weighed her choice carefully before selecting the ballet. Later she was coached by the great actor and director Evgeny Vakhtangov (Stanislavsky's outstanding pupil), which helps account for the unusual expressiveness of her dancing. Not long ago, she began rehearsing a part in a well-known Moscow theatre, but the constant interruptions for ballet performances and tours convinced her that a dual career was not feasible.

There are signs that when she does stop dancing, she could have a successful dramatic career. In the late 1960s she played the difficult role of Princess Betsy in a Soviet screen version of *Anna Karenina*. Although the film itself was a failure, a string of flashy camera effects underscoring hollow direction and buffoonish over-acting, Plisetskaya outshone all the famous professional actors. Even *Pravda* waxed enthusiastic over her performance. The film was directed by Alexander Zarkhy, who, it is well known, rarely makes a casting decision without his wife's approval.

'I need a special kind of woman for Betsy,' he told her one evening. 'Not a round Russian woman, but a tall elegant woman. A woman with a neck. Like Maya.'

'Why *like* Maya? You chump, why can't you ever think big? Why not Maya herself?'

He telephoned Plisetskaya that very evening, and she passed her screen test the following morning. On the day after, however, she left for a three-month tour of America, returning to Moscow only when the film was well advanced. From the boat to the ball, as the Russians say: on the following afternoon, she was rushed to location for the shooting of the famous scene at the races. Someone handed her a card with her lines. She had five minutes to read them, no time to rehearse. Rehearsal turned out to be unnecessary, however, as did repeats of the shooting. Professional actors on the set were stunned at Plisetskaya's flawless handling of the very first take.

When the film was released, Plisetskaya gave an interview to

Screen magazine, responding irreverently to the interviewer's solemn questions. 'Ballet is work,' she said. 'Making movies is fun.' The Soviet cinema world was appropriately scandalized, to Plisetskaya's pleasure. Nevertheless, she was offered a small role, requiring singing and dancing, in *Tchaikovsky*, the joint Soviet-American film produced by Hollywood's Dmitry Tiomkin. She accepted it, and will happily consider future film offers.

She is difficult to interview, even as Russians go; the very notion of someone gathering information about her life is alien to her. (Even *Izvestiya*, which like other Soviet newspapers takes scant interest in celebrities' private lives, complained of her dislike of the press. 'My business is dancing,' she told *Izvestiya*, which grumbled that a meeting with her could not be called an interview, 'so capriciously does she change the theme, subject and sometimes whole meaning of the conversation.') On the other hand, she is unaccustomed to keeping her opinions to herself. After a week with her, topics with political overtones are still strictly taboo, but she begins to talk freely about some of her interests, habits and idiosyncrasies.

On sleep: 'I've taken sleeping pills every night for the past thirteen years. Because I've never slept through an entire night, not once in my life – and won't until I die ... The one night I actually slept tolerably was in 1964, on a train from Rome to Vienna. Otherwise sleep and I just don't mix. Sleeping pills – I'm killing myself with them.'

In time, several explanations for her insomnia emerge: she's never been able to find a comfortable mattress or pillow; for twenty years, from the age of twelve, she lived in a flat directly overlooking the Bolshoi's freight entrance and was kept awake by the all-night clangour of crews dismantling and delivering sets ... The obvious cause goes unmentioned: her relentless surges of nervous energy.

On babies: 'As a ballerina, I don't have the right to have a baby. A baby's never improved anyone's figure. Of course, my mother's disappointed; she can't have grandchildren at all because both my brothers married ballerinas too. So no babies – but there are nice compensations ... '

On Asaf, Ra and other Messerers: 'I take Asaf Mikhailovich's class simply because it's by far the best. He seems to be very casual and have no strict system. But in fact all his exercises are carefully and creatively planned to produce a tight, extremely logical and artistically meaningful pattern. The purpose is to exercise each group of muscles, with all their special needs, in a definite progression. This is very rare: most teachers preside over a random collection of exercises, lacking continuity and inner purpose. Asaf Mikhailovich's class is different every day, but each one is a perfectly engineered *unit*, from first exercise to last.

'The value of this approach is most apparent after an interruption – after illness or a holiday, when it's hard to get started again. Asaf Mikhailovich's system not only prevents sprains; it's also marvellous therapy. Dancers go to his class after an interruption to "take the cure". Only someone who's danced for years can appreciate his extraordinary virtues as a teacher. And he's always a choreographer at heart, so the classes are also aesthetically satisfying. Everyone's sorry they only last an hour.'

Maya Mikhailovna and Asaf Mikhailovich have a quietly affectionate relationship, but do not take pains to spend free time together. For although the entire Messerer family is on close terms, they see each other often enough at concerts and other cultural events not to bother with family reunions.

Plisetskaya's immediate family is another matter, however. Alexander, her well-dressed dancer brother (the one who has remained in Moscow), sees her every day, either in the Bolshoi or her flat. And she is as close to her mother, who lives between Plisetskaya's flat and the theatre. 'Mama adores me, of course, like any mother. She hardly misses a single showing of a film I'm in, or a performance. She's a hero, that woman. Among other things, for putting up with me as a kid.'

On Plisetskaya as a child: 'I was an outrageous *hooliganka*. Always, from the very beginning. That was one reason I went to [the Bolshoi] school so early. I was brought there at eight: the director said

I had possibilities but was too small, I should come back next year. Then Auntie Sulamif said they couldn't cope with me any more at home and begged them to take me off their hands. It wasn't automatic: the examiners saw I didn't have perfect physical qualities for ballet. Then I did a curtsey, a deep one, and with such flair, such movement of the arms, that they decided to take me immediately.'

Bolshoi School pupils are taught the normal school curriculum in addition to ballet. Excellent at history and at Russian, a difficult language for children to write without mistakes, Plisetskaya found chemistry and physics 'Greek to me – I didn't even understand what they wanted. Anyway, I never opened a single text-book.'

In ballet classes, she continued to be the 'wild one'. 'I loved to dance but hated class, despised the discipline and repetition. I used to mock the exercises: make faces, screw up my arms into impossible positions, anything to gall the teacher. Even when another pupil misbehaved, I always took the blame on myself. I was constantly being kicked out of class – and loved it. Why? I don't know. Because unless I created the excitement, life was too *dull*.'

On what she believes in: 'Nothing. Talent. I believe in *taste*.'

On what she admires in people: 'I've always loved kindness and warmth in people, and always hated "good" types. If a person's consciously – meaning self-consciously – "good", he's usually unendurable. What I seek out, on the other hand, is hard to define; my friends are all different kinds, I admire many different qualities in people. But I've always been, always will be, attracted to talent. In all its manifestations; I respect and adore it.'

On the old and the new in ballet: 'I love the classics, always have, and always will. Not long ago a hack critic – English, of course – wrote that it was time to bury the old bird "The Dying Swan". I can only answer with the old Russian saying: "There are no old jokes, only old people." If a work of art is great, it will always be great. If it becomes obsolete, it wasn't great. Works of genuine genius – Rembrandt, for example – never grow old.

'I know far from everything about the ballet. But I believe that "Swan Lake" and "Giselle" will be performed for many, many more years. It's the performance that must be new; each Giselle must add something – do something *alive*. In other words, if the performers are creative, the ballets will endure. Dancers must remember: it may be stale for them, but not for an audience that's seeing the ballet for the first time.

'So the classics will live and I'll continue to love them. But having said this, I can't pretend I want to dance *only* classics. I want something new in art, as in life. *Something new*. I've always loved contrast; life dies without it ... '

On climate and travel: 'I hate the cold. Moscow winters kill me; I'll never get used to them. I'd love to spend a winter some year in Italy or California. Why don't I just go? I can't just leave the Soviet Union for a holiday, can't set foot outside the country except when I'm on tour – the tours that the Ministry want me to take; otherwise I'm "advised" to reject this or that foreign offer. I never even hear of some, because my mail, of course, is carefully censored ... I have as much chance of taking a holiday in Italy on my own as flying to Mars on a broom.'

On women's liberation: 'The question bores me, I don't like to waste time discussing nonsense. If a woman has something to offer – *and is willing to work* – she'll achieve what she deserves. Some women who have nothing start hating themselves and join one of those screaming "movements".'

On how she spends evenings: 'You know, I never know what to answer when people ask me that. There is absolutely no schedule. We go to an occasional play or concert, but rarely entertain and rarely visit friends. Because time is precious; we don't want to waste it rushing here or there, or on a horde of guests.'

At home, she plays patience with a miniature pack of cards and works at her hobby, the collection of a scrapbook of curious and absurd names. She finds most of them in newspapers, especially among the columns of people seeking divorces. The names are indeed amusing, and sometimes, as Russian names can be, implausibly rude: there are Messrs 'Nosedroppings', 'Corpse', 'Bitch', 'Threestomach', 'Broadchaser', 'Fart' and others that Plisetskaya feels would be better not mentioned abroad. 'Crazy, isn't it? I just can't get over people with these ridiculous names.'

On her attitudes towards work and creativity: 'All my life, I hated to study and train – I just wanted to *dance*. I hated the routine of the same exercises to the same music every day for forty years. Only recently have I begun to get satisfaction from training. I've just now learned to appreciate its needs and inner meaning – the value of training as such, and its creativity. Certain older ballerinas have helped pass this attitude on to me.

'Still, I don't work very hard, you know. Not in comparison to other dancers. I concentrate hard, but spend much less time training than most Bolshoi soloists. I have a different approach: for me, the critical aspects of art still come from inside. Art is an expression of feeling, not a demonstration of having worked hard to master something difficult.

'Some people believe that success in art depends ten per cent on talent and the rest on work. I've never seen it that way.'

On the essence of herself: 'I'm totally normal. Ordinary in every way. Don't bother looking for something unusual in me.'

There is also the matter of money. It cannot be avoided, any more than it could in a story about a Rockefeller, and in Soviet terms, Plisetskaya and Shchedrin are that rich.

The most conspicuous evidence of their wealth is the ownership of two cars, a stunning extravagance for private citizens in a country where few doctors and lawyers, say, entertain serious hopes of buying even one. Moreover, the Plisetskaya-Shchedrin machines are both imported (with a two hundred per cent duty) and one, a new Citroen, is driven by their own chauffeur. (Plisetskaya herself is wary of driving: on the road, she says, her excitability frightens even her.) The other car is a Land Rover, one of two in private Soviet hands, which is used primarily to negotiate the rutted, muddy roads leading to her country cottage. The delightful dacha is located some thirty miles north-east of Moscow in a beautiful, unspoiled tract reserved for artistic celebrities. The routine of class six days a week makes Plisetskaya's trips there infrequent, but she loves the clean air and legendary soul-cleansing powers of the Russian countryside.

In Moscow, she lives in a comfortable flat in Gorky Street, the capital's grandest avenue. Together with her furs and imported dresses, these quarters put her among the handful of wealthy Soviet citizens. But she should not be imagined to be rich in Western terms, any more than Gorky Street should be imagined as being like Fifth Avenue. The tiny top circle of moneyed Russians are no better off – at least live in no grander style – than tens of millions of middle-class Westerners.

Indeed, in Western terms Plisetskaya's rewards have been both meagre and slow. In the mid-1950s, for example (when she already bore the title 'Honoured Artist of the Russian Republic'), she was living with her mother in one room of a communal apartment in which twenty-two people shared kitchen and bath. When she married in 1958 (as a 'People's Artist of the Russian Republic') she was assigned a three-room flat in a modern building. Her days of relative luxury began, in fact, with her marriage, but it was not until 1963 – when she had long been a 'People's Artist of the Soviet Union', the highest title, and had won immense international acclaim on foreign tours – that she and her husband, whose income is also considerable, were able to buy their present co-operative flat.

Plisetskaya's ruble income is now handsome indeed. Her basic salary is the equal of a high government official's, and, as a People's Artist, is supplemented by a system of bonuses for every perform-ance over four each month. Her average monthly earnings equal those of six or more highly skilled engineers – but not much more than, say, an American college professor's. It is their opportunity to earn not rubles but foreign currency that makes a small clique of Russian writers and performers fantastically rich by their own country's standards. But these earnings too are a fraction of their counterparts' in Europe and America. What reduces this part of their income is not the Russian standard of living in general or the ruble's minuscule purchasing power, but confiscatory government policy.

Although the Soviet booking agency, StateConcert, demands standard fees for the Bolshoi's Western appearances, it pays Plisetskaya no more than fifty per cent, and often as little as ten per cent, of what similar artists would command for similar work. I did not determine the precise percentage on any specific tour, for although Plisetskaya talks about money with her usual candour – no qualms about asking the price of this or announcing what she paid for that – she declined even to hear out a question about her foreign earnings. Once again, this was a reluctance to involve herself in delicate political subjects: as in the case of her own family history, she is not free to comment on the state's disposal of her earnings.

Despite Plisetskaya's silence, however, it is known, if never mentioned in print, that when the Bolshoi is on tour in America members of the corps de ballet are paid five dollars per performance* – substantially less than the Metropolitan's cleaning ladies employed for those four-odd hours. Leading soloists can earn four or five times as much, and it is said that Plisetskaya commands double the fee of the next highest dancer – but still under one hundred dollars a performance. Since Margot Fonteyn's fee is roughly $2,500 per performance, StateConcert's profit on Plisetskaya can be imagined: not the ten per cent agent's commission usual in the West, but over ninety-five per cent.

Plisetskaya's case is not unusual: StateConcert pays Sviatislav Richter, for example, roughly two hundred dollars from the fee it demands for his foreign appearances. Certainly no Western performer would tolerate this exploitation, but Soviet artists have no choice; eager to travel, they humbly accept the conditions. 'Plisetskaya herself would go on tour for nothing,' whispered a Bolshoi colleague. 'She loves the things money can buy as much as anybody, maybe more than most, but she'd *pay* the rotten State-Concert to go West. Because if – or *when* – they stop her travelling

* This is in addition to their hotel room and one meal a day – a huge one, when the company is touring under contract to the Hurok Agency. While touring abroad Bolshoi personnel continue to receive their ruble salaries in Moscow, but this too is astonishingly low in most cases: new members of the corps receive some 120 rubles a month, just above a bare minimum urban wage.

abroad, she's going to tear out that famous mop of hair.'

On a snowy Friday evening, a new film is premièred to a large, august audience in Moscow's most prestigious cinema. It is a wide-screen, gorgeously coloured stereophonic spectacle called 'Ballerina', the latest and most imaginative of eight attempts over eighteen years to transpose Plisetskaya's virtuosity to the screen. Together with the director, producers and cameramen, Plisetskaya mounts the large theatre's platform in a stagy black dress for the pre-screening ceremonies. 'I hate giving speeches,' she says ironically when summoned to the microphone, 'but in the ancient tradition of saying those "few words" at film premières ... I hope you'll like this picture: it's very important to me for reasons you'll see.'

When she makes for her seat amidst the public, the heady fragrance of Bandit precedes her by a dozen rows, subduing even the heavy odours of Russian cinema audiences in winter. 'Maya, over *here*,' calls Rodion Shchedrin from many yards away, and she pushes unceremoniously through the aisle to join her husband. Like many Russian celebrities, she is unselfconscious and unaffected in public, and she engages throughout the running of the film in a noisy discussion of his music and her dancing.

I have already seen 'Ballerina' at a special preview for film personnel, but Plisetskaya virtually ordered me to see it again this evening. The preview had used a bad print with improperly synchronized sound; in this form, she felt, I could not appreciate the movie. The print provoked her fury: 'Nobody gives a *damn* unless I myself beg, scream and plead to put things right. And that miserable print, that hack rubbish, will be shown in cinemas all over the country. That's the way our lazy film industry works. Slovenliness and incompetence. They'll only make a decent print for export, damn them. For us, they'll grind out any kind of shit.' (She said the last word in English – 'sheet' – in case my colloquial Russian was not adequate to her sentiment. Her English, acquired by her musical ear on brief trips abroad, is surprisingly useful.)

The outburst was provoked not only by Plisetskaya's customary intolerance of 'interference' in her dancing but also, predictably, because most of the film is devoted to 'Carmen-Suite'. Again, only hints and clues suggest the obstacles she overcame to achieve this coup; but her friends are convinced that the 'Carmen-Suite' episodes could not have been made at all without her fiery determination – and cunning. Plisetskaya worked on the film as if possessed, often assembling the supporting cast after the Bolshoi curtain had fallen, and urging them into take after take, late into the night. She was not only the subject of the film, but also a kind of assistant director, contributing generously to the choreography, direction and general conception.

I wish I could be enthusiastic about the result. But although the film is occasionally interesting and Plisetskaya was right about the deleterious effect of the bad print, as a whole it is saved from laboured, secondhand mediocrity only by Plisetskaya's dazzling flamboyance and technique.

Plisetskaya watches with the absorption she devotes to all her films. For the first time, her excessive make-up makes her appear more than her forty-five years. When the audience applauds during a resplendent scene, she fumes over the disrespect to the music, and shouts, 'Stop that!' over the blaring stereophonic sound. When the film ends, she and Shchedrin push their way through the crowd like ordinary spectators. They find their car outside the theatre, and while other celebrities in the audience are making plans for the evening, drive directly home.

Plisetskaya and Shchedrin own one of Russia's grandest 'private' flats, as opposed to the quarters allocated to Party and government officials. Their five rooms in a large co-operative building for Bolshoi personnel are the Soviet equivalent of a Park Avenue triplex. Aside from its solidity and the round-the-clock porter at the lift, the building itself gives no outward indication of luxury, but Muscovites know it as one of the residences of Russia's super-rich.

In the case of Plisetskaya and Shchedrin, life at the top includes a Steinway grand in the bedroom, together with an immense double bed. A second bedroom which serves as Shchedrin's studio* contains a second piano. The kitchen is fitted out with an imported stove, refrigerator and dishwasher; the wallpaper is Canadian throughout and the telephones American. Bookcases in almost every room are crammed with expensive coffee-table art books and a substantial library of music and the plastic arts. None of this would be surprising in Chelsea or Manhattan, but what makes the flat sumptuous by world as well as Moscow standards is a collection of drawings, paintings and lithographs – gifts to Plisetskaya from some of the most celebrated twentieth century artists. There are Picassos, Braques, Légers, and a stunning series of Chagalls, signed in Russian 'To Mayechka from Marc': enough to fill a large room in a museum of contemporary art. Priceless artifacts complement the pictures, among them an early Picasso dish which is a treasure in itself, and a superb Léger rug. These too were gifts to Plisetskaya and Shchedrin by the artists or their families.

Plisetskaya is particularly pleased by the recognition from these inventive – and spiritually French – artists. Not, however, that she is particularly in awe of her modern classics: dotted among them are Woolworth-like portraits of herself in oil and watercolour, together with framed prints of her beloved, highly flattering Avedon photographs. As if to make the oil portraits of herself feel at home, she has displayed in glass-topped cases a garish collection of cheap souvenirs gathered on trips abroad. The casual mixture of masterpiece and carnival doll adds an air of artlessness to the flat, a lack of pretension, even order, which is characteristic of many poorer Russian homes. Riches should not interfere with 'life'.

A four o'clock on a frigid March afternoon, guests arrive as Plisetskaya and Shchedrin are preparing to take their main meal of the day. In trousers and slippers, Plisetskaya greets her guests nonchalantly and shows them some of the flat's memorabilia.

* One reason why Plisetskaya and Shchedrin were permitted to buy a flat of this size was that one room could be shown as necessary for his work.

Adorned by bottles of Campari, Black & White, Schweppes and Macon Rouge (presumably bought at the hard-currency food shop with Plisetskaya's foreign earnings), the dining-room table itself is striking evidence of extraordinary wealth: few Russians have ever heard of these trade names, let alone seen a bottle. The large plates of salad, tomatoes and spinach on the table are at least as extravagant. Fresh vegetables are an exceedingly uncommon luxury between October and June. Plisetskaya takes the pains to find them, and spends the fortune – one big plate of greens and tomatoes is a worker's weekly wage – because of her concern for diet. 'Of course I love to eat, what a stupid question. But I don't have the *right* to get fat. Who wants a ballerina with a fat arse?'

Rodion Shchedrin, too, is fussy about what he eats, and his slight, former-boxer's figure is obviously trim. In general, he seems a fastidious fellow, and he prohibits smoking in the flat. It is clear that he lives far from Plisetskaya's shadow, within his own professional commitments. He is a lively man in his late thirties, with sandy hair, a boyish face and quick grin: a Steve McQueen with a sideline in composing.

Confirming Plisetskaya's description of him as the family's 'sensible' side, Shchedrin occasionally pulls her aside for whispered consultations, presumably to counsel her on what not to say before a foreign journalist. He seems to be cautioning her about her frankness, and tries to nip in the bud some of her comments about Soviet life.

'We never argue,' explains Plisetskaya. 'Our marriage is fantastically strong in that sense. In my entire life, I've only liked one man enough to get along with him – to actually want to live with him.'

'That's interesting, dear,' answers Shchedrin. 'Who was it?'

Plisetskaya then volunteers that she has never cooked for him because she's 'not the type'. 'You always exaggerate,' Shchedrin answers, reminding her of the time, several years ago, when their maid was on holiday and she prepared a 'superb scrambled egg'. Plisetskaya laughs and removes her slipper to scratch her foot.

Later, 'Robik' (which Plisetskaya alternates with 'Shchedrin') summons everyone to the table and pours the drinks. The meal has been prepared, and is now very informally served, by Katya, his imperturbable servant of seventeen years who has become a trusted member of the family. After the luxury of the fresh raw vegetables served with caviare and other hors-d'oeuvres, there is a superb fish soup, followed by a main course of delicate, uncommonly fresh perch – both courses provided by Shchedrin's catch of eighty-two fish the day before, from a river where he first had to drill through four feet of ice.

'When I begged for Maya's hand,' announces Shchedrin puckishly, 'I promised her I could always feed her as a fisherman if not a composer. She likes fish; that did the trick.'

The food is attacked in the Russian manner, to the accompaniment of tumblers of vodka and wine. Plisetskaya eats with gusto and with her hands, gesticulating, shouting to others not to shout because there is nothing wrong with her hearing, and in general behaving so artlessly and arguing so frankly that her guests feel they are paying not their first but their hundredth visit to the flat. A friend of hers recently told me that at a Moscow dinner given in her honour by the ambassador of an important Western country, Plisetskaya left abruptly after the second course, saying simply that she had to. 'I was so *bored*,' she told her friend. 'That awful diplomatic twaddle.' But if she is unaffected in public, she is superingenuous at home.

The conversation is also 'Russian' in its randomness and spontaneous variety, ranging unpredictably, as at a Chekhov table, from questions of Grand Philosophy – Is Human Civilization Perfectible? – to hard practical detail – how best to clean a fish. Discussion of Hemingway's *A Moveable Feast* and the cause of Beethoven's deafness are mixed with rapid personal banter, gossip about current Moscow cultural life, mild dirty jokes and improvised political quips. When a 'Prague tart' is served for dessert, someone asks wryly whether the others have noticed how many more of them there are these days in Moscow. A fleeting pause descends, in memory of the Prague Spring.

It is ended by a ring of the telephone, the dozenth in an hour.

The instrument is in almost constant use – professional calls about rehearsals and conferences for Plisetskaya and Shchedrin, Plisetskaya's mother with personal news and questions – but the interruptions do not impede the conversation, which rushes on in the direction anyone is strong enough to take it. Plisetskaya remembers her last evening dancing at the old Metropolitan Opera in her beloved New York, when the house cried out for her, cheering and weeping with its unique, uninhibited emotion. Shchedrin practises his respectable English, joking, grinning and giving an impression of considerable caution beneath his wit. Over tea – Twining's Earl Grey – there is a discussion about birth control and the varying hours of sleep people need.

At Shchedrin's prodding, Plisetskaya moves her glass aside and demonstrates a favourite trick illustrating her extraordinary co-ordination. With a pencil in each hand fixed at a single starting point, she simultaneously writes one of the guest's names normally and 'inside-out', as if one side were a mirror reflection of the other. Born left-handed, but taught to write with her right, Plisetskaya chuckles merrily at her feat and whispers something to Shchedrin, provoking a roar of laughter from him.

After tea, Plisetskaya shows her guests more of the flat. Although all the rooms are adorned with stacks of old magazines and pervaded by a homey ambience of absentminded disarray, one room is devoted *wholly* to disorder. Again with a certain self-satisfaction, Plisetskaya calls it 'the dump'. The smallish chamber is crammed literally from floor to ceiling with a vast assortment of odds and ends bordering on junk, ranging from old clothes, yesterday's dirty shirts tossed atop the nearest pile, used bottles of cosmetics, Shchedrin's old manuscripts to yellowing stacks of fan mail (which Plisetskaya rarely answers: 'Life's just too short, there's simply no time'). A profusion of ancient ballet costumes has been shoved haphazardly into a wardrobe. Elsewhere, several years' supply of American hairspray stands in unpacked cases, together with foreign brands of more intimate items of the feminine toilet unobtainable in Russia. Altogether, 'the dump' is like a costume storehouse of some defunct theatre, and one is not surprised, by this time, to hear

Plisetskaya declare that it is her favourite room. Most of all, however, she likes the miniature classroom in one corner, equipped with a small practice bar and a large mirror. Here, alone with the mess and junk, Plisetskaya does much of her work.

Afternoon becomes evening; the conversation continues to leap from aesthetic theories to the latest Moscow jokes. Returning from another telephone call, Plisetskaya describes how she and Shchedrin disconnect the instrument when they are desperate for a few hours of peace. (On foreign tours, she often ignores the telephone in her hotels, sometimes resorting to cutting wires with manicure scissors or to yanking sockets clean from walls.) Although she seems faintly depressed, Plisetskaya is in a voluble mood and tells a longish story about Katya's mother, who has never set foot outside her native village – a fact that Plisetskaya finds both amusing and astonishing. She herself, she hints, would suffocate if she were again not allowed to travel abroad. At the moment, she is thinking ahead to her next tour – of Australia, in the summer – and hoping for final permission from the Ministry.

During Plisetskaya's monologue, one of her guests cannot take his eyes off her paintings. The collection of Chagalls, he mentions, includes some of his most superb and subtle work. Rising in mid-sentence, Plisetskaya strides to 'the dump' and returns with a large, distinguished Léger lithograph.

'Do you like this?' she asks him.

'Of course I do. It's clean and forceful.'

'Take it along, then,' she says, casually. 'Sorry I can't give you a Chagall – they're all inscribed to me.'

'You're not serious,' stutters the guest. He is genuinely puzzled because he does not know Plisetskaya well and may never see her again. Under the circumstances, it is embarrassing to be offered, out of the blue, a gift worth hundreds of pounds. 'I can't take this,' he repeats. 'It's not right, I wouldn't know how to respond.'

Plisetskaya pushes a clump of hair from her face and appears distracted while he repeats his protestation. Her explosion is sudden and angry.

'For the love of God, stop that genteel crap. Someone gave you something. Because she wanted you to have it. Otherwise she wouldn't have done it. Hang it on a wall and stop your feeble prattle.'

In a way, I wish I had not witnessed what took place next. For it raised, more sharply than anything Plisetskaya had said or done before, the conflict between my professional duty to report and my moral obligation not to cause my subjects distress. No one need convince me that she may be questioned about what follows, I report it – with some tempering – because to say nothing seems worse in the long run, for her as well as for everyone else in Russia; everyone else on earth.

Plisetskaya's invitation to visit her flat was neither spontaneous nor voluntary. At our first meeting on the February morning, I had told her that more than anything I wanted to see how she lived; but she shook her head. Foreigners could not visit her flat without permission, she muttered bitterly. 'I don't have the right to invite whom I want – even see whom I want. And listen: my telephone is tapped, don't ever say anything important over it. And my mail is opened. Sometimes I don't get letters from my Western friends visiting Moscow until weeks after they've left.'

Nevertheless, Plisetskaya promised to campaign for permission to invite me – not out of love at first sight, but because I'd come to her not only through Novosti, but with a personal recommendation from a trusted friend. At the same time, I intensified my own crusade with Novosti. I do not know precisely what reports were made and signatures required to sanction this visit to a celebrity's co-operative flat. But after weeks of waiting I was triumphantly informed that the undertaking had been organized.

Naturally, I was not to go alone. The man who accompanied me, and sat by my side throughout the meal, was the Novosti official who, several weeks before, had ordered Plisetskaya first not to see me, then to proceed. He was an educated, relatively worldly man who qualified for membership in Moscow's intelligentsia and, as it happened, was an old acquaintance of Plisetskaya. However, in case I did not know that his work at Novosti (where he often deals with foreigners) entailed supplementary functions, Plisetskaya herself hissed a warning the first moment he was out of earshot. 'Don't say anything important in front of him. He's an informer, everything goes straight to the K.G.B.'

Throughout the afternoon and evening, the Novosti official maintained his usual bonhomie. Whispers, pauses and political jokes had caused a few awkward moments, but as a whole the potentially risky operation had gone well from his standpoint. But as we made noises about leaving, he excused himself to go to the lavatory. Shchedrin had retired to his studio to work; Plisetskaya and I were alone again and I, still embarrassed after the Léger gift, asked more questions about her childhood. Not answering, she stared moodily into the strings of the bedroom Steinway. Before I understood, before I had time to think, she was in a rage of fury and sobs.

Moments passed before I deciphered her splutterings. There were references to terrible pressure, a filthy press conference and sadistic penalties. Slowly – yet always conscious of the lack of time – I pieced together a story: a press conference was to be staged tomorrow morning to denounce Zionism, Israeli imperialism and Jewish warmongering to national and foreign journalists, and declare whole-hearted allegiance to Soviet support of the Arabs. The participants were to be fifty prominent Soviet Jews, including many, like Plisetskaya, whose Jewishness was hardly known to the general public. In violation of everything she knew, everything she felt, everything she believed in, she had signed the statement. The truth was that she deeply admired Israel and wished it well with all her heart.

Her signature on the document to be exhibited tomorrow was a monstrous fabrication, a sickening lie. She had tried not to sign, but resistance was futile: she had been summoned to the Ministry and told that future permission to travel abroad, starting with her Australian tour that summer, depended on her 'co-operation'. She hated the people who had made her do this; hated the regime and its filthy lies. No crime was too low for Russia's rulers. They cared for nothing but suppression and power.

Unwilling to doubt her, I yet could not fully believe. I had always thought that a small charmed circle of Russians, no more than a dozen of the most illustrious celebrities, were immune to such pressure. I told Plisetskaya that even some of my knowledge-able Russian friends assumed that her international reputation made her a kind of 'independent government' in full command of her professional and personal life. I mentioned Graham Greene's phrase: the 'non-torturable class of Soviet citizens', to which Westerners were certain that she belonged.

'You're a naive fool after all,' she snapped. 'There's no such circle of "celebrities" in this country. There's not a *single* such person. Brezhnev is afraid of Kosygin and Kosygin is afraid of Brezhnev. They are both afraid of Podgorny. Not one man or woman in two hundred and twenty million can take a free breath under Soviet rule.'

The next moments made Plisetskaya's fury against English critics seem mild by comparison. She told of a vicious anti-Israeli article which she had not so much as known about until she opened *Pravda* one day and saw that the author was 'Maya Plisetskaya'. She cursed the fate of Soviet artists. 'It's hell to live like this. You can't imagine what it does to a person – the frustration, the hatred, the overwhelming self-disgust. All of us must perjure ourselves.' She insisted that the Ministry's threats were wholly real: she had been prevented from going abroad before, and they would do the same to her again without a moment's hesitation. 'My work's the only thing I live for – and they don't give a damn about that. They do what they please with the country and people's lives. Ruling and lying, smashing and corrupting. What they care about is one thing: their own power. To resist is useless; you only ruin yourself – and it can change nothing in this wretched country ... '

My Novosti 'colleague' was returning from the lavatory. 'I'll tell you the one thing that explains everything about Soviet rule,' raced Plisetskaya. 'It is the *lie*. Every word here is a lie. Big or little, depending upon *their* needs. Sometimes you can even tell the truth if it happens to suit *them*. Ungodly lies, vicious and cynical lies ... I hate them. There was no dignity for individuals in Russia in the seventeenth century, and there's no dignity in the twentieth. There will be none in the twenty-first. Read Russian history. Nothing important has improved here, nothing will.'

Rejoining us, the Novosti official could not fail to notice Plisetskaya's agitation. Controlling it as best she could, she showed us more memorabilia before we said our goodbyes. On her night table next to her current reading (Gogol stories and a biography of Bruno Walter) was a bowl of china carnations given her by Robert Kennedy. His birthday was hers – November 20th, 1925 – a coincidence that became the spark for their fast friendship. She was on tour in New York when he was assassinated; they were to have had supper a few days later, upon his return from California. The tragedy still affects her deeply.

In another room, she showed us a drawing of the Swedish-Italian ballerina Marie Taglioni that Anna Pavlova owned until her death. Ram Gopal then acquired it and gave it to Plisetskaya; and she was as proud of it as anything in the flat, obviously because it linked her sentimentally to great personages in dance history ... But her manner was distant now, perhaps because she was tired, and it was obviously time to leave. I had not expected to learn from this visit that one of the world's greatest ballerinas had fewer civic rights than any English school-girl.

The next day, the press conference was duly mounted before television cameras and the statement published in all national newspapers. 'As Soviet patriots and internationalists, we hold in contempt the laughable pretensions of Israel's rulers and their Zionist accomplices in other countries to speak in the name of all Jews ... Zionism is motivated by imperialist, predatory interests alien to the popular masses ... ' Plisetskaya's name leapt from the dense list of signers, titles and accomplishments. She refused to come to the conference to exhibit herself, but even this limited resistance, she had told me, would provoke retribution.

The incident had several curious minor aspects. For one thing, several of the signers were revealed for the first time as Jews – a cruelly ironic reward for a lifetime of concealing their Jewishness. Later it was learned that other prominent Jews, notably members of Moscow University's mathematics faculty, successfully resisted the pressure. Of the fifty-odd signers, only a handful were known as 'liberals'; the rest were Soviet 'house' Jews, many of whom had extremely unsavoury pasts. Before this, Plisetskaya herself was considered one of the more daring liberals, having signed (unpublicized) petitions against trials of Soviet writers. Was it, therefore, some special pressure that made her succumb in this case? Was her fury partially self-directed for having done so? Unless Plisetskaya writes her own memoirs, only her closest friends will know.

But it is now widely known that she did not exaggerate the threat of punishment and interference with her professional life. The superb cellist Mstislav Rostropovich who, like Plisetskaya, used to be thought of as a member of the charmed circle of illustrious Russians, was punished for a similar transgression by the unceremonious cancellation of his permission to travel. Subsequently, other great Soviet musicians failed to appear for engagements in Europe without so much as a telegram of regret. And shortly after my visit to her, Plisetskaya herself was refused permission to travel to West Berlin – because, according to her friends, Rudolph Nureyev was there at the time her performances were scheduled.

During the next week the Novosti official hung at my heels, uncharacteristically generous with his time and advice. 'You're a big boy now,' he repeated genially. 'You may have learned some things that would be rather sensational in the West. But they're not the important things about Maya. It's best not to write about them. If I were you, I'd concentrate on her dancing and some personal details ... And remember: you're going to leave Moscow next week. The rest of us – Maya as well as me – must stay here.'

He is not an unpleasant man. Somewhere, he is revolted by this aspect of his work, but he wants to enjoy the satisfactions and privileges of his position, which lift him out of the drabness of Soviet working-class life: permission to read English newspapers, and the satisfaction of a Sunday dinner of chicken. No more than I want myself. And since he has but one life, and resistance to the dictatorship is in any case futile, he does what is necessary to earn himself a reasonable standard of living.

But where does the bribery and pressure stop? When Plisetskaya was called to the Ministry, the threat to her was put in precisely the same terms as the Novosti official had used to me. 'You're a big girl now, you know nothing can be done, you understand that the people up above won't stop at damaging you.'

In a way, I wish I had not learned of Plisetskaya's part in the press conference. My work would have been easier – but not, I believe, her life. Not, at least, in the long run ...

I saw her only once after my visit to her flat: two days later in the Director-General's salon at the Bolshoi. Once again, I'd barely got into the building – a new guard demanded my papers and refused to hear even a word of explanation – and I was late for our appointment. Maya Mikhailovna was even later: she'd been rehearsing a new role, while Ulanova watched. Against the background of crimson and gilt she appeared in a fitted, floor-length black mantle that protects her against chill after sweating. She had only a moment, and, in the presence of several Bolshoi officials who were conversing nearby, seemed uncharacteristically formal.

I'd come to say goodbye and to return the June 1966 issue of *Theatre* which she'd lent me at dinner – her last copy, which she wanted back. It contained a prose-and-verse portrait of her by Andrei Voznesensky, about which both she and Shchedrin had enthused, insisting that no one had captured her so well as the gifted young poet. Their recommendation, however, was accompanied by comments I did not understand: something about 'reading between the lines' and revised editions of the poem because Voznesensky had changed his mind about something. Was he forced to re-write lines for political reasons? Had he been infatuated with Plisetskaya?

The version published in *Theatre* shimmers with alliterations and

illusions that are untranslatable and/or unintelligible to people
unfamiliar with Pushkin, Dostoyevsky and the poetry of
Tsvetayeva and others in Russia's largely unpublished avant-
garde. But the more obvious passages also suggest the portrait's
tone. It is entitled 'Maya':

There are ballerinas of silence,
Ballerinas like snowflakes; they melt.
But she's like some kind of infernal spark.
When she perishes, half the planet will be incinerated!
Even her silence is frenzied, the roaring silence of
      expectation,
The actively tense silence between lightning and
      thunderclap ...
She is tortured by her own gifts –
Inexplicable even to herself, but nothing to joke
      about ...

What can be done with this weightless creature in a
      world of ponderousness?
She was born more weightless than anyone.
In a world of heavy, blunt objects.
Better able to fly than anyone,
In a world of clumsy immobility ...
The splendour of genius amidst the ordinary – that's
The key to all her roles.
She blazes brilliantly; it's brought on by her boiling
      blood.
This is no ordinary mythical fairy.
She suffers from too little spark, fire and light
In this half-way world ...
She cannot bear half-measures, whispers, and
      compromises.
Her answer to a foreign lady correspondent was
      cunning.
'What do you hate most of all?'
'Noodles!' ...

Yes of course, noodles are the most repulsive of all
    things:
A symbol of standardization, of things boiled to mush,
    of commonness;
Of subjugation, of anti-spirituality.
Wasn't it about noodles that she wrote in her notes:
'People must stand up for their convictions.
Not by use of the police and denunciations,
But only through the strength of their own inner "I".'
And further: 'I don't particularly respect people who
    live
By the maxim: "If you don't repent, you won't be
    saved."'
Maya Plisetskaya doesn't like noodles!
She creates ...
We've forgotten the words 'gifts', 'genius',
    'illumination'.
Without them, art is nothing. As the experiments of
    Kolmogorov proved,
Art cannot be programmed; two human qualities
    cannot be derivative:
The feeling for religion and the feeling for poetry.
Talents cannot be cultivated by agricultural systems
    invented by Lysenko.
They are born. They are part of the national wealth,
Like radium deposits, September in Latvian woods,
    or medicinal springs.
Plisetskaya's lines and movements are miracles like
    these,
As much a part of the national wealth.

What a feeling Plisetskaya has for poetry!
I emember her in black, sitting on a sofa;
She looks as if she's put a wall between herself
.. d the rest of the audience.
She sits in profile, leaning forward.

Like the famous statue with a pitcher*
Her eyes are switched off.
She listens with her neck.
With her Modigliani neck, with the curve of her spine,
    with her skin.
Her earrings tremble, like nostrils ...

She is the most modern of our ballerinas.
Poetry, painting, physics have their time in terms
Of style – but not ballet.
She is a ballerina who lives in the rhythms of the
    Twentieth Century.
She should dance not among swans, but among cars and
    jets.
I see her against the background of
The pure lines of Henry Moore and the chapel of
    Ronchamp ...

Her name is short,
Like those of other girls in tights,
And as thunder-like as that of a goddess
Or pagan priestess: Maya.

I handed her the magazine; she stuffed it into her bag together
with her ballet shoes. She was slightly breathless from the rehearsal
and clumps of thick reddish hair lay across her still-moist face. The
salon's soft semi-darkness would have been flattering to any
woman, and Plisetskaya never looked more beautiful. I wanted to
thank her for helping me to see her – very great help, under the
circumstances. But she had work to return to and wasn't in the
mood for sentiment. She kissed me, pressed my hand and gazed
penetratingly at me in the Plisetskaya manner. She wished me good
luck and withdrew. The black mantle danced behind her over the
crimson carpet. All afternoon a bitter March wind blew the smell
of Bandit from my cheek.

* In the park of Tsarskoye Selo, near Leningrad.

3. *Afternoon in a People's Court*

People's Court, Leninskii District, City of Moscow. The court-room is small, sagging, stuffy. The grey of a late December afternoon seeps through two double-paned windows; one bare light-bulb is burning. Three spectators wander in. Behind the desk, a judge with a factory-foreman's face and light grime on his open collar slowly puts down his glasses.

'Defendant Zaitsov, stand. Do you understand the charge against you?'

A small voice, matching the boyish face and faintly dandyish blond hair, searches for a convincing tone.

'Yes, Comrade Judge, I understand.'

'And do you admit your guilt as charged in the indictment?'

No answer. The defendant wrinkles his handsome young brow.

'Zaitsov!'

'Of course, I know I acted wrong. Yes, I admit I'm guilty, and I'm ashamed of myself. But the indictment is wrong too. All wrong. I can't admit to everything it says.'

'So you don't fully admit your guilt?' The judge makes a fleet-ing grimace of impatience. 'Exactly what do you admit and what do you deny? Tell us the whole story. The court wants to hear everything you have to say about the charge.'

The defendant assumes a pose: the picture of innocence. His gestures and features are younger than his thirty-three years. He is – the judge has established – Russian, a bachelor, a construction worker earning 105 rubles a month; he was born in a village north of Moscow, received five years' schooling, is not a Party member, has never been convicted of a criminal charge. Under his overcoat he sports the only tie and white shirt in the courtroom.

'I admit I let him into the queue, Comrade Judge. I'm sorry about that – though, you know, everybody does it. But I took no money; there was never any talk of any money. I only did it as a favour, to ... '

'There was no talk about money? Did you take three rubles from him or did you not?'

'Comrade Judge ... ' (pause) ' ... yes. I took them. Just to have a drink afterwards. He told me ... '

'You took the money. You admit that. Three rubles from the victim. And in spite of that you deny your guilt? Defendant Zaitsov, we want the whole story. Start at the beginning and explain exactly what happened.'

'It was on the twenty-first. I had just got through working ... '

'The twenty-first of what month?'

'Of October, Comrade Judge.'

'Go on. What happened on the twenty-first?'

'On the twentieth, I'd worked a double shift on our construction site – you know, we're building blocks of flats. Then I went to my sister's. Just for a little relaxation after the week's work. I stayed overnight. In the morning I told my sister I was going to the *yarmarka'* (an outdoor bazaar of stalls and booths) 'to buy a raincoat.'

'The Luzhniki *yarmarka* alongside Lenin Stadium?'

'That one, that's right.'

'And the raincoat – was it intended for your own use or for resale?'

'For me. Honest, I just needed a new raincoat for myself. The only thing I got for somebody else, Comrade Judge, was for my sister. She gave me twenty-five rubles to buy her a sweater. So first I stood in a queue for that. The queue was very long – for those nice red sweaters they had. There was this tremendous crowd and I waited a long time. Then I realized I was standing in the wrong queue – I'd forgotten to look at the sizes – and I had to go to the tail end of another even longer one. Finally they started selling sweaters but the queue moved very slowly, and when it got to my turn there were none left. Oi, what a waste of two hours – and on Sunday, my day off. And to disappoint my sister! That's when I saw this girl near the booth – she'd just bought herself a sweater. I said, "Miss, please sell me your sweater, there's none left in stock." She didn't want to at first, but finally changed her mind. So I gave her twenty rubles for the sweater: she'd paid eighteen rubles fifty kopeks for it. And that was that.'

Zaitsov stands shyly, earnestly, unblinkingly before the judge, telling his sad little story with plaintive intensity and the fullness of his heart. The spectators seem persuaded. The judge is unmoved.

'All right, Zaitsov, enough! Nobody's accused you of anything about any sweater. Get to the raincoat, will you?'

'Of course, Comrade Judge, the raincoat. You see, then I stood in a queue for a few hours for a raincoat – the queue for *my* size this time. They were selling these new belted Polish raincoats, and you can imagine that the queue was pretty long again. Plus lots of people who were butting in. You know how it works. Well, I'm standing there pretty near the front finally, and suddenly this man comes up to me, this stranger, and says he's in a terrific hurry. He says he's got a car waiting for him – to go to the Black Sea on holiday. He's been to the *yarmarka* three days in a row, he tells me, but can't get a coat, and it looks like another whole day shot because he's Number 465 on my queue and he doubts he'll *ever* get to the booth. He tells me all this and I feel sorry for him. So I let him in – in my place. That's the whole story. It's just that he was in a hurry to go on holiday.'

'And the socks?'

'Yes, the socks, Comrade Judge. That's simple. After he gets his belted raincoat, he suggests we go buy some socks, he's running clean out of them. So he gives me ten rubles and goes to tell his driver to wait and I find that queue and ask a girl to let me in. I explain to her that I'll repay her kindness. Then I buy a few pairs of socks.'

'What size?'

'Twenty-five.'

'And what's your size?'

'Twenty-three.'

'So the socks were no good *for you*. You couldn't use them *yourself*.' To convict of speculation, it must be proved that the defendant bought an article intending to resell it for profit, not to use it himself.

'I gave one pair of socks – they were good ones, with genuine elastic tops – to the girl and offered two pairs to that man. He agreed to buy them. And that's all there was to it, Comrade Judge. Then we separated and he thanked me warmly. He said, "I'm very grateful; you helped me very much with my shopping."'

'How much change did you give him?'

'Er ... ' (pause) ' ... I ... forget.'

The judge fumbles with his glasses again and glances at the dossier. 'You gave him four rubles change, isn't that right? When you had just bought the socks for two rubles and fifty kopeks a pair the minute before. That makes five rubles but you charged *six*. You made a ruble profit on the deal. Is that or is it not correct?'

'Er ... yes.' Zaitsov hangs his head.

'Plus three rubles for selling your place in the queue. Disgusting! You *know* it's disgusting. You deliberately milked a stranger, a Soviet citizen, a man of the working class just like yourself, of four rubles. Just like that. It's a plain case of intentional cheating. And you had it all planned, Zaitsov. Isn't that right?'

'Absolutely not, Comrade Judge. Oh no, I didn't mean to sell him anything.' Zaitsov fairly trembles with conviction; his innocence seems beyond question. 'It just happened that way, Comrade Judge. When we separated, he said, "I must thank you, I'd be happy to treat you to a proper drink, as they say. But I'm in a great hurry. So take this instead" – he handed me three rubles – "and have a drink on me as a token of thanks." At that moment a citizen rushes up to us shouting, "I'm a detective, show me your papers and come with me." That whole *yarmarka* is crawling with these plainclothes types, snooping around, just waiting for someone to make one false move. So this one arrests me and takes me to the station house. That's how it happened; the rubles were pressed on me, if you know what I mean. I didn't even want to take them.'

'Then what made you?'

'Can you insult a man who offers you a drink?'

The judge clears his throat, surveys his shabby courtroom and sighs, preparing himself for a distasteful task. He has the hands of a manual labourer, steel teeth and a leathery face. His voice is colourless: typically lacking compassion, untypically free of anger. His wits are obviously keener than his appearance.

'Do you really expect the court to believe that? Your story is a farce. Never mind; we'll hear the witnesses. But first I must find out something more from you. Now, Zaitsov, this isn't your first time with this same thing, is it? It's the third time – at least the third. You have been warned. Good people – the authorities – have tried to reform you. The third time. The same disgraceful business. Why did you do it again? Why? How can you, a Soviet worker, allow yourself to decay into a rotten little swindler, a petty speculator? Do you know what you're forcing us to do with you?'

Zaitsov's game is up: a blank look of defeat spreads over his face. 'I didn't *want* to take the three rubles ... '

'And on October 6th, just two weeks before – what happened then?'

'Oi, Comrade Judge ... that was a mistake. Honest it was.' It turns out that on October 6th, the defendant had been fined twenty rubles for selling his place in a queue for Czech woollen underwear. (An administrative fine, it was not entered on his record as a criminal conviction.)

'Yet you failed, you refused to learn any lesson from that fine. Well, you are forcing us to treat you less leniently. Now tell the court: aside from October 6th, did you ever engage in petty speculation before?'

'No, Comrade Judge. Just those two mistakes.'

'Never?'

No answer.

'There's no point in hiding the truth from us. We know it anyway.'

'Maybe something very minor – very long ago.'

'When?'

'Could it have been 1959? On May 1st, I think.'

The judge sighs. 'Tell us about that.'

His composure vaporized, Zaitsov stammers through a lengthy narrative, obviously embellished during scores of tellings. The court learns that years ago, Zaitsov had worked in a construction crew that won the title 'Brigade of Communist Labour'. The award was an expenses-paid May Day trip to Leningrad – on which he had sold his place for thirty rubles to a worker from another brigade.

'And this was in 1959?'

'I don't remember with absolute certainty, Comrade Judge. My memory is bad.'

'1959. Now strain your poor memory and tell the court about the other incidents.'

'I can't remember. I don't think there were any more.'

'None? Think! In 1959, a few months later – do you remember now?'

'Yes.' Zaitsov makes another simple story complex. In 1959, he bought a camera and resold it almost immediately, pocketing a twenty-five per cent profit. Then he bought and sold a rug. Later he dealt in jazz records.

'Don't you understand that there have been too many of these incidents? It's no longer a joke. You're on your way to becoming a dangerous criminal. Why? What makes you cheat like this?'

'Comrade Judge, I don't even know how it happens. I'm sorry.'

'Was it necessary for you to cheat? Was there something you needed? Something lacking? Were you in difficult straits? We want to hear your motive.'

No answer. The defendant rests his head on his chest and covers his eyes.

'Maybe you'll think it over and tell the court how those three rubles *really* changed hands. Your story is weak. Don't think I'm talking you into anything. But we'll give you a chance to think it over. If you've made mistakes in life, you yourself must be the first to recognize and correct them. You must judge yourself honestly; then things will go easier for you. Your job is to reform yourself, to make yourself an honest, upright Soviet citizen. Because, young man, you simply cannot go on like this, cheating like a bourgeois moneylender, scavenging for profits, filling your pockets with filthy money squeezed from the toilers. Living like a parasite, a fungus, a blemish on our Soviet society. A society building Communism cannot tolerate spots of rust like you. We must scrape them away. But unless you reform, unless *you* see the folly of your ways, the punishment won't do you any good. You've got a skill: "construction worker" is a proud title in our land. Yet you go around dreaming only of rotten little profits. Disgusting! Intolerable! Are you a son of the working class, or some capitalist scum? Your greed will only destroy you. We are trying to help you control it, but first you must tell the whole truth and explain *why* you continue with this ugly cheating.'

The defendant has no answer to this sermon. Finally he looks up at the judge. 'I'm truly sorry, Comrade Judge. I swear it will never happen again. Give me a chance to show I can be a useful member of Soviet society.'

Three witnesses are called. The first is the 'victim' (according to Soviet law) in the *yarmarka* deal. A swarthy, moustached Georgian in a ragged work-jacket, he has stared fiercely at both judge and defendant throughout the trial. Now he testifies, sullenly, that Zaitsov solicited the sale of both his place in the queue and the two pairs of socks. The judge berates him only slightly less vehemently than he did Zaitsov, for 'participating in a disgusting violation of Soviet morality'. 'You knew it was wrong to buy your way into queues, yet you bribed the defendant to do it. You're hardly less guilty than he is.'

His sense of himself as a tough operator obviously offended, the 'victim' is furious – at the judge for his lecture and at the defendant for allowing it to be known that a Russian had got the better of a Georgian. He shouts at the judge in thickly-accented Russian: 'I needed the stuff and I paid for it. You do the same when you need things. Stop making a murder case out of this, all I wanted was to get something decent to wear on holiday. I haven't been home to Tbilisi in three years. This guy knew how to operate in that lousy *yarmarka* of yours and I didn't – what's the big crime?'

A middle-aged woman who was behind them in the raincoat queue testifies next. She heard the two men talking and witnessed the exchange of socks and the place in the queue, but heard no details of the transactions. The third witness, the detective who made the arrest, does not appear; the judge reads a statement he made for the pre-trial investigation. His deposition repeats the charge of the indictment – that the defendant wilfully sold his place in a queue and two pairs of socks for motives of profit – adding that Zaitsov is a known 'operator' whom detectives in that *yarmarka* and others had been warned to keep under surveillance.

Now the judge moves quickly to the trial's conclusion. 'Any other questions or comments? Anything unclear? Nothing from anyone? Defendant, what have you to say as your last word to the court?'

'Comrade Judge' – Zaitsov's voice now rings with painful contrition – 'I have committed too many shameful acts. I am not worthy of the great title of Soviet Citizen. But I have learned my lesson at last, I have learned how ugly my greed appears in the eyes of others. I have no excuse. But I promise, I swear that I am already on the road to reform, and therefore I beg the court not to make my punishment too severe.'

'Is that all? The court will retire to reach the verdict.'

The winter evening's blackness now shows through the windows, although it is just five o'clock. The hearing has lasted an hour and the writing of the verdict in the cubbyhole that serves as the judge's chambers takes another half. When the court returns, it brings no surprises. 'In the name of the Russian Soviet Federated Socialist Republic' it is found that the defendant Zaitsov, Viktor Mikhailovich, committed the acts charged in the indictment, that is, crimes specified by Article 154 (III) of the criminal code: petty speculation, committed by a person previously convicted of the same offence. In determining measures of punishment, the court took into consideration the defendant's long history of speculative activity and obvious unwillingness to learn from administrative warnings, and also his apparently genuine promise to reform. The sentence is a year of 'corrective labour' without deprivation of freedom: Zaitsov will continue to work at his construction job and forfeit 20 per cent of his wages to the state.

'Defendant, is the sentence clear to you?'

'Yes, Comrade Judge, it is clear and I thank you; you will never see me in court again.' He shuffles out quickly, trying to suppress the grin of relief that almost breaks through his tragedian's frown of remorse.

The courtroom empties in a minute. Rising stiffly, the judge lights a *papirosa* and puts away his glasses. 'Fat chance we won't see him again,' he mutters, not quite under his breath. 'Oi, these speculators, these good-for-nothings. How can we teach the young generation proper socialist morals?'

The secretary yawns, giving the judge the minimum pretence of attention.

'Good night, Inna Filipovna,' he says. 'Don't forget to send a copy of the sentence to Zaitsov's trade union. We've got to break him of his greed somehow or next he'll be in here for stealing. What I'd really like to do is shut down that *yarmarka*. It gives us more trouble than all the rest of the district combined. Now Polish raincoats and elastic socks. There's altogether too much temptation in that place.'

4. *The Rossiya Hotel*

On a Friday evening in February, it is nearing ten o'clock. The Moscow River is a solid band of ice, despite steaming discharges from factories on its banks. The Kremlin's electric stars show as distant daubs of red through the gelid mist. In Red Square, nothing moves; silence stalks the cobblestone pavements and walls of sepia brick. Only purple lips and puffs of frozen breath indicate that the two motionless figures near the centre of the square are alive. They are sentries guarding Lenin's mausoleum.

The immense new structure that dominates this scene intensifies the pervading ambience. Its vast, inert mass towers over the river and Kremlin accenting the relationship between human frailty and nature's crushing forces at this latitude; providing the same associations with Russia's vastness, coldness, harshness and houses-sealed-tight-against-the-elements way of life. Although depressingly out of proportion to everything around it, one is reminded that Red Square has the same effect on the individual who traverses it. This is a triumph for the building's designers, for their cardinal concern was not to spoil the unique atmosphere of Russia's epi-centre. By enthusiastic newspapers and its own proud architects, the building is sometimes called the 'Crystal' or 'Marble' Palace, in honour of its glass and marble façade. But most Muscovites call it simply 'the big box'. It is the Hotel Rossiya: pride of the Soviet Union and flagship of its modest fleet. Its name, 'The Russia', is as symbolic as its size and weight.

Inside, the ponderous structure is blessedly warm and glaringly lit. With their flickering fluorescent lights and dented polishing-machines for the great sea of floor tiles, the lobbies have all the cosiness of a passenger airport at midnight. No less than three generous lobbies – on the western, northern and eastern sides of the almost square 'box' – minister to the Rossiya. Each offers a full range of services, and operates virtually as an independent hotel.

At this hour, the action is centred in the ground-floor restaurant off the western lobby. Although all three lobbies are theoretically equal, this one – which faces the Kremlin – is manifestly more so than the others. The restaurant's two burly doormen are turning away hopeful guests with less than customary surliness. But the lucky thousand-odd diners inside are thoroughly enjoying their evening in one of the capital's smartest new attractions.

It is a wondrously garish place, even in its subdued lighting and heavy cigarette haze. Synthetic gold columns soar to a ceiling of synthetic silver; thick dandruff from both alloys has already begun to flake to the floor. Elsewhere, the furniture, staircases, balustrades and draperies are in a flamboyant style most flatteringly described as pseudo-Miami Beach. The hotel management is gushingly proud of this decor, which is featured not only in its own leaflets, but also in a hundred Soviet magazines, as graphic evidence of the consumer economy's miraculous growth. And the hotel is indeed a new development in Russian life. Only in Russia, however, could so many furnishings put together at so great a cost in money and effort have deteriorated so quickly. The tawdry carpets are already grimy and threadbare; the plush-looking dining-chairs heavily stained with food droppings and grease. The despoliation screams of the false economy of inferior synthetics. The Rossiya is to Miami's Hotel Fontainebleau as that comically vulgar imitation is to the exquisite country retreat of the kings of France.

Decor seems irrelevant, however, as the evening's merriment approaches its climax. The band is executing a medley of Gershwin and soulful Russian ballads at a volume to match the size of the room. Over the clangour, the staccato of an argument swells in angry crescendo: a customer is distressed because, the menu notwithstanding, there is no sturgeon. Or smoked salmon or zander – not even cod. No fish, in fact, of any kind. (Moscow is suffering a severe shortage again, caused by the vagaries of the system of supply.) With his greater practice, the waiter quickly surpasses the outraged diner in vitriol. 'What the hell do *I* care what you eat?' he spits scathingly, and stalks away, leaving the order untaken. A moment later, he is exchanging shrill insults with a neighbouring waitress.

At an adjacent table, a group of stout middle-aged men and women celebrating a birthday have linked arms and, in competition with the band, are cawing sentimental ballads of the 1930s at the top of their pleasantly tipsy voices. Toasts resound throughout the room, accompanied by the popping of corks and clanking of thick-bodied glasses. An army officer in a uniform as ill-fitting and unpressed as those of the waiters asks a blushing young blonde from another table to dance, and they make their way to join the happy, sweating couples already jamming the dance floor.

The new couple are badly bounced about and the young blonde suffers a painful bruise on the leg – which she receives, however, as if it were her just deserts. Like the service, food and table manners, like the young orchestra's music, the standard of dancing would provoke winces in any European restaurant remotely comparable in prestige and price. Yet there is more old-fashioned fun here than in a dozen of Europe's most elegant restaurants combined. The waiter who has wrangled with the customer about the missing fish returns to his table; soon the two are pumping hands and exchanging family snapshots. Behind them, a grinning Russian with silver teeth – he is a provincial engineer summoned to the capital for discussions in the Ministry – is delighted to discover that his tablemate is an American tourist, the first 'real' one he's seen in his life. Painfully reviving his text-book English, he makes the happy discovery that neither wants war and that all men – except them murky Africans, greedy Arabs and treacherous, yellow Chinese – are brothers. His conviction becomes firmer upon discovering that the American, too, is fond of children, swimming and evenings with his family, and that television is boring in both countries. He orders more vodka (bribing the waiter to ignore the new rule limiting each diner to one hundred grammes) and insists that the American drink with him to peace and friendship, their own *private* kind ...

The restaurant's mood of abandoned, almost deliberate splurging swells in proportion to the approach of its midnight closing.

Encouraged by vodka – or Armenian cognac or Egyptian rum – strangers sharing tables swap jokes, confessions and life stories. Busty women dance with well-oiled men or other busty women. Two skinny teenagers have spent a week's factory wages on shashlik with all the trimmings – and leave it untouched because it pleases them more to smoke. One of the escalators to the kitchens below has broken down again, causing intervals of fifty minutes between courses. But the confusion and arguments provoked by the insouciant staff matter less and less, and generous tips are bestowed even by men recently apoplectic over the service. When the chanteuse – a large woman in a metallic dress, whose warbling unintentionally parodies the entire genre of the romantic ballad – has completed her final song, the diners provide their own entertainment. Soon the cavernous room echoes to the soaring refrains of folk tunes ...

This is the Rossiya, the first Soviet 'international' hotel on the Western model. Except for a few native details, the building might easily be one of a large American chain; except for the occasional portraits of Lenin, the decoration is modern and anonymous enough to fit in anywhere, from Chicago to Cairo. But within the bricks and mortar are a million-plus cubic yards of Soviet procedures and unyielding Russian attitudes.

Next morning, the Rossiya goes about its business much as any new hotel. By the cold light of day, massive bulk is its predominant feature. It is not only the largest hotel in Europe, but is seen and felt to be the largest from every vantage point, inside and out. This too is typically, if not exclusively, Russian. Size *per se* is a virtue in this country; the Rossiya is the latest of a long line of biggest-in-the-world and largest-in-Europe industrial and commercial projects. One of the funniest comic novels published in the Soviet Union (in 1927, before Stalinism drove the author from print) was about a bureaucrat obsessed with the dream of building a cafeteria on the Rossiya's lines. It was to be 'a giant, the greatest cafeteria, the greatest kitchen ... It will be, if you like, the industrialization of all kitchens.'

The Russian word that describes this passion is *gigantomaniya*. The Rossiya's plot measures no less than thirty-three acres, and it is a measure of the building's gargantuan appearance that it seems to use every inch of this space, although there are in fact many acres of open air and landscaping. The hotel is twelve storey high, with five basements and a separate ten-storey building to house some of the service operations. The main structure's perimeter is almost nine hundred yards; its volume exceeds that of several giant aircraft hangars. This cavernous space is divided into, among other things, three thousand two hundred rooms which can accommodate some five thousand five hundred guests. A fetishist who changed rooms every night would take eight years to complete his rounds.

More than half the hotel's guests can be fed simultaneously in its nine restaurants. Two of these are among the Soviet Union's largest, seating almost a thousand diners each. Six bars, a rare novelty in Russia, are scattered somewhat timidly throughout the vast building, as if on a troopship hastily converted for cruising. But the self-service snack bars called 'buffets' are easier to find: every wing has five, one on every even-numbered floor. Ten thousand eggs, nine thousand pounds of bread and six thousand pounds of meat are among the victuals consumed daily.

In addition to the eating places, there is a ballroom believed to be the world's largest, providing more exhibition space on a single level than in any other hotel. Its freight lifts can deliver large, loaded trucks directly into the hall. Forty barbers are employed in four barber's shops; a medical clinic is supplemented by a small pharmacy; a large hard-currency shop serves foreign tourists. Two eight-hundred-seat cinemas are part of the complex, as well as a larger auditorium called the 'Cine-Concert Hall'. This seats three thousand on stands that fold away automatically to provide open space for dances and exhibitions.

The machinery which supports these vast numbers of people in modern comfort is as impressive as everything else about the hotel – even more so, perhaps, in the context of the country's relative backwardness in consumer services and comforts. The Rossiya is a pioneer in several aspects of mechanization and automation, a kind of Hilton plunked in a still underdeveloped land. Air conditioning, for example, is virtually unknown in Russia except in military installations, but twenty-four giant devices serve the hotel, helping maintain a constant sixty-five degrees in winter and seventy-one in summer. The building is also served by no less than ninety-three lifts and a fifty-pump air-compressor system providing enough suction to vacuum-clean five floors of all wings simultaneously. The food refrigeration capacity is equal to fourteen thousand large domestic refrigerators; the ice-making machinery can produce twenty-five tons daily. The internal telephone system is large enough to service a town of thirty-five thousand people, and the hotel uses as much electricity – one and a half million kilowatt hours per month – as a city of fifty thousand inhabitants.

These statistics pertain primarily to the main twelve-storey building. In addition, there is a twenty-three-storey tower rising from the courtyard in the centre of the hotel. Known as the 'Presidential Wing', it can accommodate guests of almost that stature (though not Richard Nixon during his 1972 visit) in luxuriously furnished suites of up to five rooms. Notables just below the very highest state guests are expected here.

Size, of course, is a virtue in a hotel whose principal functions include accommodating congresses and conventions. The five-thousand-odd delegates to the congresses of the Soviet Communist Party – that most august gathering in the land, whose ceremonial importance exceeds that of the Tory and Labour Conferences and Democratic and Republican Conventions combined – are quartered conveniently and prestigiously here, overlooking the Kremlin. Participants in smaller international gatherings – the biennial Moscow Film Festival, for example – are swallowed up by the structure. Many guests staying in one wing of the hotel are unaware of an event taking place in another.

But if a hotel's role is to provide a haven of homey rest in a world already full of anonymous uniformity, the Rossiya will never win its way on to lists of friendly little inns. To accuse it of being less than cosy is surely unfair at this moment in international architectural history; but the Rossiya may be unique in offering a million cubic yards without a single snug nook. The hotel's hugeness often distresses in other ways. Every day, exasperated guests and guests of guests wait hours for appointments that are never kept; some never discover that they have been in a restaurant below the east lobby instead of the west, or a snack bar in the north wing instead of the south. Even members of the staff occasionally make these mistakes; foreign tourists sometimes lose heart and beg Intourist to move them. To some, the near symmetry of the 'box' and the identical decor of its lobbies make it a rat-maze. At the risk of walking a quarter mile or so in the wrong direction, one must think carefully every time one sets out along a corridor. And if one lives in the south wing, as a young Belgian girl recently explained, and has business at the post office in the north, one does not set out at all unless a good twenty minutes remains before closing time.

Not long ago, a distinguished American scientist arrived at the hotel with the usual entourage of Russian guides, interpreters and representatives of government institutes. To everyone's consternation, his reservation could not be found. A frantic search was set in motion; overwrought telephone calls were made. An experienced traveller to Russia, the scientist took a long walk to give the Russians time. In fact he walked the approximate mile of the hotel's outer circumference – but the accusations and counter-accusations were still in progress when he returned to his lobby. At last, the puzzle was unscrambled; his reservation had indeed been made, but in another wing. The search had lasted an hour. 'Just one of those things,' said a girl behind the desk. 'It happens every day.'

The *patron* of this huge enterprise – the Rossiya's General Director – is a short, thrusting man in his middle fifties named Vasily Andreevich Zashibkin. The picture of the Soviet 'big businessman', Mr Zashibkin seems about to burst through his expensive, obviously imported brown suit. In social origin, education and professional experience, not to speak of political attitudes, Zashibkin is the successful Soviet executive *par excellence*.

And in his rise to the top. Mr Zashibkin was born of solid peasant stock in a village some hundred miles south-east of Moscow. An able, energetic student, he graduated from the Moscow Communications Institute in 1940. During the war, he distinguished himself in the aircraft industry, and also in Party affairs, where he was a trusted stalwart with obvious leadership abilities. The Party favours men of village background and bustling energy, and liked Zashibkin particularly. Soon after the war, he was transferred to full-time Party work, serving tours in Moscow's Directorate of Tall Buildings and Hotels and later in the Municipal Council. When he was selected as the Rossiya's Director – in 1966, while the building was still under construction – he had had no experience in hotel management. But it is not unusual for Party functionaries, especially those with engineering backgrounds, to be entrusted with the operation of vital enterprises. In Russia, ideological trustworthiness and Party discipline take precedence over professional expertise. Moreover, it is in Party work far more than any other that a man's leadership and administrative talents are recognized.

Mr Zashibkin had no more ambition to become the Rossiya's General Director than knowledge he was being considered for the job. 'I used to drive past this huge box of a building and whistle, "Yes sir, that's some piece of construction." But it never crossed my mind that I'd be connected with it, let alone be Director. And I'll tell you a secret: it's a tough job. I wouldn't envy someone else behind this desk.'

The desk is in a spacious office with sheeny wood panelling, emerald carpeting, a large conference table and a private entrance: the Hollywood image of a corporate executive's headquarters. There is a white telephone with forty buttons for communication with Mr Zashibkin's highest subordinates, of whom he can speak to seven simultaneously. A closed-circuit television system transmits panoramas of the three lobbies at the flick of a lever. And, of course, there is a case filled with portraits and statuettes of Lenin.

'I hope you don't spoil your article by describing an old fogey like me,' said Mr Zashibkin, with the smile of a self-made tycoon. 'For goodness sake, save your words for this big, beautiful hotel. Don't forget: it's still young.'

By the nature of things, Mr Zashibkin faces many of the same economic imperatives and pressures as his capitalist counterparts, and the fact that the Rossiya's profits go to the Moscow Municipal Council rather than to stockholders does not appreciably diminish his desire to make them. He is gratified that the hotel's operation is becoming more efficient: last year the costs per bed per day were shaved by fifteen kopeks. But his satisfaction is far from complete. The Rossiya cost over ninety million rubles, and Mr Zashibkin is naturally concerned to reap a respectable return from this huge capital investment.

'We're hoping to recoup our investment in twelve to fifteen years. Last year, our net profit was one million nine hundred thousand rubles (roughly two per cent). This doesn't justify the great capital outlay. Profits should – and could – be higher.'

One reason why profits are not higher is the general Russian tendency to work less hard than Westerners – and, contrary to common assumption, for their employers to demand less of them. For example, each of the Rossiya's chamber-maids is responsible for eight rooms, in contrast to the fourteen at the London Hilton. For all its incessant propaganda about labour productivity and discipline, despite its frenzied exhortations to work better and faster, the Soviet Union rarely drives its workers hard in ordinary jobs. On the contrary, the general policy seems to be to hire and maintain supernumeraries wherever possible. And except when there is a crash effort to meet production norms near the end of a month or quarter, few Russian workers show any real anxiety about – or interest in – getting a job done. Why should *they* worry if the work drags on until tomorrow, or next week?

Coupled with the generally indulgent attitude towards employees, there is a chronic problem of overstaffing; in most organizations and economic enterprises, the presence of extra, idle bodies is what one notices first. At the Rossiya, this takes the form, most glaringly, of teams of operators for self-service lifts – usually bored, faintly insolent girls who look up from their novels only long enough to jab the buttons designed for passengers to push themselves. As if this were not enough, superfluous supervisors are posted on the ground floor of each lobby, supposedly directing the superfluous lift operators. The presence of the supervisors serves only to slow the service slightly, since they are fond of gossiping and joking with the operators while guests wait impatiently to be delivered to their rooms. No doubt there is also a general supervisor of the supervisors.

Mr Zashibkin knows his hotel is overstaffed, and speaks hopefully of reducing the payroll soon. But once hired, Soviet employees are virtually immune from sacking for redundancy; indeed, protection for one and all, in needed jobs and concocted ones, is one of the unspoken principles of the Soviet economy. Streamlining the Rossiya's personnel will be a protracted process.

Another reason why profits are not higher is the remarkably low charge for rooms. Soviet hotel prices are among the lowest in the world. Even in the Rossiya, a single room – spacious enough to include a convertible sofa in addition to the bed and other furniture – costs three rubles, about the price of a moderate restaurant lunch, a seat in the Bolshoi Theatre balcony, or a pair of coarse nylon stockings. A double room costs but five rubles, and a superb five-room suite in the Presidential Tower – with piano, two television sets, stereogram, refrigerator, and three telephones – only fifteen rubles, the price of a good cotton shirt. All this is superb value for money (assuming the extremely unlikely possibility that a Russian could take advantage of it; more about this later).

Prices are so low partly because of the primary function of hotels in the Soviet Union. Very few Russians can use them for private travel; almost all rooms are reserved for personnel, usually managers and scientists, travelling on official business. And with rare exceptions for the most exalted officials, everyone travelling on official business is granted a per diem allowance of two rubles sixty kopeks for their hotel (an allowance, incidentally, which has not changed in over twenty years despite the steady deflation of the ruble's purchasing power). Since both giver and taker of the per diem allowance are *au fond* state agencies, hotels cannot reasonably charge anything in great excess of the allowance. It is a tangled system that prevents hotels from operating as profitable business enterprises – as all Soviet economic units have supposedly been encouraged to do over the past five years – because they cannot set their own prices. And it is typical of the grave obstacles facing Soviet economists in their efforts to rationalize the economy.

'It's a difficult situation,' says Mr Zashibkin. 'We'd like to charge more for our rooms. They're certainly *worth* more, as everybody knows. But at three rubles a day, we're already "taxing" the man who's here on official business – which means almost everyone. So we just have to make the best of it.'

There is no such hindrance to raising prices for foreigners, however; and in catering to them, the Rossiya literally does 'make the best of it'. For the single room which costs a Soviet citizen three rubles, Western tourists pay about ten pounds, or twenty-five dollars. On the official rate of exchange, set arbitrarily by the Soviet government, this is worth about twenty-one rubles. But the official rate is meaningless; on the free market in Europe and black market in Russia, twenty-five dollars fetches one hundred and fifty rubles. Notwithstanding the inclusive breakfast and such services as transportation to and from airports, Westerners are charged astronomically more for the same room. Not double, as under an 'obsolete' and discarded system, and not triple or quadruple, but roughly *thirty-five times* as much!

Few foreigners are aware that they are being so mercilessly fleeced. Some who do discover it are soothed by the Soviet standard reply to their puzzlement: that ten pounds is not, after all, an unreasonable price for a hotel in London. This is a specious answer, however, and not only because in London one would expect a considerably more elegant room in a considerably more elegant hotel for that price. It also implies that Russian tourists who hurry to Marks and Spencer upon arrival in London should be charged six pounds for a pair of tights – the equivalent of what Muscovites pay when they are lucky enough to find them on the black market. But if an outraged foreign guest of the Rossiya persists in his questioning, the Soviet official is likely to answer with his own question – probably about imperialist aggression in the Middle or Far East. The conversation is closed. 'A thief believes that everyone else is a thief,' goes the old Russian saying.

However, these arguments are irrelevant in any case. For if the Western tourist does not like paying thirty-five times as much as a native for his hotel room, he can always ... stay at home. There is no alternative. It is the time-honoured technique of the monopoly exercising its prerogatives and the consumer liking or lumping them.

Although the monopoly in this case is technically not the Rossiya itself, but Intourist – the infamous, exclusive, inescapable agency for foreign tourists – the Rossiya's executives are not embarrassed by the surcharge arrangement. On the contrary, they speak proudly of their special charges. 'Yes, we've learned how to price our rooms for the foreign trade. Yes, they do make us a tidy little profit.' The executives feel they have mastered the workings of capitalism – exploit the customer! – and since the victims are themselves only capitalists, no pity need be wasted on them. On the contrary, squeezing them is performing several services simultaneously for the Motherland and socialism.

The motive for all this is of course the Soviet government's great and growing craving for hard currency, which increases relentlessly as the ruble's real worth devalues. The appetite is now so great that a foreigner will be charged in dollars for a telephone call made from his room in the Rossiya to, say, Leningrad, even though the call had nothing to do with anything abroad. The Rossiya is no less interested than Intourist in hard currency; the two institutions work hand-in-glove, if the metaphor is not too pointed, in parting Western tourists from it. Intourist is assigned a block of the Rossiya's rooms, but the arrangement is flexible; foreigners get preference, of course, as the quest for hard currency dictates, and during the summer may occupy almost the entire hotel. Over the course of the year they account for about a third of the Rossiya's quarter-million guests. A double book-keeping system is maintained, one for Soviet citizens, the other for foreigners. Accountants' skills are not needed to see where the big money lies.

Mr Zashibkin is served by a full management staff, to whom he has, or should have, instant access. Besides the usual internal telephones, the top forty officers are linked by the English-invented Multiphone System. Outside his office, each executive carries a small plastic box which beeps futuristically when he is wanted. The signal tells him to contact the switchboard operator, who relays his message to him. If this sounds too much like arrangements for some General Staff, it should be remembered that, as in the Pentagon, reliable communications are essential – and a Rossiya official can easily be lost in the corridors or bowels of his vast building. And besides, the top Rossiya staff, like officers with new weapons, like to play with their new gadgets.

In the Rossiya, however, Multiphone apparently works better in theory than in practice. A proud executive proposed to show a foreign journalist how the clever invention works by arranging for himself to be paged. As so often happens in Russia, the system broke down through human fault: laziness, lack of interest, or a distracting telephone call from a friend reporting the appearance of woollen socks in an unlikely shop. In this case, the weak link was the switchboard operator in charge of sending out the beeps. Having told her that he himself was urgently needed, the eager executive waited a full five minutes for the signal to sound in his pocket. Finally he rang the operator in exasperation. Oh, she had forgotten all about it, she said – but promised to send out the beeps 'very soon'.

In the Soviet tradition, Mr Zashibkin's management staff is enormous. Almost fifty officers serve him, including some ten heads of departments and four assistant directors (all of whom, unlike the General Director himself, have had considerable experience in hotel management). But a second, and in a sense higher, directorate also functions in the Rossiya, as in every Soviet theatre, restaurant, factory and farm – in each and every economic, social and cultural body in the country. This is the Communist Party captainship.

The term 'Party control' seems so caricaturish on the one hand and textbookish on the other that most strangers to the Soviet system have understandable difficulty picturing it. The example of the Rossiya is not very helpful in unravelling the mystery, for Party secrets remain Party secrets in the vast building, and the essential elements of control are not the business of outsiders. But acquaintance with the hotel reveals, at least, that the concept is not an abstraction. The Party not only has a local headquarters, hierarchy and chain of command, but also maintains agents in every branch and sub-division of the hotel's operations, where they are expected to exercise the leadership which is the Party's *raison d'être*. Three hundred and fifty of the Rossiya's three thousand-odd employees are members, a somewhat greater ratio of Communists to population than in the country as a whole. Almost all the leading executives are members of considerable standing.

In another sense, too, the Rossiya can help one grasp the abstractions of 'the Party' and 'Party control'. It is, of course, simpleminded to assume that all Party functionaries are alike, any more than all bank clerks are. But a certain type of man gravitates to this work, and only men with certain qualities are successful in it. The men entrusted with the Party's operations in the hotel are entirely representative of the Party worker carrying out similar functions everywhere in the country.

The command centre of the Party organization in each economic and cultural enterprise is called the Party Committee: 'Partcom'. The Rossiya's Partcom is represented by the 'Partorg' (Party Organizer): Viktor Illarionovich Savitsky, a small man in a green suit, green tie and green enamel Lenin badge. His office is crammed with mass-produced Woolworth-like pins, medals and postcards of Lenin which are being evaluated, with befitting gravity and thoroughness, as souvenirs for distribution to the Rossiya's guests. 'The Party Committee supervises everything,' declares Mr Savitsky with the solemnity of the organization itself. 'We issue instructions on all matters.'

Yes, but what does the Party actually have to do with the running of a *hotel*? Again, this is a complex question involving the inter-relationship of the Party and management – indeed, the Party and government – everywhere in the Soviet Union. The difficulty in defining the Party's role precisely is illustrated by the fact that Director Zashibkin himself is a longstanding, trusted Party member: what need has he of guidance, not to speak of instruction, from the obviously less dynamic (and almost certainly less capable and powerful) Mr Savitsky? Yet the Partcom meets, deliberates, gives advice and issues directives to the Rossiya's three hundred and fifty Communists, and presumably guides the executives in the management – at least the overriding moral and political principles – of the hotel as a whole.

In any case, one function of the Rossiya's Partcom is well known. Like Partcoms everywhere, it is primarily responsible for the moral rectitude of the entire 'collective' of workers, both Communists and unanointed. This means, first of all, political and ideological instruction. The titles of the latest lectures delivered to the Rossiya's collective speak for themselves about the content and tone of this catechization: (1) 'Left-wing Communism: An Infantile Disorder' (the title of a famous polemic by Lenin); (2) 'The Sharpening of the Ideological Struggle between Socialism and Capitalism Today and the Tasks of Communist Rearing of the Soviet People'; (3) 'The Leninist Plan for the Building of Socialism in the U.S.S.R. and its Realization'; (4) 'Vladimir Ilich Lenin: Leader, Comrade, Man'.

'Our present lectures centre around Lenin,' revealed Mr Savitsky. 'A new decree was recently promulgated on how everyone should prepare to celebrate the Leninist Jubilee. This' (he waved a green booklet in the air) 'is our inspiration and our law. Oh yes, and we're all busy studying the Central Committee's Theses in connection with the Lenin centennial.'

In addition to lectures, the Party Committee organizes pilgrimages to places where Lenin lived, worked and walked. Trips are arranged to 'Leninist places' as far away as his Volga birthplace and the former capital of Leningrad. There are lectures on international politics, in which capitalist evils are exposed, and Soviet rebuffs to imperialist plots analysed and celebrated. The Party also helps arrange courses on 'aesthetics' for the Rossiya's staff: how to dress attractively, behave in public, appreciate music. 'We're responsible for people's cultural development. Not only their moral strength and the correct political attitudes.' But the Partorg takes pains to emphasize that the Partcom is not 'in the clouds'. On the contrary, it is battling with all its energy and resolve for something tangible: successful fulfilment of the hotel's plans and norms. 'What we want to inspire is a *rise in productivity*. Not just slogans, but more work – that's the best gift we can give the Motherland.'

The Party Committee claims great success in inspiring the Rossiya's employees to give such 'gifts'. Not less than six hundred and fifty of them are 'Shock Workers of Communist Labour', and to the last man and woman, the remaining two thousand three hundred and fifty are fighting for the coveted title – which includes an obligation not only to work well but also to behave decorously in private. Moreover, Mr Savitsky divulged, every employee without exception has pledged to contribute his own personal 'socialist obligation' in honour of the Leninist year. And a few Saturdays ago, the Party Committee organized what is known as a *subbotnik*, in which citizens are permitted to volunteer their labour, usually with a shovel or broom, to some project on a day off, without pay. The project was helping with the Rossiya's unfinished construction and 'every single employee volunteered – to give something personally to the Motherland and Five-Year Plan'.

'Everyone was singing, it was a real celebration,' hummed Mr Savitsky. 'So you see, Lenin's jubilee is not a holiday where you sit around all day guzzling vodka. No, no. It's a time for giving the Motherland your labour. Remember, Lenin himself worked on *subbotniks* – I'll show you his photograph. There, Lenin. That's the inspiration and teaching of our Party.'

With this evidence of intrepid moral leadership and building-of-Communism zeal, a stranger to Soviet life might feel confidence in the Rossiya's immunity from scandal. Yet even in its brief existence, and despite its exalted position in Soviet society as the official hotel for Party Congresses, the Rossiya has been afflicted with a degree of bribery and embezzlement that can only be called normal in Russia. Greed for private profit has penetrated literally to the Kremlin's walls.

The most celebrated affair took place – according to knowledgeable Muscovites; it was not mentioned in the press – in the late 1960s. It concerned lemons, love of luxury and Georgians. Among other treasures of a warm climate and appropriate soil, lemons are what make Georgians by far the richest of the Soviet nationalities, and love of luxury lies deep in their bones. Soviet conditions played their part in this combination, too: without astounding consumer shortages Georgians could not have grown rich in the ways they have; and perhaps they would be less inclined towards conspicuous consumption – in this case, their great urge to stay in the Rossiya, and only the Rossiya, on their frequent Moscow trips.

In any case, soon after the Rossiya opened, it was noticed that wealthy Georgians were flocking to the hotel and securing accommodation by bribing members of the administrative staff. Many of these not-entirely-welcome guests were 'businessmen' who had flown to Moscow to peddle suitcases of lemons and other exorbitantly expensive fruits and vegetables grown on their own private plots. An uncomfortable situation became progressively worse: by late 1969, almost half the hotel's Soviet guests were said to be Georgians. The Rossiya became the Moscow headquarters of Tbilisi tycoons: *mutatis mutandis*, the status symbol was as indispensable as the Hilton to a certain category of Americans in London. Finally – so the story goes – an investigation was launched in the Central Committee of the Communist Party, and when the scope of the bribery was revealed, many of the Rossiya's administrative staff were discharged.

The account usually concludes with an observation that far fewer Georgians subsequently made use of the hotel. Apparently the scandal had simmered down by the time of my own visit, however, for my neighbour for several days was a large, obviously well-heeled Georgian with luggage packed with fruit, a strong predilection for expensive cognac, and a habit of gathering a dozen countrymen in his room for midnight suppers. Guttural songs and raucous laughter rang in my ears late into every night, proving, if nothing about the Georgian Affair itself, that the Rossiya's walls are no more soundproof than those of most of its Western counterparts. When the Georgian finally vacated his room, it was with a smile of huge self-satisfaction under his luxuriant moustache, and a large collection of cardboard suitcases. Emptied of fruit, they had been stuffed with hundreds of rubles-worth of GUM purchases.

One of the principal causes of the Georgian Affair – and of the chronic bribery in order to secure rooms even in far less desirable hotels – is the general shortage of hotel beds. Like most goods and services in Russia, hotel space is wildly inadequate: less than a third of the requirements, according to a recent Soviet trade journal. This is presumably a conservative estimate, in keeping with the tendency of Soviet statistics in such matters. Moreover, the demand is kept artificially low because potential customers, knowing that their wants cannot be met, do not even express them. Beyond this, there is the usual frustration for Russians arising from the allocation to foreigners of 'deficit' goods and services in exchange for the Holy Grail of hard currency.

Moscow is incomparably better off for hotel space than other Soviet cities, for it is here that the international conferences and seminars are held, and supreme efforts are made to accommodate foreign tourists in the country's principal showplace. Still, despite impressive plans for expansion, the capital has only fifty thousand hotel beds, a fraction of the number in Western cities of comparable importance. Elsewhere in the country the shortage is far severer, causing a mad scramble for a place to sleep, and the familiar, permanent NO VACANCIES sign at hotel counters. In the lobbies of Moscow hotels not catering to foreign tourists, a dozen or more weary travellers are almost always encamped on lobby chairs or benches through the night, hoping against hope – not for their own room, or even a shared double, but for a camp bed in a dormitory, for which the charge is a ruble a day. This type of accommodation accounts for many of the beds available in non-Intourist hotels.

Hard as it is, however, the scramble for hotel space would be far worse did not the Soviet people tailor their demands to the shortage. Unless they have friends or relatives who can put them up, many Russians simply refrain from travelling to another city, whether for private business or pleasure; and unless they have good contacts or 'influence', those who do make a trip avoid the bother of inquiring at hotel counters only to be snapped at by surly receptionists. Tourism and travelling are understandably among the least developed Soviet industries.

Like most first-class Soviet hotels, the Rossiya takes *no* private citizens 'off the street'. All rooms are carefully allocated through official channels. To procure one, a request must be made by a state agency, usually a Ministry or research institute with adequate prestige and 'pull', for a person arriving in Moscow on official business. Ivan Ivanovich from Odessa, in other words, will not so much as apply to stay in the Rossiya if he is simply visiting Moscow with his wife.

Neither, however, can Viktor Viktorovich apply if he is a Muscovite – no matter how famous he is and how solid his ministerial contacts. For it is a nation-wide Soviet rule that no citizen may stay in a hotel in his own city. And the rule defies evasion, since Russians must present their papers – in which their authorized place of residence is recorded – when registering at any hotel. Thus, except for its public rooms, the Rossiya is 'out of bounds' for some eight million Muscovites. Once again, shortage is the rationale for this rule; but many Russians feel another factor is also involved: a persistent moral disapproval of hotels and their purposes. What business would an honest citizen have in a hotel room, the Party would want to know, when he has his own flat, room or dormitory bed in the same city?

Hotels and restaurants are still considered twilight places smacking of bourgeois decadence and insidious influences;

upstanding citizens, whose thoughts naturally centre on Strengthening the Motherland and Building Communism, will not care to spend much time in them, except for an occasional celebratory fling or when on official assignment in a distant city. Untrustworthy elements are likely to lurk in the lobbies and eating places: sybarites, black marketeers and 'cosmopolitans' – people with time and money to waste. And this kind of company honest hard-working citizens naturally want to avoid.

This attitude manifests itself most strongly in lectures by judges and prosecutors in Soviet courts and 'people-gone-astray' articles in the Soviet press. The setting of these socialist-morality sermonets is often a hotel: the speculators, 'parasites' and dissolute elements are described planning their deals and spending their free hours and filthy lucre here. Hotels are indeed the centres – and in many Soviet cities, the only places – for wining and dining. In the absence of bars, pubs, cabarets and coffee houses, not to speak of discotheques and night clubs, Russians who crave a few hours of high life can only gravitate to hotel restaurants.

Unless they happen to read Russian, foreign guests will not notice this suspicion of hotels. For them, however, another property of Russian hotels sets them apart from Western ones: the dominant role of an institution called the Service Bureau.

The Service Bureau is the outpost of Intourist in hotels to which foreigners are admitted. The large, prominent office near the lobby deals with foreigners' passport registration, travel arrangements inside Russia and abroad, requests for tours, cars, reservations, theatre tickets – in short, with most of a traveller's requirements, including coupons for food and drink. It is a thoroughly 'Soviet' organization because it combines the functions of hospitality and control. For no arrangements, above all no travel arrangements, can be made except through and by the Service Bureau. This has become so much a part of the Soviet system and psychology that many Russians cannot imagine travelling abroad without Service Bureaux. 'Just like that? Just freely? You mean people wandering around another country without any itinerary or place to go? You can't fool me: that would be anarchy for the country – and hell for the tourists themselves.'

There is misapprehension on the side of foreign tourists too. The Service Bureau is the office with which most travellers in Russia have their closest, if not their only, contact; through it they form their impression of Soviet institutions in general. A foreigner whose ticket has been lost or flight changed without being consulted, or who encounters the dictatorial arrogance with which Intourist often makes its maddening ineptitude law, will have a very poor opinion of the Service Bureau. And indeed a large number of Western tourists spend much of their extremely expensive holiday time pounding desks in frustration and futile rage. Nevertheless, these people have been served incomparably better than Russians who must deal with ordinary Soviet organizations, for as agencies of Intourist, Service Bureaux are far more efficient than most Soviet offices. Enormous pains are taken to please foreigners: arrangements are made overnight that would mean days or weeks of waiting for Russians; smiles greet their requests instead of barked refusals; tickets and seats are procured for which most Russians know it is pointless even to apply.

All this is done for the despised but greedily coveted hard currency as well as out of impulses of Russian hospitality. At the same time, foreigners are relieved of the searing inconveniences of ordinary travel in Russia: the day-long queues and sleeping in railway stations; the scrambling, snarling and fighting at ticket counters. The advantages are obvious of being delivered from one's hotel in Intourist cars to special Intourist waiting rooms at airports and major railway stations, from there to be escorted to planes and trains on the strength of Intourist reservations while the hoi polloi scrambles. The disadvantage is that most foreign tourists catch but a glimpse, literally, of local conditions.

The Rossiya's Service Bureau – to return to the particular – corresponds to the size of the hotel itself, which is to say that it is outsized. Each of the three lobbies has a sweeping office housing complete facilities and services for its own wing of the building. Among office staff are forty-six skilled interpreters offering all the world's major languages, including Turkish (but not, at the moment, Chinese). Some thirty thousand theatre tickets a year are procured for the hotel's guests, even though most Moscow theatres are closed over the summer, the hotel's busiest season for foreigners. And the requests for tours, plane and train tickets, taxis, rented cars and reservations in Moscow's hugely over-crowded restaurants are correspondingly profuse.

Not a few of the requests put the staff on their mettle. Recently, for example, a tourist checked into the hotel with a pet monkey. This curious travelling companion urgently needed bananas, but most fruit is exceedingly rare during Moscow's six or seven winter months. The enterprising Service Bureau employees were able to find a small supply – possibly through the shops that serve foreign-ers for hard currency, or that are reserved for high government, Party and secret-police officials. Other requests, best described as eccentric, reflect some of the odd notions entertained in the West about supposed Russian scientific and medical breakthroughs. One elderly lady arrived from Australia soon after reading there about a 'fountain of youth' with a life-giving elixir developed by Soviet scientists. From the check-in counter she proceeded immediately to the Service Bureau for details about where to purchase the tonic. Remembering their exhaustive training *not to insult or ignore guests*, the girls on duty patiently telephoned Moscow's medical research institutes: was a fountain of youth in operation there, they asked, and if so, what were the hours for foreign visitors? 'We try our best always,' said the Director of the Service Bureau wryly. 'Unfortunately, we weren't able to help in this particular case. Too bad; I'd have liked a glass of elixir myself.'

Such good-nature is part of his stock in trade. Boris Vasilievich Ionov is a thin, slightly stooped man in his late fifties; he has a ready boyish smile, and nervously lights a fresh cigarette from the stub of the last. This key executive has had even less hotel experience than Director General Zashibkin. An army officer, he was retired in the 1960s, during Nikita Khrushchev's contraction of the military establishment. Feeling too young and vigorous for retirement, he cast about for work to supplement his pension. The idea of running the country's largest Service Bureau appealed to him the minute he heard of it. 'This hotel job is mostly working with people, after all. And I worked with people all the time as an officer – that's what the army's all about, isn't it?'

It is a moot question whether a military background is ideal for hotel management, but if Mr Ionov is a fair example, extensive military training might be the solution to Russia's management problems. The difficulties of decision-making in the Soviet economy constitute a separate subject, and a very large one indeed. Here it is enough to hint at the mountains of documents and authorizations required to take the most minor decisions, and the extreme rigidity and sluggishness this system, together with the infinity of rules and regulations, breeds into executives at every level. (One small example from the area of hotel management. I once had a heated exchange with a Leningrad hotel manager who later apologized and sent a bottle of mineral water to my room. The gesture was at her own expense, for use of hotel – i.e. state – funds for this purpose would have required authorization at three or four levels, involving days of telephoning and massive documentation. The bottle cost twelve kopeks.)

Mr Ionov, however, is a thrilling exception to the rule of inertia, languor and red tape in Soviet offices. Although his office was but a few floors below my room, I had been waiting ten days in the Rossiya while Novosti tried to make an appointment for me; this was one of those one-telephone-call tasks that seemed too much for them. Time was running out for this stay in Moscow, and at last I decided to ring Ionov myself. The results were astounding: with an amicable greeting, the ex-officer invited me to his office immediately to outline what I wanted to see in the hotel. In all my years of reporting in Moscow, this was the first and only time that an official of any rank reacted spontaneously, opening his office door without days of prevaricating. The reflection on the Soviet Army is flattering: if Mr Ionov is in any way typical, one can assume that in military affairs, if nowhere else in Soviet life, executives are efficient and willing to listen. Or is it that Mr Ionov's long years of military training have made him courageous enough to see a foreign journalist on the spur of the moment? In either case, he is that rara avis in Soviet officialdom, a man of *action*.

Apparently men of action were sorely lacking when the Rossiya was being built. Or perhaps, on the contrary, only men of uncommon energy and determination were able to overcome the bureaucratic inertia of a project of this size. In either case, the story of the building of the Rossiya is a virtual primer of the Soviet construction industry, with all its economies of size, innovative labour-saving technology and monumental losses caused by waste, delay and muddle. 'Story' is not the word, however; as so often with important Soviet projects, the Rossiya's construction became a saga.

The hotel's site is one of old Moscow's best known regions, the home of petty craftsmen and vendors who participated in the open-air carts-and-stalls trade that thrived for centuries in and near Red Square. It was called *Zaradye* – 'behind the rows' of Red Square booths. During the sixteenth and seventeenth centuries, *Zaradye* became a jumble of stalls, shops, markets, flats, workshops and twisting lanes with evocative and colourful names. Shoemakers and saddlers, tailors and blacksmiths eked out a living in their tiny quarters and workshops, squeezed among dismal warehouses, grain dealers' depots and taverns. In the twentieth century, *Zaradye* was still picturesque but had become one of the city's worst slums, with the dosshouses and low life Gorky liked to describe. In 1947, to commemorate the eight-hundredth anniversary of the founding of Moscow, the Soviet government decreed its reclamation. Demolition began some two years later.

The U.S.S.R. Council of Ministers, highest body in the government, decreed the construction of a building for its own administrative offices on the site. It was to be thirty-two storey high – immense by Moscow standards – and crowned by a giant red star. The building was designed in the well-known 'Stalinist' skyscraper style of the Ministry of Foreign Affairs and the Hotel Ukraine which now dominates Moscow's skyline. Seven of these encrusted behemoths were already built; this was to be the eighth and largest. Plans were drawn up with the necessary care and duly approved by the necessary governmental agencies.

Work began in 1950. The foundations required heavy expenditure, but as a giant, high priority project it was allocated appropriate resources in men and material. Construction progressed for three years, then everything was discontinued and the building abandoned.

It was a huge loss of labour and money, but reversals on this scale and at this cost are not uncommon in Moscow history of the Soviet period. The vast outdoor swimming pool less than a mile upriver from the Rossiya is in fact the abandoned foundation of what was to have been the world's tallest building, the stupendous 'Palace of Soviets'. After construction of that leviathan had begun, however – to the accompaniment of corresponding publicity about socialist architecture, the socialist system and Stalin – it was found, among other miscalculations, that the clay subsoil would not support the weight. And it was also reckoned that the giant statue of Lenin which was to crown this structure would often be obscured by Moscow's low-hanging clouds – a covert insult to the Leader of Mankind and a blow to Soviet morale. These errors, it is said, led to the shooting of a group of prominent architects and engineers for 'subversion'. (A man who worked on the project, luckily for him in a minor capacity, also says that the fingers of Lenin's outstretched right hand – the left was to be gripping a tome of Marx – were to conceal secret anti-aircraft armament for the capital's defence. Although this story sounds specious, it is fairly typical of the kind that still circulate about this bizarre period of Soviet rule.)

The Rossiya's abortive predecessor, however, was abandoned for happier reasons. It was realized that the huge building would have left the Kremlin and Red Square both literally and figuratively in its shadow, devastating the scale and flavour of Russia's most famous square mile. The site lay abandoned for a biblical seven years while governmental and professional bodies debated its use. Various proposals were advanced and supported – somewhat timidly, it is said, because of the fate of the Palace of Soviets engineers. At last Soviet history came on easier times, and in 1957 the concept of a hotel was approved. The architect Dmitry N. Chechulin was commissioned to draw up the plans.

Chechulin was an authoritative figure: a member of the U.S.S.R. Academy of Architects and, if the metaphor is excusable, a pillar of the Moscow architectural establishment. Through him, one gets a hint of the workings of Soviet architecture at the highest level. He was the architect of several of Moscow's most prominent, if not most distinguished, buildings, including the Tchaikovsky Concert Hall and Hotel Peking on Mayakovsky Square, and a huge block of flats on the Kotelnicheskaya Quay. Immediately after completing the Rossiya, he was commissioned to design the extremely important *new* House of Soviets, soon to be built on Krasnopresnenskaya Square. Two of his earlier structures are among the seven 'Stalinist' skyscrapers that glower down upon Moscow. Indeed, Chechulin was the architect of the very red-starred giant which was to have been built a decade earlier on the Rossiya's site!

Thus the leading practitioner of a crushingly unattractive, almost universally disliked style remains in high favour and continues to re-build Moscow to his own taste. How can Chechulin's remarkable durability be accounted for? Political considerations would seem to play a significant role: it appears that the important architectural decisions in Moscow are strongly influenced by a tight little group of 'elder statesmen' who have friends in high places and get the plum jobs. That Moscow's present Chief Architect was the creator of at least one of the remaining Stalinist skyscrapers strengthens this assumption. There is nothing necessarily sinister in this, of course; it follows the pattern of professional relationships everywhere. But since every major building in Moscow – and the Soviet Union – is by the nature of things an affair of state, this arrangement drastically curtails variety and creativity. Or perhaps the high government officials who take the decisions about prominent buildings are fond of the heavy, orthodox style of the Chechulins, so faithfully reflecting the tone of the Soviet government. But the explanation of the Chechulins' survival and prosperity may be simpler still: they have shown themselves to be reliable.

In any case, Dmitry Chechulin and the organization he headed – Shop No. 16 of MosDesign-One – went to work designing the Rossiya, fully conscious, as he was later to write, that it would be one of the capital's most important buildings. Some twenty-five architects of Chechulin's team worked on the initial plans, which were completed in 1960.

A chronicle of the meetings and forums, seminars and synods, conferences and colloquiums devoted to reviewing these plans would fill the better part of a textbook. The proliferation of architectural councils and city-planning units with at least a consultative voice in matters of this nature seems even greater in the Soviet Union than in most Western countries. The city of Moscow alone has a clutch of city-planning and architectural agencies, not to speak of committee upon committee of the City Soviet (Municipal Council). In the end, the plans were examined and approved by all of them at all required stages.

But not without opposition. Disapproval came principally from what might be called 'left-wing' architects and city planners, whose professional standing was often distinctly higher than Chechulin's. They argued that a structure of the Rossiya's monolithic mass would forever destroy the harmony of the Kremlin and Red Square, Russia's unique, symbolic centre. Its crushing bulk would so dwarf the surroundings, as well as clash painfully with them, that all scale and sense of proportion would be lost. At least part of the site, they pleaded, should be a park, Russia's most glorious, with perhaps a small museum of history, art or architecture – something that would let the existing structures live, rather than suffocate them.

The conflict was a classic one. Chechulin argued in terms of Moscow's urgent need for hotel accommodation and of the close correlation between hotel size and profitability, which everyone wanted. 'The construction of large hotels in preference to others', he wrote, 'is necessary for many reasons, above all, economic ones.' In other words, his was the language of the developer. His opponents spoke for the conservationists and lovers of history, visualizing St Basil's Cathedral, an incomparable masterpiece of Russian design, lost against a background of vulgar aluminium and glass instead of the sky for which its evocative shapes were intended. St Basil's and all of Red Square would become a cheap toy, and the Kremlin, the country's greatest architectural treasure, would be callously violated by the giant box with its disregard for existing proportions. Especially when viewed from the Moscow River or its opposite bank, urban Russia's most glorious ensemble would be forever destroyed.

The controversy is familiar to virtually every major city of every nation. The difference was that it took place, as do most Soviet conflicts involving governmental decisions, largely in secret; the myth of unanimity in the Soviet government is preserved with great pains. Nevertheless, arguments of this kind, which do not directly challenge the Party's authority, are not entirely suppressed, and protests against the building of the Rossiya did achieve a modicum of publicity. The most prominent took the form of a letter to *Moscow Pravda* in October 1961. Signed by sixteen celebrated architects, artists, city planners and other intellectuals, including many Lenin Prize winners, it quoted Lenin on the need to make the banks of the Moscow River green, called the Rossiya an 'architectural crime', and begged for reconsideration of the entire problem. A gigantic building on the site, the letter said, would mock eight centuries of Russian history.

Objecting to the general idea of a hotel on this site, the distinguished artists and architects were also scathingly critical of this building in particular. The Rossiya, they said, was no more than a squashed version of Chechulin's thirty-two-storey skyscraper abandoned almost ten years before. 'It may be massive but it is not monumental, and far from majestic.' The letter also pointed out that when the building's plans were discussed in the U.S.S.R. Union of Architects, the majority voted against them.

Why, then, were the plans later approved? The most satisfactory answer seems to be that the final, affirmative decision was made not by architects or city planners, not even by the Moscow City

Council, the site's nominal proprietor, but by no less a body than the Central Committee of the Soviet Communist Party. Most informed Muscovites feel certain that a structure of the Rossiya's importance – not to speak of the significance of its location, overlooking the Kremlin – required the endorsement of the very highest political authority. And since the Central Committee itself had originally initiated the idea of a hotel and selected Chechulin as the architect, it was naturally disposed in favour of the end product of its own decisions. 'It's the Central Committee's hotel, make no mistake about it,' a Moscow artist put it recently (and quietly). 'Everything in it reflects the Central Committee's style. Not exactly Stalinist like the old skyscrapers but a stubborn rock, like the Committee. Ponderous. Pompously solemn. They try so hard to be "stately", as understood by their own lower-class tastes and perceptions.'

The opponents were not appeased by the rescue of half a dozen of *Zaradye*'s more memorable old churches on the outskirts of the Rossiya's site. The Rossiya's designers offer this preservation as proof of their own good intentions and remarkable imagination. 'It's a fantastic and unique idea: a dazzling combination of an ultra-modern hotel against the background of our national cultural treasures. We think it's unequalled for sensitivity and beauty by any modern hotel in the world.' Rumour has it, however, that the task was forced upon the architects because the excavation of the site and construction of the substructure had badly undermined the old buildings. This provoked a new wave of protests from the 'left-wing' architects and conservationists and this time the Communist Party's Central Committee intervened, ordering the builders not only to stop damaging the churches, but to restore them at their own cost.

Whoever saved them, the restored churches – and the thirteen hundred trees and shrubs planted on the grounds with obvious care – are an enchanting sight, especially when viewed from an angle which excludes the massive monolith itself. (And one must of course remember the horrific destruction of architectu treasures during the crudest Soviet anti-religious campaigns of the

1930s. In that decade, the desecration and dynamiting of chapels paralleled the destruction of human life. Among the losses was the celebrated Cathedral of the Saviour, on the site chosen by Stalin for the Palace of Soviets. In all, according to one expert, 'some four hundred and twenty-six of the best specimens of classical Moscow ecclesiastical and secular architecture were obliterated'.) Many of the surviving buildings have important historical, as well as aesthetic, significance. One housed an old guild-cum-club for English traders who helped reopen Russia to the West in the sixteenth century. Nearby is an ancient house where Romanov boyars lived before the family became Russia's ruling dynasty. Looking down on the river, on the opposite side of the hotel, stands the church of Anna Zachastiye ('The Constant Visitor'), where childless couples prayed for the blessing of fertility. Ivan the Terrible was married in the Church of St Maxim, another of the restored structures.

The opponents of the Rossiya admire these restored buildings only grudgingly because, they say, the hotel has robbed them of all proportion to their surroundings. Preserved and painstakingly restored, the previously crumbling old churches and chapels, tiny by comparison to the hotel, now serve as decoration for it, circling the square structure 'like bits of jewellery around a bath tub', as one young architect put it. These critics feel that there is something self-consciously cute about the clean, brightly painted churches which now so obviously provide 'local colour'. 'They've not only lost their social and architectural meaning,' complained an artist recently. 'They've also become distasteful. In the way a pretty little lap dog is vulgarly indecent in the arms of some bulbous matron.'

Nevertheless, even the disappointed and the cynical prefer the preservation and restoration of the churches to the alternative. The old buildings reflect an intimacy, style and sense of 'values-in-proportion' and 'national roots' which appeal strongly to 'left-wing' intellectuals, with their new-found love of old Russian folk culture.

After the final decision to build had been taken, the Rossiya's opponents came to terms with their defeat. One cited an old Russian saying – 'After a fight, you don't wave your fists about' – to illustrate the futility, and perhaps danger, of continued protest against the Central Committee's will. When the construction was nearly completed and the building's 'glaring' and 'tragic' effects on its surroundings had become clear, they were more than ever convinced that their opposition had been justified. But although criticism at this stage might have helped improve some minor details, further struggle wasn't worth it. Here another old Russian saying was quoted: 'When your head's been cut off, you don't cry over your hair.'

'We've put a Hilton in Red Square,' moaned a young architect recently who has access to Western magazines and knows about such things. 'No, an *imitation* Hilton. And a mediocre imitation. The biggest hunk of pretension on earth.' This accusation would not offend the Rossiya's designers. On the contrary, Hiltons were high on the list of hotels they studied before turning to their drawing boards. 'We familiarized ourselves with Western hotel technology,' they say proudly. 'Hiltons. And in many capitalist countries. It was our solemn duty to examine and incorporate the best of foreign design and experience.'

The Rossiya's designers paid earnest lip service to the concept of harmonizing the building with its unique surroundings. 'The beauty of the Kremlin-Red Square ensemble is as important as its supreme historical significance,' said the project's Chief Engineer. 'This is the centre of world revolution. All progressive peoples of the world consider it sacred.' (He glanced quickly at his colleague, a vigorous young man who had mysteriously appeared, as a 'colleague' usually does, just before the interview.) 'Our hotel had to blend organically with these surroundings and, in keeping with the site's historical and political significance, express the highest possible taste.'

At the same time, hotel economics required a contemporary building with all the latest equipment and services. Every room in the hotel was to have a bathroom containing bidet and shower in addition to the usual conveniences. There were many unusual features, such as heating between the double windows of the public rooms to make them comfortable during Moscow's seven-month winter. 'Russian hospitality was another of our goals,' said the Chief Engineer, 'but you can't have *any* kind of hospitality in a draughty room ... ' And, of course, there was the profit motive: the designers were determined to make the hotel pay.

These considerations and others made the Rossiya an unusually challenging project. After four years of work, the designers themselves were extremely pleased with what they call their 'baby'. 'I can honestly say we're delighted with the way the building has worked out,' the Chief Engineer beamed. 'How it's run, of course, is something else; that's out of our hands.'

Construction began in 1961, undertaken by Trust No. 2 of Chief-MosConst, the universal consortium responsible for all building in the capital. The 'Cine-Concert Hall' made use of a part of the foundation of the abortive 1950 skyscraper. By 1963, the Rossiya's shell was rising behind wooden fences, like some great industrial project on the Volga.

It was an immense undertaking, involving massive earth-moving machines, thousands of workers, the use of explosives and many of the mechanization-industrialization-automation techniques in which Soviet engineers excel. Almost all manual work by skilled craftsmen was confined to the public rooms on the lower two floors. For the upper ten storeys housing the three thousand two hundred guest rooms, standardization and prefabrication were the central elements of construction. On factory conveyors, *two* storeys at a time were manufactured in the form of prefabricated concrete structural members, and the components shipped to the site for erection. 'The entire hotel was built on this pattern,' explained the Chief Engineer. 'Maximum prefabrication, minimum wet-work at the site. It's what we call the "industrialization" of construction.'

With these ultra-modern methods, the Rossiya's entire frame was completed in less than a year: from spring 1963 to spring 1964.

Then, typically, the structure stood virtually abandoned during the following year while a search was made for the necessary plumbers, plasterers, electricians and carpenters. Thus the handsome savings in time and money were lost while the great capital investment lay fallow. It was a classic example of the rush-to-wait pattern common to most armies and the Soviet construction industry.

Even when the necessary craftsmen were delivered to the site, progress was slower in almost every area than had been hoped. This too was a reflection of a general Soviet pattern, for 'finishing' work, requiring attention to detail, is almost always more slowly and less satisfactorily accomplished than heavy, basic excavation and structural jobs. The Soviet construction industry – indeed, Soviet industry generally, with a few exceptions such as watches and cameras – excels in brawn over finesse. This is why Russians can export, say, some of their massive excavating machinery, but must import equipment, furnishings and even workmen in the rare cases when they take the pains to finish the interior of a building to Western standards. In the Kremlin's Palace of Congresses, for example – setting for Communist Party Congresses and other exalted gatherings – the parquet flooring is said to derive from Italy, the air-conditioning from Britain, much of the furniture design from Scandinavia, and the glass from Germany. Similarly, Czech and East German designers and craftsmen were imported for the more exacting work on the Council of Economic Co-operation skyscraper.

Nevertheless, the fitting out of the Rossiya's rooms, restaurants, bars, air-conditioning units and greenhouse (where the hotel raises its own plants) pressed slowly forward, and most of the equipment was Soviet, except for the Finnish-made furniture and other especially sophisticated items.

The next three years of struggle, until the Rossiya welcomed its first paying guest, were reported to the Soviet people in unlimited detail by detachments of correspondents from the construction site. 'Struggle' is the appropriate word: press descriptions were phrased like dispatches from the front. As with all major Soviet construction projects, the Rossiya was treated as a do-or-die, victory-over-all endeavour whose success, which was vital to the Motherland, was threatened by the forces of indifference, sloppiness and neglect – with always a suggestion of more sinister enemies lurking in the background. The huge red banners of the construction site itself suggested the tone of this period: FORWARD TO VICTORY! COMPLETE THE PROJECT AHEAD OF SCHEDULE! SOVIET CONSTRUCTION WORKERS: FULFIL YOUR DUTY!

Whether this strident crusade mentality is a function of the Soviet system or of something more deep-seated in Russian life is a matter for speculation. Soviet economics, with its goal of making every citizen a conscious warrior in the struggle for the national welfare – and the concomitant tendency towards laziness and indifference through lack of incentives and consumer goods for rewards – is unquestionably a factor. But so too is the Russian national character, with its well-known capacity for exuberant self-congratulation after successful achievements and profound suspicion about Russia's ability to compete with the West – in building hotels, evidently, as in most other undertakings. At any rate, the articles about the Rossiya in the Soviet press expressed that singular Soviet combination of self-satisfaction over the construction – 'Hurrah! Look what *we've* done!' – and whining dissatisfaction that the construction was not going well enough. This fuss over a project that would be taken for granted in the West can only be described as childish. It is one of the aspects of propaganda from which cosmopolitan Russians feel a powerful urge to escape.

In the case of the Rossiya, progress at the 'construction front' was reported not only wing by wing but floor by floor and craft by craft to a nation presumably holding its breath. *Item*: 'Next week, the electricians will be moving up to the eighth floor of the north wing. Brigade Leader N. V. Belkin has promised to complete the work there within two weeks. His brigade is battling for the title, "Brigade of Communist Labour" ... ' The movements of the carpenters, plasterers, plumbers, painters, tile-layers and furniture movers were reported in like detail.

Together with news of this level of interest – the Soviet public is enlightened by similar items not less than a thousand times a day, *every* day – there were equally interesting accounts of individual workers and brigades who had pledged themselves to voluntary new targets for the sake of the Rossiya, Lenin and the Motherland. Usually these 'socialist obligations' were assumed in honour of one or another of the most important national holidays. Thus in the months preceeding May Day and the Anniversary of the October Revolution there was a rash of pledging by zealous workers. 'The plumbers, led by Brigade Leader I. F. Silonov, have pledged themselves to install all bathroom fixtures in the eastern wing before the May Day holiday ... ' This was repeated twice a year – year after year. It was supplemented by socialist obligations for other important days, such as Construction Workers' Day and Lenin's Birthday. And for the fiftieth Anniversary of the Bolshevik Revolution, the pledges were more numerous, solemn and impressive than ever.

Only someone who has worked on a Soviet construction site or in a Soviet factory can know what 'socialist obligations' actually signify in terms of producing more real work. The outsider must suspect that they mean very little beyond the niagara of stupefyingly boring copy they provide for national, local and wall newspapers. The hundreds of thousands, perhaps millions, of these declarations made at regular intervals during the revolutionary calendar seem to change nothing. In most cases, the 'socialist obligation' involves work that would ordinarily – or hopefully – be completed without it. And when they are abrogated, nothing seems to happen except, inevitably, new pledges for the next anniversary and nagging newspaper articles which, when analysed, suggest that roughly half the old pledges were not kept.

Soaring costs and unmet deadlines are hardly peculiar to the Soviet construction industry. What made the Rossiya's case typically Soviet was the urgent nationwide ballyhoo that accompanied the protracted years of building. When the hotel received its first paying guest in December 1966, a thousand sighs of relief were surely heaved by as many construction executives and foremen. A small ceremony marking the date was held in the west wing facing the Kremlin, whose lobby has been regarded as the main one ever since. Construction workers pledged to complete the remaining wings by November 1967, to honour the fiftieth anniversary of Soviet rule. Parts of the south wing were in fact opened on time, but the east wing was not completed for another four months and the north wing until late 1968, a full year after the solemn pledge. This still left the 'Presidential Tower', parts of which were ready a full year after *that*.

And construction still dragged on. Workers assumed socialist obligations to complete the Cine-Concert Hall by April 1970, to honour the centennial of Lenin's birth; but once again unforeseen complications caused delays. Among other things, a large swimming pool and a sauna remained to be built. According to a later schedule all this was to have been completed in 1971, some ten years after construction had begun, and almost a quarter of a century after the decision was taken to rehabilitate the site. Then yet another deadline was established. The Rossiya's construction lasted almost half as long as Soviet rule.

The end product of this quarter-century of effort leaves most Western tourists, especially architects and professional hoteliers, with mixed feelings. In some respects, the Rossiya is far superior to any other hotel in Russia: many of the conveniences of a modern hotel are available to guests, and most of the equipment works most of the time. The frustrations of Moscow's older Intourist hotels – no hot water for hours at a time, dead telephones, switchboard personnel who behave like enemy radio operators and manage to wake guests every other dawn with wrong-number calls – have been largely eliminated. It is a relatively smooth-working enterprise, where obvious pains have been taken to build the equipment correctly and keep it maintained.

Beyond this, the very generous accommodations – even a single room easily takes two people – are well heated and kept reasonably clean. And, rare luxury in a modern hotel, the windows open easily, allowing guests fresh air instead of air-conditioning's chilled imitation.

On the other hand, the hotel's appointments are exceedingly cheap and vulgar. Although unusual care was taken with the construction (as with all high-priority projects largely for foreigners), the woodwork has begun to warp, the plaster to crack and the paint to peel badly. The furniture and carpeting of which the Rossiya's managers are so exorbitantly proud is nothing more than mass-produced, mail-order stock in anonymous 'inter-national-modern' style, indistinguishable from the furnishings of slap-dash Mallorcan and Yugoslavian resort hotels, except that the Rossiya's units are marginally more tawdry and badly veneered. The shiny alloy bedside lamps might have come from Wool-worth's. Western hotels often resort to cheap items because of theft; here they appear to reflect something about Soviet styles. As Soviet tourists in Western cities rush to the tawdry bargain shops, so the Rossiya's designers gravitated to meretricious wares. Economy must have been a factor, but bad taste also played its part. Because the Russian people in general have a poorly developed sense of style, and because the Soviet economy is so retarded, most Russians are easily tempted by the gaudy, especially if they believe it is 'in' in the West. This is why trashy nylon garments have a higher value than cashmere on Moscow's black market.

However, the management is preoccupied with problems other than furnishings. If the builders heaved a sigh of relief when the hotel finally opened during the last days of 1966, the management uttered a gasp at the task before them. The hardest years still lay ahead. Their goal was to make the building a hotel in spirit as well as structure: to concentrate on personnel, rather than the relatively easy problems of material. In other words, to develop – out of thin air, as it were – an esprit de corps and tradition of service. This would require nothing less than iron determination and super-human perseverance: a typical Soviet crusade.

'Frankly,' confides Mr Zashibkin, 'my hardest job as Director has been assembling a competent staff, people who know something about hotel work. And then training our three thousand personnel in the habits of a fine hotel. Educating them in the spirit of looking after our guests. In a word, instilling the concept of *service* in them.'

The reason for Mr Zashibkin's intense emphasis on training and service will be obvious to anyone who has lived in Moscow more than a few days. The foreign tourist may be lucky enough to be served, in his hotel, by one of the delightful old ladies who brings him an unsolicited glass of tea and sews a button on his old shirt – and is genuinely offended by the offer of a tip. (A tip in coin, that is; a chocolate bar, almost the equivalent of their daily wage, is always appreciated in the same truly friendly spirit as their services are given.) But these bustling old grandmothers are the rare exceptions to an extremely unpleasant rule. The general level of service in Moscow can only be described as horrendous. In restaurants, shops, ticket offices and department stores the public are almost always ignored, snarled at or reviled. Approaching the person behind the counter or desk in Moscow one expects not service, but nastiness or bald arrogance.

Why this is so is a subject for a separate inquiry, again involving the confluence of Russian history and the Russian national character with the distinct pressures of Soviet socialism. To confirm that it *is* so, however, requires no more than a morning's shopping – during which bored or acid salesgirls will do their best to repel you from their wildly overcrowded counters. Later, you may attempt to have a bite of lunch – and the maître d'hôtel or waitress will insult you while providing the most appalling service you've ever encountered, many levels below New York's worst. The antipathy to the customer is so strong that many Soviet personnel, even in the rare cases where the establishment is uncrowded, try to turn prospective clients away in a kind of parody of normal business practice. Besides, waiting on people is degrading; and whoever waited on *us*?

To deal with the drastic problem of personnel training (aggravated in the case of the Rossiya because ninety-five per cent of the staff had had no previous experience of hotel work), courses were inaugurated. Mr Zashibkin likes to call them his 'school of Russian hospitality'. 'I can't overemphasize the stress we put on training people in *service*,' he says. 'Every phase of hotel operation, from maid's work to how to clear a table after a meal, is taught and re-taught. All our people have had preparation at special classes, and every two years they're sent back for re-training. Because our standards are getting higher and higher. It's a difficult job we have – but satisfying when you see the results.'

Even Partorg Savitsky waxes enthusiastic over professional training, echoing the management view with the Party's inimitable moral overtones. 'Our Party is the Party of Lenin. Our task is the task to increase production everywhere in the economy.' After a pause he adds a thought of faultless logic. 'But since we don't actually produce anything in a hotel, the task of *our* Party Committee here is the task of improving service everywhere in the hotel. That's what we mean by a Communist attitude towards labour ...'

Has the crusade succeeded? Mr Zashibkin is certain it has. 'Frankly, we may still lag behind Western standards here and there. But I honestly don't see a significant difference in the general level, and in some areas we're actually ahead. When a guest arrives in one of our rooms, for example, he doesn't have to ask for water as he would in most Western hotels. The water pitcher is already filled. Because that's the way we train our staff. It's a reflection of our socialist attitude towards people ...'

Despite this optimism, however, many foreigners feel that the Rossiya lags well behind the standards it has set for itself. Soviet trade literature claims, for example, that the large bank of lifts serving each floor guarantees no guest will wait more than forty-five seconds to be whisked to the lobby from his floor. In fact the wait lasts anything from four to ten minutes; one or two of the bank of six lifts are invariably out of order, and others stalled because the operators – young girls who have already developed the traditional Russian antipathy to work – are chatting with their colleagues in neighbouring lifts, or have reached an interesting passage in their novels.

Similar obstacles hinder the operation of the registration desks in the lobbies. The much-vaunted computers frequently break down – some have not yet been properly installed – and the traditional mêlée often develops at the counters, with dozens of despairing guests pleading for service from bad-tempered clerks and assistant managers. The public lavatories nearby display other traditional shortcomings. The soap or towels are missing, together, of course, with the toilet paper.

But it is the Rossiya's service that is weakest, falling well short of what one expects from a hotel with luxury prices. To watch a single delegation of fifty Japanese businessmen arrive at the hotel is enough to estimate the extent and cause of the problem. At the counter, one girl who speaks Russian only, plus ten English words, takes an hour to check in the enthusiastic businessmen. Two of the girl's colleagues flank her, idle, but refusing to lift a finger: the customer be damned. A recent article in the newspaper *Literaturnaya Gazeta* hints that professional Russians themselves recognize the shortcomings. It was written by a young Intourist interpreter-guide who begins by introducing herself and her good intentions.

My name is Vica, meaning Victoria, meaning victory. Mama wanted me to be victorious in life, and therefore chose this name for me. I love life very much, and many things have worked out well for me. I love my work, too. As I see it, no other kind of work can give a person so much as mine does – and demand so much knowledge, feeling and love of people. I'm always meeting more and more new people; I have acquaintances in all parts of the world. Perhaps they've forgotten me, but they remember my country, where I was their guide. I very much want them to admire my Motherland and the heroism of my people deeply, and to believe in our future. I consider my work extremely important ...

After the ritual praise of the Motherland and Intourist that follow, Victoria Vershkova-Sdobnova approaches the substance of her article: recommendations for improving Intourist's services. Although she, or her editors and censors, keeps her criticism within the limits of the Soviet press, the implications come through. She begins by describing some of the inconveniences suffered by foreign tourists from the moment of their arrival in the country, including inexplicably long waits for the ramp to the aircraft cabin, snarling replies to requests for information at the airport and the impossibility of arranging a snack for hungry travellers ...

Finally our coach approaches the hotel Rossiya. 'Goodness, what a magnificent building!' people exclaim ... The tourists are pleased that they're staying in a beautiful new hotel in the centre of the city, adjoining Red Square, the Kremlin and GUM. They're given their room numbers and, in a much improved mood, make for the lifts.

Happily, the lift problem is not as severe in the hotel Rossiya as in certain others. Wonderful new hotels lose their prestige in the eyes of guests because travelling up or down becomes a complicated affair involving 15 or 20 minutes. I wonder who planned hotels so that 2,500 to 3,000 people are served by two or at best four lifts? ...

Having received his key from the duty matron in the corridor, the tourist enters his room: clean, comfortable, with modern furniture and a pleasing combination of colours ... The tourist would now like to take a bath and change his clothes. But why hasn't the luggage arrived yet? Two hours have already passed. 'Whatever's happened to my things?' the tourist begins to wonder. Imaginations are set to work, and all sorts of unpleasant ideas entertained. Finally his nerves give out, and the tourist hurries back to the lobby. There stand 140 valises patiently waiting their turn. And the two duty porters somehow can't manage to find the time to get to any of them. Besides this, the luggage was delivered from the airport with a full hour's delay. Sometimes the guests themselves take hold of their heavy valises and drag them upstairs ...

My tourists, whom I've gathered here in the lobby to take to supper, look very elegant: the men in dark suits with snow-white shirts and the women in revealing dresses, festooned with jewellery. But I'm upset, knowing I'm faced with the unpleasant duty of ruining this festive mood. I must tell them that the supper will be in an entirely different restaurant, on the opposite side of the hotel. If one goes there by the outdoor route, the restaurant is easily found. This will take 10 to 15 minutes. But it's cold and raining outside. So I suggest walking to the restaurant by way of the inner corridors. This way it will be warmer. However, here the tourists will be faced by other difficulties. The corridors are like a labyrinth, with steps and slopes, snack bars, barbers' shops and beauty salons, various working quarters – this whole long route in the dark to the restaurant reminds you of an obstacle course. Is it to anyone's advantage that a group of tourists is housed in one wing, and fed in another, diametrically opposite? ...

Oh, corridors of the Rossiya! You are mute witnesses of how sixty-year-old Miss Smith, having lost her way, wept inconsolably, certain she'd be stranded in the Rossiya forever and never again see her sweet mother in California ... As in all other hotels, fine women are on duty in the corridors of the Rossiya. But they speak no foreign languages. They can't understand foreigners without an interpreter, and it may take the woman on duty a good hour to decipher a tourist's wishes. God forbid a Soviet guest of the hotel should appear during this time and remind the duty woman of his own right to some service. He'll be rewarded with a cascade of reprimands and accusations of irresponsibility and lack of manners. 'Can't you see I'm talking to a foreigner!' Where did this fawning upon foreigners come from? Who has indoctrinated us with it?

And apropos of this, one more observation. A person who is rude to our own Soviet guests is a person who can be inconsiderate towards foreigners as well. A polite person is always polite – with everyone, whether Russian or foreigner ...

The need to make this elementary point about elementary

courtesy – one that is repeated daily to the Rossiya's staff in the endless exhortations *to raise the standards of politeness* – speaks for itself about the level of service. One can never guess in advance whether the response from a lift operator, floor attendant or desk clerk will be the delightful, unaffected Russian congeniality or an angry bark. A restaurant meal is unlikely to pass without the accompaniment of a shrill argument among the staff or between staff and guests. A doorman will often simply not answer when you ask his help in finding a taxi.

All this having been said, however, the Rossiya deserves high marks for effort. On the whole, and considering its size, it operates with greater efficiency and graciousness than most Moscow establishments. In the hotel's most elegant restaurant atop the Presidential Tower, the service can be quick and pleasant enough to make one forget one is in Moscow, but for the spectacular panorama. Even when an unpleasant encounter takes place with a member of the staff – as when a (seated) maître d'hôtel removes a cigarette from his lips to abuse a prospective diner – the employee then seems to remember his extensive training. He apologizes, shows the guest to a seat, opens the menu and actually wishes him *bon appetit*. More cannot be realistically expected in Moscow now.

And although the Rossiya at first seems a monument to everything that is standardized, insipid and dehumanized in twentieth century design and construction, it is less oppressive and characterless than its architecture and appointments suggest. After a week in the hotel, a distinct personality begins to make itself felt: a reflection less of 'industrialization' and socialism than of the colourful old slums of *Zaradye* on the hotel's site. If the awkward giant has a single dominant motif, it is the survival of Russianness behind a façade of anonymous aluminium and glass.

Each floor of the hotel is presided over by a manager. Stout women in shapeless old dresses, they issue directions to their assistants with a profoundly Russian combination of bossiness and maternal warmth. When a reprimand is necessary, it is often accompanied by indignant squawks and trembling denunciation on both sides, and followed by tearful reconciliation.

The chamber-maids are alternately jolly and carping. At the slightest invitation, they will exchange views with the guests about the best way of cooking herrings and the optimum age for marriage. They will also chronicle their life stories including, if you are interested, their views about the world – which are extraordinarily naive, provincial and pro-Russian, despite the dazzling comparative wealth of the Westerners whose rooms they clean. Their incessant squabbling, giggling and squealing is more like a farm crew's shouts and songs than anything encountered in a Western hotel.

In the half-kilometre corridors outside the rooms, the maids' children – who are often brought along to work on school holidays – play hopscotch or pedal tricycles. At the head of the corridor stands a strategically placed desk commanding a view of all doors to all rooms. A twenty-four-hour vigil is maintained here by duty assistant-managers; they hand guests their keys and guard against Russians entering foreigners' rooms or hanky-panky of any kind. The young daughters of these women are likely to be playing house or banging on the piano supposedly there for the guests' entertainment.

It is the Rossiya's personnel who provide its 'organic' atmosphere and continuity with Russian life. The salesgirl at the newspaper counter who whispers an offer to buy your tie for her boy-friend's birthday. The plumber who comes to repair your sink and spends the morning talking about his six lorry-driving years in Siberia, where he pursued a highly profitable sideline in black-market furs. The fat lady barber with the tangerine hair who is angry because 'it's bloody miserable to work all day', but bubbles over with admiration for her own amorous exploits. The gentle, world-weary doctor who appears in your room four hours late to treat your cold with traditional mustard plasters as well as modern antibiotics, and for another hour shares his dream about the trip to the West he knows he will never make. The assistant manageress with the disintegrating marriage and passion for Nabokov who *promises* she'll never tell (the authorities) if you give her a copy of his autobiography ...

Of all these colourful people, the most interesting may well be your own chamber-maid, a large woman somewhere between forty and sixty with several silver teeth. She much prefers talking to working, and if you strike up an acquaintance with her, she will tell you, implicitly and explicitly, as much about the Rossiya – and Russia as a whole – as a dozen interviews with architects, managers and Party organizers.

She will get into the habit of joining you in your room when she wants a rest or gossip, sinking into your armchair and happily munching your chocolates, or a biscuit from her uniform pocket. Her bulk looks amusingly incongruous in the grey chamber-maid's dress with the dainty white cap; and whatever the regulation about shoes, she has got on her comfortable, floppy old slippers.

'Yes, my son,' she sighs, returning to a frequent lament. 'Yes, that is my sorrow. An old maid's sorrow. No husband, no children ... Only God knows why I was put on this earth.'

'It's not your fault, Svetlana Filipovna. It couldn't be helped.' In her generation of Soviet women this is a common misfortune: half their men were killed in famines, purges or on battlefronts.

'I'm not fooling myself. If I were a good woman, a man would have taken me. No man did – that proves everything, doesn't it? What good is a woman like me without a man?'

Svetlana swallows a chocolate and rolls her eyes. The picture of an ageing milkmaid, she was in fact just that before moving to Moscow. During her first years in the capital, she worked as a factory hand, but she likes the Rossiya job better because she can supplement her salary with laundering for the guests. And because her 'bosses aren't strict'.

Svetland crosses herself from time to time like a doting granny and she's not clear whether England and France are 'ours', meaning Soviet satellites. But she is nobody's fool. She knows, for example, about security. Not that she has any secrets that would interest a foreign journalist. But when she agrees to wash *this* journalist's shirts and asks to be paid not in cash but in a small garment from the hard currency shop, she makes sure never to discuss the 'deal' in the journalist's room, but in the corridor, several steps away.

For the arrangements are slightly shady, if not actually criminal:

hotel employees should not be asking foreigners for sweaters or stockings. And no one need tell Svetlana about the Rossiya's microphones. Muscovites say that 'ears' are planted in each of the three thousand two hundred rooms, and that the system of tuning in, taping and co-ordinating – together with the equipment for tele-taping in a selected number of bedrooms – is the most advanced of all the hotel's technological developments.

A pretty Intourist guide swears that a large, 'off-limits' section of one of the basements is devoted to this purpose, and that its fitting out was a major cause of delay in the hotel's construction. Svetlana herself never talks about this, and probably doesn't know the details – or care to. But when she has something 'of that kind' to say about our agreement, she looks up at the ceiling where the microphone is presumed to be hidden and waits for me in the corridor.

And this too is the atmosphere of the Rossiya. The microphones and hidden television cameras are common knowledge; what most Westerners find harder to believe is that teams of K.G.B. officers in the guise of casual visitors or guests circulate around the clock in the lobbies, restaurants and shops, keeping watch on foreigners. Often their poses are so poor and their faces become so familiar that a Western tourist does indeed recognize them once they have been pointed out, and falls into revulsion or faint panic. In fact, however, shock is as inappropriate as naïveté in these matters. For tourists who have no reason to be blackmailed and have engaged in nothing 'anti-Soviet', microphones pose little danger; merely a soupçon of excitement. For those who travel frequently to the country and have Russian friends to protect, the habit of saying nothing of any consequence in one's room quickly becomes second nature. Naturally, the hotel's Big Brother aspects some-what undermine General Director Zashibkin's campaign for Russian hospitality. But in this matter guests should not feel significantly more oppressed in the Rossiya than in the rest of the country.

As for Moscow as a whole, the saga of the Rossiya may be but a prelude to an epic now being plotted. In the spring of 1973, a government decree ordering the rebuilding of the entire city centre was considered imminent. To transform the capital into a 'model Communist city', sixteen boulevards radiating from the Kremlin were projected, each wider than the Champs Élysées and flanked by uniform skyscrapers in modern style. Among the buildings scheduled for demolition were the century-old Lenin Museum (the former Tsarist municipal hall) and Museum of History at the top of Red Square; the Moscow Art Theatre and Mali Theatre, Russia's oldest; and virtually all the architectural landmarks that survived the Revolution – including some which had also escaped the great fire of 1812, during the Napoleonic invasion. At this prospect, the protests of the left-wing intelligentsia were even more forceful and anguished than during the planning of the Rossiya* – but they will probably be no more effective. Although prestigious academics and leading cultural figures won a year-long period of grace, the city fathers and national government were apparently determined to proceed with the grandiose undertaking. No doubt they will – and much of old Moscow will acquire the glass-and-concrete façade of the Hotel Rossiya, the big box.

* The opponents' strongest argument was Lenin's dictum to the Moscow city council in 1918: 'Do not touch a single stone. Preserve monuments, old things and documents. All this is history – and our pride.'

5. Demimonde

Its feeble night life extinguished, Moscow at midnight settles into provincial gloom. Two or three hotel restaurants, reserved principally for foreigners, still operate, together with Intourist's sorry hard-currency bars; but Muscovites themselves are shut into their flats for the long, dark night, and the sprawling city smacks of black-out.

Only at the major railway stations does a faint pulse continue beating. In vast Komsomolskaya ('Young Communist') Square, three great terminals stand almost shoulder to shoulder; the graceful Leningradsky Station is often the liveliest. Talk your way past the policeman at the entrance (posted there precisely to cool the 'nightspot' by barring visitors without tickets), and one gets a glimpse of how the masses travel.

Ragged peasants sleep on the waiting-room's hard benches, hunched in positions suggesting both that they have been there for days and that they can leap to attention at the appearance of a wrathful official. Impassive, submissive, shabby to their bones, they wait for a place on a train as Russian peasants have always waited: the pawns of Nature's hard forces and of human superiors. Backwardness and drudgery show even on the faces of the children asleep in their arms.

Railway stations are the night depots of the homeless and stranded. Clusters of people from provincial cities stand out among the rustics, their city clothes, however dishevelled, contrasting with the quilted jackets and felt boots of the peasants. The benches are crowded. There are young men and women left in the lurch until a parental telegram delivers their fare to Kiev or Smolensk; there are older people, even petty officials, who have sought out the waiting-room's warmth for the night – they can afford a hotel, but their rank does not rate a reservation, and they prefer not to waste time searching. At the dingy snack counter, a red-faced woman dispenses hunks of unhealthy-looking chicken and a liquid called coffee, berating an even larger granny, her wheezing dish-washer, when no customers, the preferred target, are within earshot.

Seated on a bench opposite the waiting-room door is a woman of strikingly distinctive appearance, the only animated being in the hall. At first glance she seems an attractive twenty-five, but a closer look reveals that her ruby cheeks are a coarse counterfeit of the Russian maiden's admired outdoor flush: lipstick smears topped by a layer of *vazeline*. The calculated angle of her cigarette and her method of rouging her cheeks establish her profession beyond reasonable doubt, and all her features and mannerisms, from the tight, six-month permanent wave to the bored and faintly alcoholic smile, fit into place. A full-bodied woman, her coat is grimy at the collar and she herself may be diseased. Like so many of the bit-player 'types' of Russian cities, she seems slightly larger than life, and therefore caricaturish, against the lacklustre *mise-en-scène*.

Our subject has been strolling about the station, stopping one man for a cigarette and the next for a light. Now she sits on the prominent bench with her coat unbuttoned, bosom revealed in a garish green sweater and legs crossed in a faintly racy posture rare among Russian women. The figure 10 chalked on the sole of her right shoe is her asking-price in rubles.

The official Soviet position on prostitution – that, like illiteracy, beggary, smallpox and indeed all major causes of unhappiness, it has been eliminated by Marxist-Leninist socialism – is among the regime's better known shibboleths. For decades, Western observers sympathetic to Soviet social goals have furnished the gullibility to believe it. On fact-finding trips to Russia, distinguished philosopher after energetic social scientist has inspected model institutions, digested guides' statistics and become convinced of the 'oldest profession's' virtual disappearance. Western experts on the Soviet family conclude that 'the Soviet claim to have eliminated the sexual exploitation of women [is] justified by the facts' and even old-hand ghetto correspondents stress, in confirmation, that not since the

1930s have prostitutes solicited on the streets of Moscow. Common sense alone might make one cautious of accepting this optimistic view, but Soviet sanctimony on the subject is the clearest giveaway. Apart from officials, no Russian I know refers to 'the line' except in joke; a forty-eight-hour tour with a hep private guide is enough to demonstrate its speciousness.

Nevertheless, all official agencies uphold the dogma: as a disease of exploitative societies, sired by the conditions and mentality thereof, prostitution does not – almost *cannot* – exist in the Soviet Union. Defining and describing the phenomenon as it thrives in the capitalist world, the *Large Soviet Encyclopedia* states that 'prostitution has been liquidated in the Soviet Union, since the conditions engendering and nourishing it have disappeared.' Fuller pronouncements in textbooks and popular pamphlets are like a Peter Ustinov burlesque of the fatuity and Philistinism of modern dictatorships. (Perhaps only masturbation provides richer material for spoofing Soviet self-righteousness. Warning of the direct and potential dangers of 'self-pollution', a prominent Soviet authority recently wrote, in praise of Soviet society's power to purify, invigorate and heal, that 'the experience of doctors shows that under Soviet conditions masturbation is no longer the mass phenomenon it used to be in the [pre-revolutionary] past.')

As for prostitution, a rather more mature attitude than that of the textbook and political manifesto is expressed in a recent five-volume study compiled by the Academy of Sciences' Institute of Philosophy.

> In capitalist conditions, sexual problems exist which society cannot resolve. Begotten unhindered, they are deepened by that social system's antagonistic economic, social and human relationships. The socialist system eliminates such ulcers inherent in bourgeois society. In our country, the deep social flaws which give birth to prostitution in exploitative societies have disappeared, just as crude exploitation of female labour in intolerably difficult working conditions is a thing of the past. Together with women's dependent position,

deprived of social and family rights, their backwardness and
ignorance, downtrodden condition and oppression – and, not
infrequently, moral breakdown – all the inhuman conditions
forcing women to sell their bodies, driving them to the abyss
of prostitution, have gone. However ... the resolution of
society's sexual problems does not yet mean a full and final
liquidation of all survivals of the past in human relations.
Because this sphere involves much that is profoundly personal
and intimate, inasmuch as the influence upon it of social morals
and the effect of public opinion does not take place as openly
and directly as in social-political life, it has a tendency to
keep alive more survivals of the past than any other sphere of
social relations ... This is one of the causes engendering
individual cases of sexual dissoluteness and irresponsible liai-
sons. We must not forget Lenin's words that 'Lack of self-
control in sexual matters is a bourgeois characteristic, a sign
of demoralization.'

This cautious hint that prostitution 'survives' here and there
despite elimination of its causes represents the outer limit of forth-
rightness for the general public. Most publications adhere more
strictly to the traditional canons: the socialist revolution led to the
freeing of the Soviet people from this burden as so many others;
and while women under capitalism continue to sell themselves in
despair of their living conditions, Soviet womanhood rejoices, in
gratitude to the Party.

However, the official dogma has more than a grain of truth:
prostitution in Russia is indeed a feeble plant. The concerted efforts
of a totalitarian government to root it out, and the practice of
exiling convicted and suspected practitioners to distant settlements,
clearly help account for this. But there are other reasons, deriving
from some of the strongest elements of Russian life.

To begin with, popular sexual attitudes and practices reduce the
demand for commercial transactions. To say that Russians are less
neurotic about sex – that the society is less 'sex-crazed' – is of
course oversimplified but not misleading. Less aggressive and

guilt-torn about relieving urges, less driven to demonstrate virility, less tense and less needful of a quick lay to ease anxiety, the average Russian (obviously there are exceptions) has less want of prostitutes. The total absence of external stimulation – from magazines to popular songs, the country is thoroughly sanitized – both reflects and reinforces the muted sexual atmosphere. This freedom from commercial titillation cannot be attributed to Soviet priggishness alone. Whatever the behaviour of individuals in private, pre-revolutionary Russia too was distinctly more delicate than Western Europe – even in its otherwise deeply probing literature – in all public reference to sex.

A principal source of this relaxed, 'natural' attitude is the easy availability of sexual outlets. This explanation confounds many Westerners, for one of the most unedifying and widespread mis-conceptions about Russians – perhaps second only to the notion that they are diligent, self-disciplined workers – is that the puritan surface of life and exaggeratedly chaste Soviet pronouncements are reliable indications of private behaviour. In fact, the Russian attitude was extremely permissive well before the word came into vogue in the West: troubled little by guilt and less about social convention, no one is particularly inhibited about going to bed. The violent contrast between political and sexual freedom is reflected in the threadbare punch-line: 'This is a free country, isn't it?'; and Moscow wits are fond of defining 'socialist realism' not in terms of ideology, but as women's pragmatic acceptance of libidinal urges. Nowhere is the gulf between the hypocrisy and cant of official attitudes and the private lives of individuals as great as in the matter of sexual relations.

Apart from the universal trend to sexual liberalism, Russians' easy-going attitudes are the product of a dozen formative influences in the country's history and traditions. The losses of the Second World War played their part: amidst the great surplus of women – no less than nineteen million more than men in 1970 – any 'marry-me-first' notions (laughable in any case to the contemporary Russian ear) can only lessen a woman's competitive chances. Decades before the war, the celebrated 'free love' movement of the early Bolshevik period had helped loosen sexual inhibitions and apprehensions. The so-called 'theory of sexual Communism'* was vigorously expounded until the early 1920s, and although it was even more vigorously suppressed, together with so many of the post-revolutionary period's enthusiasms, it contributed to an emancipation in thought and behaviour.

Lying deeper, the other sources of the Russian approach to sex are harder to isolate. If unsettled times help relax traditional notions of 'virtue', the severe, sometimes brutal dislocations of fifty-five years of Soviet rule made a significant contribution to the 'live for today' atmosphere. More specifically, the breakdown of the religious moral code plays a part – though in fact Russian Orthodoxy itself, for all the power of its ritual and its mystical grip on the Russian people, never inculcated profound guilt over sins of the flesh. For centuries preceding the high-morality line of the

---

* According to which Communist morality was one and indivisible: having renounced private property in the economic sense, the Russian people must also do away with 'detached individualism' in their sexual lives.

The free-love theories of some Russian revolutionaries are as easy to satirize as the present pseudo-humanistic Victorianism, chiefly because some workers' and peasants' councils interpreted them as primitively as so many other social ideas. In 1918, for example, women were nationalized by decree in the towns of Saratov and Vladimir. 'At the age of eighteen, all girls are declared state property. All girls achieving the age of eighteen and not having married are obliged, on pain of severe fines and punishment, to register with the Bureau of "Free Love" attached to the Commissariat of Charity. Those having registered ... have the right to choose a cohabitant, ranging from the age of nineteen to fifty ... Men also have the right to choose from the girls of eighteen or over. For those who want it, the choice of husband or wife takes place once a month. The Bureau of "Free Love" is autonomous. Men from the age of nineteen to fifty have the right to choose women registered in the bureau even without their consent, this being done in the interests of the state. Children deriving from such unions become the property of the republic ... ' Leagues of free love, marches of naked women and proposals to build cabins for sexual relations (along with public toilets) in streets and parks were seriously discussed in Soviet literature of the time. However, the works of Alexandra Kollontai, the high-priestess of sexual emancipation and propagator of the 'Winged-Eros' theory, were far more realistic and subtle than many of their detractors make them out to have been. Lenin, incidentally, was disgusted by the 'new sexual life' and the notion that under Communism sexual needs would be satisfied as easily as drinking a glass of water; to him, all this was 'a variation of the good old bourgeois house of prostitution'.

1930s, Russia was relatively untouched by the puritanism of its north European neighbours. In the most intimate sphere of life, therefore, the country is indeed free.

One social circumstance deserves special mention. Beyond the lack of anxiety and clamour that makes most Russian men appear less beguiled by sex than their Western counterparts, a significant proportion are in fact less interested. Formative influences in upbringing and outlook have made the factory hand and lorry driver seek release not in the joys of the flesh but in the oblivion – and perhaps the quasi-religious visions – of alcohol. The Russian need to splurge and forget is as strong as ever, but, as an underground writer pointed out, the white magic of vodka takes preference over the black magic of women. For men of village background – who still constitute most of the population – the manly thing is to share a bottle rather than hunt for sex. By buying vodka (extremely dear in relation to their wages) to entice young men to an evening, working-class girls confirm the subordinate place of their own attractions. Drink as a vehicle for relief and self-expression has not lost its hold on the muzhik.

For these reasons among others, prostitution in pre-revolutionary Russia was generally less important in scope and scale than in Western Europe in the same periods. Another complex of specifically Soviet restraints now limits it much more. But despite tradition, the police, the availability of women in general, and the scarcity of safe places, the demimonde of Moscow, at least, is large enough to fall into several distinct groups.

Predictably, in a country of consumer shortages and depressed wages, 'amateur' commerce is widespread, as is reflected in the hep new term *sekretutka*, a combination of *sekretarsha* ('secretary') and *prostitutka* ('prostitute'). From university students enticed by a carton of Kents to bored shopgirls seduced by an evening in a restaurant, occasional prostitution is an accepted feature of Moscow life, although too amorphous to measure or even define. Except that the lower standard of living makes it more obvious, it differs only in detail from the same practices in the West. Chocolate and Western cigarettes have less buying power than in post-war Europe, but the analogy is not farfetched. One middle-aged Muscovite with a penchant for schoolgirls finds that a large bar of the best chocolate (which costs what a secretary earns in a day) is often the price of conquest.

Of the women who can fairly be called professional prostitutes, the lowest category operate largely from railway stations, recruiting their clientele from the capital's transient, and often least prepossessing, population: provincial workers, farmers and drivers come to shop in GUM and gape at lights perceived as bright. Poorly educated, and with meagre prospects, most of these women are either very young and inexperienced or well past their better years. Bearing the marks of excessive drinking of decades in their profession, the latter include some truly fallen women: robbers and thieves, cripples and hideous hags. Black teeth, mottled skin and dirt are among their attractions. Dressed wretchedly and exuding corresponding odours (many bathe once a week in the *banya*), they smoke the cheapest *papirosi* – the cigarettes with the long cardboard filters usually favoured by soldiers and unskilled workers – and can curse men who reject their approaches in the rich Russian language's vilest epithets. In the case of one woman with a squint and filthy briefcase, this is always followed by a spine-chilling laugh. Many are alcoholics, and it is in hopes of earning vodka for instant consumption that they go to the stations to ply their trade. (Given their appearance, it is hardly surprising that most of their clients are drunk too.)

To avoid detection, some of the more enterprising of these women write their prices on their palms or inner arm – where Soviet concentration camp numbers, like the Nazi equivalent, were tattooed. The cream of this category quote ten rubles, knowing that bargaining may reduce the final figure to six or seven; otherwise five rubles is a standard asking price, which may be beaten down to two or three. A few 'railway' women will agree even to a single ruble, together with the ritual glass of vodka accompanied by bread and herring; and late at night, the genuinely desperate will accept an offer of the vodka and herring alone.

Earlier in the evening, before the metro system's midnight closing, a scattering of 'two-ruble' prostitutes establish their beats at the exits to a handful of busy stations. Taken to a John's room or flat – a relatively uncommon occurrence, since most of their trade is with provincial tourists – they may try to steal clothes or trinkets; a heedless or helplessly drunk man may be stolen blind. On the other hand, some customers take advantage of their position of strength in their own homes, forcing the girls to return the fee before departing. Crueller clients compel victims to empty their handbags and pockets, sometimes relieving them even of their last kopeks for busfare. On a moonlit night in the grip of a paralysing Russian winter I saw such a woman returning on foot from an outlying section of the city. Singing as she trudged, shaking her fists at the snowy trail of the rare passing car, desultorily propositioning hurrying pedestrians bundled to their ears, she uttered sounds undefinable as laughter or cries, revealing wide gaps in her teeth. She thought nothing of the evening's harrowing misadventure. For lower-class prostitutes, life has strong overtones of Gorky's down-and-out Moscow.

Well aware of the dangers of theft, scandal and disease, most Muscovites avoid prostitutes. The clientele consists mostly of lonely out-of-towners lacking time and opportunity to meet ordinary girls with whom to fulfil their obligation to enjoy a spree in the capital. Soldiers, sailors and, to a lesser degree, students make occasional use of the lowest harlot category; they seldom have more than a few precious rubles to spend, the price of a half-litre of vodka (which equals an Army recruit's monthly pay). But Moscow teems with non-Muscovites: on any given day, roughly a million lone-travelling men from Arkhangelsk and Kharkov, Irkutsk and Novosibirsk throng its thoroughfares in pursuit of the nylon shirts unavailable in their native cities, an audience with a Ministry official, or simply anything beguiling in a shop window or a rumour of a department store delivery. Together with the grotesque over-centralization of Soviet bureaucracies, Moscow's top priority in the system of consumer goods allocation – and the concomitant bareness of the provinces – makes it an intensely powerful attraction for the country's aspiring, desirous and rich. (But the hordes of provincial visitors also account for much of the capital's uncouth manners and appearance. It is largely they, in their outmoded clothes, who form the daunting queues besieging shops and stalls; and their rustic mien and manners, active elbows and peasant resolve to *buy* while this precious chance lasts, not only lower Moscow's tone, but help provoke Muscovites' rudeness to each other in public places.)

Among this vast daily invasion are men of considerable wealth and standing who provide the bulk of prostitutes' business: well-paid military officers, workers from northern industrial and construction sites who come to the city to spend their augmented wages and bonuses; officials of provincial economic enterprises and of regional Party and government headquarters; rich 'businessmen', sellers of fruits and vegetables, and various categories of black marketeers, principally Balts and Georgians. For these upper-middle-class travellers, the equivalent of Western executives on business trips, the choice of girls goes well beyond the frequenters of railway and metro stations.

Taxi-drivers are the usual middle-men for the prominent but unconnected visitor. They are even greater specialists than their Western counterparts in their city's illicit attractions, and it is to them that the crucial questions are put: 'Where can I get a bottle?' (the latest campaign against drunkenness has taken the form of prohibiting the sale of bottled wines and spirits after 8 p.m.), and 'Where can I find a girl?'

Enterprising drivers lay in supplies of vodka during the afternoon, and offer bottles from under their seats at double the retail price. Most drivers also know where to find a presentable prostitute after a short ride, and, in some cases, can provide telephone numbers of girls to whom they are on retainer. But some prostitutes are as handy as the bottles: much of the taxi trade is launched in the five-seater Volga itself. The driver at the wheel, the girl – from fifteen to fifty years old and attractive enough to please at first glance – at his side or on the rear seat, they cruise the streets in the city centre.

Late in the evening, a number of such cabs can be seen circling around the favourite locations, the heavy Hotel Moscow standing opposite the Central Lenin Museum and across Manezh Square from the Kremlin walls. A likely customer spotted, the taxi approaches, the potential client examines while the woman shows him a hint of a wink. In cases of mistaken purpose, dissatisfaction or disagreement over price, the taxi quickly drives off – often it has barely slowed down – for further cruising.

That these cabs do not stop for ordinary passengers is no more curious to bystanders than that they should take on a second passenger, seemingly unknown to the first. Both are normal practices. Even in the context of Soviet consumer-salesperson relationships, Moscow cabbies stand out for treating customers according to mood and whim. The taxi prostitute's standard price – ten rubles to her and ten to the driver – makes her inaccessible to almost everyone except the market she tries to reach: the same military officers, officials on business trips, free-spending Georgians and recently paid workers seeking rewards for their hard Siberian tours.

Because of Moscow housing conditions, much taxi coupling is accomplished *al fresco*. Experienced drivers know quiet side-streets and dark apartment-block entrances where they can park, get out and count on ten undisturbed minutes with lights off and only the heavy Volga's slight rhythmic undulation to betray its use. From May to September, some teams like to use one of the city's large parks, preferably Izmailov or Sokolniki. If the grass is too wet, the driver absents himself for a smoke at a distance of a hundred metres, eyes peeled instinctively for 'rubbish' (vernacular for uniformed policemen). When parks are under snow and cars more conspicuous, drivers often seek sites in the city's more dilapidated districts – the 'East End' of Bogorodskoe or Cherkisovo for example, with its considerable sprinkling of drunks – where police patrols are thought to be sparser. Sometimes the couple just stay in the back of the cab, the driver following an untrafficked route at comfortable speed – and, in such cases, demanding extra payment for the meter. Squabbles over money between cabbie and girl are not uncommon, for the twenty-ruble asking price is open to bargaining, allowing the partners to feel themselves cheated. But most Russians are liberal spenders of what they have; money is not the most serious of the team's problems.

By its nature, congress involving taxis must be brief: most of the rides are completed within half an hour. Otherwise, Moscow prostitutes are more generous with their time, and since vodka is always shared as well as carnal knowledge, the night is often spent together – providing, always, that suitable accommodation has been found.

At all levels of prostitution, the custom of client treating harlot to food and drink, in keeping with the image of the expansive Russian nature, is one of the few affecting aspects of a business otherwise abnormally hardened by Soviet conditions. 'Russian [prostitutes] drink heavily,' remarked Alexander Kuprin shortly before the Revolution. 'And they never think at all about their future.' Contrasting them to foreigners working in the same brothels, especially Germans and Balts who saved religiously to leave the profession comfortable, novelist Kuprin noticed that native girls splurged their last kopek on vodka, many giving themselves without charge in return for a good meal with unstinted drink.

Fear of famine is still relatively close to the surface. But to regard the meal – or even the snack and slug of vodka – strictly as payment, is to overlook the deep, ritual importance of food and drink in the Russian idea of getting properly acquainted, and of what constitutes celebration and well-being. In non-commercial love, too, in even the briefest encounters with the most eager, accessible girls, something to eat and drink is virtually *de rigueur*. 'Washed down by nothing' is degrading for both partners to the transaction, and even railway hags expect their shot of something 'for the right mood' or as 'food for the soul'.

The resort to taxis, back streets and parks is a reflection of prostitution's precariousness in the face of antagonistic forces. As Russia enters the motor age, perhaps chic girls will begin cruising Paris-style in private cars – but decades will surely pass before 'wheels', as the Russians say too, become sufficiently available. Meanwhile, although knowledgeable Muscovites assume that some drivers work for the police – reporting the conversations of 'suspicious elements' and even, in some cases, driving them into police station courtyards for examination of documents – the taxi is heavily relied upon. Most are little islands of privacy, relatively free of the mainland's bundle of restrictions.

In this way, prostitution is automatically limited, along with all activities requiring privacy and individual initiative. Most economic, political and social activity not sponsored by the Party is *ipso facto* illegal, and the government's monopolistic control of all social intercourse, from the renting of a flat to the operation of a snack bar, permits far fewer such dealings to pass unnoticed. Great police numbers and powers help preserve the monopoly, purging the community of all spontaneous activity. Although statistics are secret, evidence of the eyes suggests that the Soviet Union is extremely heavily policed. In central Moscow, the show-place, at least one grey uniform of the 'People's Militia' seems *semper et ubique* in sight. Although the typical acclamatory press reports rate the vigilance of these rather lumbering muzhiks unrealistically high, they are supplemented by plainclothes K.G.B. agents patrolling the city's most populous places, and by citizen-informers working 'on commission' or out of patriotic zeal.

With narrower limits of operation and fewer places to hide, the crucial test of prostitutes almost everywhere – to attract the notice of clients but not of the law – is distinctly more difficult in Russia than elsewhere. Since citizens' behaviour is observed not only in public places but also in meeting their socialist obligations in general, one of the most important rules to comply with is the one requiring every able-bodied adult, excepting only wives supported by their husbands, to work at a job considered socially useful. Even committed prostitutes must 'be on the books' of an official organization, on pain of risking far more severe punishment upon discovery of their illicit lives.

Full-time study at a proper educational establishment qualifies as socially-useful work, and several of Moscow's more successful harlots are handsome students – their bright wholesomeness in prominent contrast to the majority of common street-walkers – enrolled in degree courses at language and literature institutes. Although some thirty-five weekly class hours are obligatory for higher-education students, a good mind and memory are enough to permit preoccupied ones to coast by with a minimum of work. Less capable girls take jobs that provide wide exposure without exhausting them physically. Some are shop assistants in the large department stores (especially the pivotal GUM and TSUM), waitresses in restaurants and cafés, hairdressers (preferably in the shops for men), conductresses on suburban trains, and secretaries.

Suitable 'cover' of this kind arranged, girls may give their spare time to canvassing. The first problem is where to establish an unobtrusive yet effective beat. In Tsarist Russia, this was not a difficulty; from 1843, prostitution operated under government regulation, and most of the trade was carried on in brothels. Under Soviet rule bordellos are of course illegal, and even a very small one could not hope to escape quick detection, provoking the authorities' special anger at 'organized' unlawfulness (in which they see a threat of organized political opposition).

A test of the law took place, significantly, in the early 1960s, when many middle-class Muscovites believed that Khrushchev's tentative liberalization would soon deliver Russia to relative political normality. No doubt encouraged by the surge of (subsequently rued) optimism, a Moscow entrepreneur recruited half a dozen well-groomed local housewives, assembled an album of their photographs to show potential clients and adapted his flat as the business premises. His staff were said to include the wives of influential Party and government officials, motivated, as in Buñuel's 'Belle de Jour', more by upper class boredom than by financial need. The enterprise was extremely successful, but the house was exposed by informers, and its proprietors severely sentenced; since then, at least according to Moscow gossip, no emulators have appeared. The handful of madames who do operate in Moscow – almost

exclusively for the upper crust of the Georgian travellers, prominent officials and captains of private trade – have no houses, merely
small lists of reliable women to telephone, and of convenient,
available flats. The women are of good social standing, a large
proportion of them being 'prominent' housewives. ('Housewife'
is almost by definition an indication of upper-class status, since only
the best-paid husband can afford to support a non-working wife.)

These exceptions aside, almost all prostitutes operate independently, although for company they may stand in pairs against a
street railing outside a crowded metro station. Even working
alone, however, girls have very few places to display themselves.
In the absence of nightclubs, bars and cabarets, the capital's night
life takes place in restaurants – of which only the rarest use can be
made. Quite apart from the general difficulty of gaining entrance
to the handful of better ones – it is chiefly celebrating couples or
groups who brave the hours of queuing – social custom, surly
doormen and churlish maîtres d'hôtel exclude unescorted women
after six p.m.

To win their way into hotel restaurants such as the prestigious
National, Metropole and Ukraine, some prostitutes go escorted
by their ponces, who absent themselves for lengthy periods once
the couple have a table. Called *souteneurs* in Russian, procurers and
pimps play a relatively minor role in prostitutes' affairs, perhaps
because the profession is so insecure, but among those who do have
women in such servitude are 'bitter drunkards', as the Russians say,
proud of their criminal connections, as well as an occasional husband who compels his wife to sell herself for his daily vodka.
Because of the attitude to women in restaurants, ponces can make a
real contribution to their vassals' mobility. Because of this attitude,
too, interested men may reasonably assume that an attractive
woman staring or crossing her legs provocatively – as uncommon
for Russian women as smoking on the streets – is approachable.

The smarter cafés, of which the National, Metropole and several
on the new Kalinin Prospekt offer the best opportunities to meet
moneyed tourists, can be visited by women alone – but only in the
afternoon, by the small percentage with enough grooming and

polish not to attract suspicion in the relatively plush surroundings. And since centrally located cafés which attract 'unreliable elements' – especially foreigners – are constantly under watch by plainclothes agents posing as customers, even women most skilful in varying their dress and make-up risk the wrong kind of notice by appearing in any one café more than several times a month. Under the circumstances, no such establishment can serve as a prostitute's base; those who frequent the more outlying cafeterias, snack bars and the few, tumbledown beer halls – and even here, steady attendance is imprudent – can expect only the disinterest, flat pockets and coarseness of local customers, slim pickings even in comparison to the travelling men in railway waiting-rooms.

Outdoors, too, prostitutes must be careful: leaning against a doorway with a dangling cigarette, let alone strolling a likely street with swaying hips and swinging handbag, would quickly deliver the novice to a police station. Crowds offer a measure of safety as well as opportunity, one reason for the popularity of busy metro stations and the ticket-halls of large central cinemas, especially the Metropole in Revolution Square and Rossiya in Gorky Street. Detectives cannot easily distinguish harlots from other women waiting for friends or otherwise milling about in the little clot of urban excitement. Later in the evening, the subway passages beneath main thoroughfares, especially the busiest ones at Manezh, Sverdlov, Arbat, Revolution and Mayakovsky Squares, are casually patrolled, and during the day the crowded *yarmarka* alongside Lenin Stadium is visited by girls taking time off from their regular jobs, together with a sprinkling of pickpockets and speculators.

Her customer attracted, a prostitute's concern shifts from Where to Be to the marginally less difficult Where to Go. A hotel room for herself is impossible, because of the prohibition against using hotel accommodation in one's city of residence. Providing she departs before midnight, however (the hour when anyone visiting a registered hotel guest must leave the building), the room of a man visiting Moscow can be used. She must take care, in this case, not to attract the notice of the matron on every floor who keeps the keys and watches the doors; but if the woman recognizes her, she might perhaps bribe her with a ruble or two. Women who visit travellers' rooms, especially Georgians', are *ipso facto* suspect, but in the absence of proof, they can hope to spend an evening undisturbed unless they break a hotel regulation or flaunt some article of clothing given in payment.

A handful of the capital's most successful prostitutes, *mutatis mutandis* the equivalent of elegant Western call girls, have their own quarters, some even in co-operative flats – which, because the pretexts for eviction are somewhat fewer, and the neighbours are generally better educated and less inclined to snoop and snitch, are fractionally safer than the far more common municipally-owned housing. One of the few prostitutes well enough known to enjoy something of a name among Moscow's small 'swinging' set lives in a well situated, relatively luxurious co-operative building. A svelte Siberian girl of uncommon poise and Nordic beauty – 'Bardot's lips with Monroe's tits' in the description of an admiring Muscovite – she married an official for the sake of a Moscow residence permit. By the time he was fired (for drunkenness in a job involving foreigners) she had saved enough money from her fees to divorce him and buy her own flat – which allowed her to increase her earnings still more.

But only the aristocracy of the profession ever aspire to such working conditions. The quarters of the rank and file are far humbler – and often unavailable, since many occupy a room in a communal flat, where neighbours in adjoining rooms know of every coming and going; and even if the neighbours are not police informers, a parade of unknown men visiting a healthy woman would prompt an expeditious visit from the Inspector responsible for the sub-district's every resident. When a prostitute does risk bringing a customer back to such a flat, he waits outside the building, controlling his passion in a much-practised acceptance of difficult conditions, while she runs up to check the neighbours. If they are asleep or otherwise out of sight, the man tiptoes into the girl's room and has an hour or two of careful whispers behind the locked door – not the most stimulating environment, whatever the girl's charms. Afterwards, the man will sneak sheepishly down the stairs again, shoes in hand.

To improve on such arrangements, many prostitutes have standing agreements to rent rooms for the required hour from a trusted acquaintance with a 'safe' self-contained flat. Whether by coincidence or because they are unlikely to be suspected, these rooms are frequently rented by elderly widows, archetypal Russian grandmothers with stooped shoulders and kerchiefed heads, who are glad to supplement their subsistence pensions. Their recompense is rarely less than two rubles, one from the client and one from the girl. Although unlawful use of government-owned flats is cause for eviction – an additional discouragement for anyone thinking of opening a brothel – lonely old *babushki* usually escape full punishment, unless they persist after several warnings.

Perhaps because old grannies are the last to be moved from such quarters, the rented rooms are often in Moscow's old wooden houses, many of which, scheduled for replacement by new prefabricated apartment blocks, are in the last stages of dilapidation. In these cases, the setting for the sexual embrace is more joyless than even a parked taxi. Opening her front door no more than an inch, the old woman scowls at her visitors, leads them to a sittingroom-bedroom smelling of ancient poverty and soiled linen, and shuffles off to the grimy kitchen to wait, leaving the door ajar to guard against theft. Such boudoirs represent far from the minimum in comfort, however; sometimes children can be heard stirring behind a blanket rigged up as a curtain, or the muffled cough of a husband waiting for his wife to finish and hand over his vodka money. And there is a yet lower level of cosiness: a substantial percentage of all transactions are five-minute, stand-up affairs in the doorway of a dark apartment-house courtyard or behind a tree in a deserted corner of a park. Most 'two-ruble' prostitutes know suitable sites for these very brief encounters, and the exigencies of time and place encourage them to perform a service called the 'speciality of the French tongue' – which a certain number of customers prefer in any case because of the women's primitive hygienic standards and the likelihood of disease.

Because ordinary arrangements may fall through on any given day, making Where to Go an acute problem – and because for all their onerousness, Soviet regulations often have some inexplicable gaps – prostitutes sometimes resort to curious refuges, of which Moscow River excursion boats are the best known. Since cabins cost little and, in contrast to hotel rooms, may be hired without papers of any kind, the neat river cruisers invite a happy mixture of 'the profitable with the pleasant', as the Russians say. They leave from the River Terminal at Khimki, conveniently served by a metro station and an inexpensive fish restaurant where the man can treat his lady to suitable refreshment before boarding for the four-hour trip (few take the full-day outing) upriver to the picturesque Klyazma Reservoir. Even during the evening excursions, the scenery outside Moscow – woods of birch and fir growing directly to the clayey river bank – evokes the unique sad-but-serene spell of the Russian countryside, enhanced by the absence of interference from the authorities. The drawback is that the 'floating whore houses' operate only half the year. Like the great Volga freighters and ore-carriers whose vast deliveries to Russia's primary industrial centres cease entirely during six months of winter, the little excursion boats are withdrawn from service in October, shortly before the Moscow River freezes over. This is precisely when they are most needed, for winter makes more difficult all aspects of prostitutes' work, from recruiting outdoors to using parks. Their plummeting business from October to May illustrates how much closer Russians are than Westerners to nature.

Prostitution is not a crime in Soviet law, probably because any mention of it in criminal legislation would contradict the myth of its non-existence.* The Russian Republic's criminal code includes seven articles defining sexual crimes and their punishments:

* Questioned about the seeming lapse in the law, a Moscow judge responded with the usual statement: 'There is no prostitution in the Soviet Union.' 'Because the law says so?' persisted his interviewer. 'Exactly!' replied the judge.

Infecting with Venereal Disease, Illegal Performance of Abortion, Rape, Compulsion of a Woman to Enter into Sexual Intercourse, Sexual Relations with a Person Who Has Not Attained Puberty, Depraved Actions, Pederasty. Since neither the code nor its detailed commentaries refer even by implication to prostitutes or prostitution – and inasmuch as Soviet law explicitly forbids punishment without a crime – the penalties awarded for such activities are theoretically illegal.

But in practice, the highly flexible interpretation and administration of the law permits some forms of punishment, often more severe than if recognized sanctions existed. One of the rare recent cases involving prostitution which achieved a degree of notoriety vividly illustrates the euphemisms surrounding most Soviet penalties. In the mid-1960s, some dozen students, most from the Institute of Road-building, were tried at Moscow City Court. This tribunal, one level above the People's Courts where such cases are usually heard, was appointed because of the importance of the scandal and prominence of the defendants' families: a K.G.B. colonel, a judge, an editor, a Party official, a writer and a well-known composer were among the disgraced fathers – a circumstance accounting for the widespread knowledge of the trial, despite its conduct *in camera*.

The testimony established that when the parents of one of the richest sons departed to their country *dacha*, a gala party was arranged to celebrate the 'liberation' of their Moscow flat. For entertainment, six young 'taxi' prostitutes were engaged after careful selection, each of the co-hosts contributing ten to fifteen rubles for the girls' services. Although this sum was roughly a third of the average monthly student stipend, it was not prohibitive to the sons of the notoriously child-pampering Moscow elite. The soirée went splendidly – until the occupants of a neighbouring flat, irritated at the boisterous laughter and resentful, like many less privileged Russians, of the antics of upper-crust progeny, informed the police that prostitutes had been escorted into their building.

The officers arrived to a memorable scene: at a long wooden table, six soup bowls had been set out, each filled with a quarter-litre of vodka. A naked girl was bent over each bowl, conscientiously racing her colleagues to lap up the vodka with her tongue. ('Here you see the influence of our "socialist competitions" in production,' wryly commented a Muscovite. 'Like all good Soviet youth, they were concerned with which girl could fulfil her plan fastest.') The young women were given no hors-d'œuvres to blunt the vodka's effects, but dill pickles were waiting to reward each one as she completed her assignment. A fine feast would follow – but meanwhile, as the contestants tried to keep their faces steady above the bowls, the students took their pleasure from behind at the conveniently angled bodies, urging their favourites to stop their rotten goldbricking and lap faster.

To mitigate their own punishment, the students supplied investigator and judge with every detail of the girls' behaviour. But they were not convicted of prostitution; it was established that they lacked steady employment, and they were sentenced as parasites. The older girls were exiled from Moscow for five years. ('Ways will be found to keep them out of the city for at least another five after that,' said the Muscovite who knew the details of the trial.) The younger ones were dispatched to 'the 101st kilometre', one of the best-known penal colonies, populated, it is said, largely by prostitutes from eleven to eighteen, the age of legal maturity. The students themselves, incidentally – although open to conviction for Depraved Actions – were merely expelled from their institutes, and their parents subjected to the disgrace and potential damage of personal Party reprimands.

In the absence of proper legislation and many safeguards of due process, prostitution is fought – as are many social conditions and circumstances which the authorities do not publicly recognize – on the basis of secret circulars to judicial police and local government officials. Inevitably, therefore, criminal punishments (although disguised under different names) are pronounced on people who could have no precise previous knowledge of the offence or its potential punishments, another serious violation of generally accepted legal norms. Prostitutes must weigh the potential rewards and risks on the basis of rumour and deduction. Together with the scanty evidence of the disposition of actual cases – most are dealt with by 'administrative measures' as hushed as the instructions defining them – these indicate that the circulars rely heavily on expulsion from major cities as punishment. The authorities want not only to cut off the errant women from their trade (there is little conventional prostitution in the villages) but also, in accordance with a venerable Soviet tradition, to evacuate the eyesores, together with 'idlers, loafers and parasites', from the pride of Russian cities – where, in addition to other embarrassments, they may be noticed by foreigners.

Many of the exile sites are in the swampy Mordovian Republic, the arctic wastes outside Arkhangelsk and the desolate plains beyond the Volga – places 'not too terribly distant' in popular Russian irony. Under local police supervision, exiles perform a full day of hard labour, often starting at dawn with street-sweeping and log-splitting; when their tasks are completed, they are free to circulate within the community – although they may not leave it without permission. To discourage escape they are deprived of their papers, without which travelling is very difficult in the Soviet Union. A ragged, paper-less woman is likely to be re-incarcerated after her first encounter with a curious policeman.

Although exile towns would seem to benefit from the forced labour of such women, there is evidence that they are not entirely happy with their part in the arrangements. A trickle of letters to editors from town and village officials complain sourly that although their work forces badly need reinforcement, they would refuse the good-for-nothing Moscow exiles if they could. And bitter squawks from local women occasionally see print too: why should *their* villages be burdened with Moscow's dregs? The insolent hussies learn nothing from exile, only lowering the moral tone of previously peaceful streets, and distracting previously faithful husbands.

Although it is designated an 'administrative measure' as distinct from a criminal conviction, a sentence of fifteen days in a city prison is also administered with wide discretion by People's Court judges. Usually awarded as a warning to first-time girls against whom suspicion exists without proof, the sentence is served together with drunk-and-disorderly offenders in physical labour on Moscow streets and construction projects. Despite the food and cells – conditions are purposely kept primitive as a discouragement to further misbehaviour – professional prostitutes are happy to escape with 'fifteen days'.

By contrast, a sentence in a labour colony, the punishment for most criminal convictions, is regarded with genuine dismay by all except oblivious alcoholics. Since it is not in the criminal code, no one is awarded such punishment for prostitution alone. But especially during the periodic campaigns against one or another form of recognized crime, theft, for example, a defendant suspected of earning immorally may be damned by broad, often unsubstantiated, implications at her trial, which invariably lengthen her sentence. In such cases a prostitute can be sent to a labour camp for years for pilfering a pair of stockings. There is no need to describe these institutions here; recent inmates' accounts smuggled to the West make clear that, quite apart from the unfairness of Soviet criminal trials in 'campaign' cases, the conditions of many camps are savage by Western standards. Gruelling physical labour on insufficient rations seems to be the core of penal policy: prisoners are 'rehabilitated' by exhaustion. Ironically, only by prostituting themselves to camp administrators and powerful prisoners can female prisoners obtain relief from the grinding conditions by getting an easy job, with extra food, in an office, hospital or kitchen. This too is an old Russian tradition: in his celebrated report on the exile colony of Sakhalin, Chekhov spoke of women prisoners going directly into brothels to serve the lonely men.

For juvenile prostitutes, there are special correctional methods and establishments. Well-informed Muscovites estimate that bored girls of fourteen, fifteen and sixteen, the progeny of the capital's large corps of 'tough' families, comprise a significant percentage of Moscow's prostitutes. This was confirmed, if only by allusion, in an extraordinary Soviet article of the mid-1960s. Published in a literary newspaper during the brief summer of expanded press coverage and candour under Khruschev, it expressed a degree of frankness about social problems unknown before or since; but even then the taboo word was avoided except in a (totally irrelevant) mention of its 'phenomenal mushrooming' under capitalism. Nevertheless, the well-remembered article was clearly about juvenile prostitution and its punishment.

The little chick was hanging about the railway station. She not only had nowhere to travel but, it seemed, no business at all in the station. Still, one might say she had business of sorts there. She bought meat patties from women hawkers, treated herself to soda water, struck up conversations with strange men, sat sideways on wooden benches in the waiting-room – and from under her short skirt her knees poked out into the wide world.

It ended with her being noticed by a man named Prilepko. He approached the little slip and discovered that her name was Marina Kovaleva, and that she was sixteen years old ... He invited her home. A fast acquaintance, a brief moment together – and having seen the chick to the door, Prilepko muttered:

'That's about the size of it – what's called love.'

The special penal facilities for girls eighteen and under begin with the Juvenile Departments (literally 'Children's Rooms') attached to each of the city's 150-odd police stations. One of their primary functions is to uncover and suppress the activities of 'adolescents gone astray', the official euphemism for under-age prostitutes. Girls found guilty of sexual misbehaviour are dispatched for extended 're-education' – for Marina Kovaleva, for example, the sentence was for 'several years' – in juvenile correction colonies. In Moscow, young *filles de joie* live in persistent anxiety about 'the 101st kilometre', the juvenile penal colony located at that distance south-west of the capital along the main railway route to Kiev. Surrounded by a high fence and watch-towers, its external appearance accords with stories of life within.

When Beatrice Webb visited a model prison colony near Moscow in 1932, she came away transported by enthusiasm. The colony, she wrote, was 'a remarkable reformatory settlement which seems to go further, alike in promise and achievement, towards an ideal treatment of offenders of society than anything else in this world'. What excited her in particular were the colony's experimental methods: ideas and practices which seemed to fulfil progressive penologists' most daring dreams and to confirm the young Soviet republic's dazzling promise. Of all the joy elicited in Mrs Webb and a host of lesser social reformers by socialism's enlightened humanitarianism, nothing surpassed that in the reclamation of prostitutes. A library of articles, monographs, scholarly papers, treatises and polemical memoirs was written about experimental colonies and homes, entreating the West to follow Russia's example.

That brief, brilliant interval of Soviet history, when Russian literature, art, music and social theories led the world's avant-garde, is remembered with a shudder by the Soviet penal system's present administrators. 'Those were the days of experiment, chaos, wild theories, hopeless liberalism,' a high penal officer told me, pronouncing 'experiment' and 'liberalism' with the usual official scorn. 'No more experiments for us; except for minor administrative arrangements, experiments are things of the best-forgotten past. Because we have found the answer to juvenile delinquency.'

I have never seen 'the answer' as applied to girl delinquents, but a three-hour visit to a boys' colony near Moscow was a depressing experience. My guide was the same unquestioning penal officer, the assistant director of the Ministry for the Preservation of Social Order's Juvenile Delinquency Division – and, simultaneously, a lieutenant-colonel in the Soviet Army: the Ministry is a quasi-military establishment, subordinate to the army's high command. The colony itself was part military school and part Siberian labour camp: discipline and gloom, gun-posts, searchlights and armed guards. Not so much as a wink or a tentative smile relieved the gravity of the uniformed, shaven-headed inmates, teen-agers with the look of convicts.

Although somewhat less severe in setting, girls' colonies are essentially the same. 'We've settled once and for all on a standard system,' the lieutenant-colonel declared proudly. 'One single system for all juvenile colonies everywhere in the Soviet Union.' As in all sister colonies, the inmates' day at the 101st kilometre is divided between classes at a school offering the standard, nation-wide curriculum and work in a prison factory; voluntary hobbies, Sunday sports and weekly films provide some relief. Since almost all the girls have an extremely low standard of education and general culture, their schooling in elementary hygiene and manners has definite benefits, much as the Soviet Army, for all its primitive conditions and severe discipline, broadens its raw peasant recruits.

Nevertheless, in practice the much-vaunted Soviet programme of juvenile re-education and rehabilitation is principally hard work, on the theory that 'socially useful labour' is the best cure. There is considerable emphasis on the factories being not mere training workshops, but genuine economic enterprises which must fulfil their plans and make a profit for the state. In surroundings depressing even by comparison to the rest of the colony, the girls work hard – five hours a day, six days a week, after a half-day of school – under strict surveillance.

'First and foremost, reform means labour,' said the lieutenant-colonel. 'If a delinquent is going to become an honest citizen, *he must work*. We teach them that – and teach them to love work. We do this by *making* them work: real work in a real factory. So that they will always know that work is paramount in their lives and the life of our socialist society. That is the only approach to rehabilitation.'

Permeating work and school hours – and even the 'free time', for evening political lectures are mandatory – is a degree of Marxist-Leninist indoctrination that surpasses even the ordinary school-children's choking ration. Campaigns to revere Lenin achieve a near hysterical pitch: LENIN IS ALWAYS WITH YOU! LENIN LIVED, LIVES, WILL LIVE! EVEN TODAY, LENIN IS MORE ALIVE THAN THE LIVING! 'Moral, political and spiritual re-education' is the second mainstay of the programme of rehabilitation. 'We teach delinquents the Moral Code of the Builder of Communism,' the lieutenant-colonel declared. 'And arrange things in the colonies so that they live by that code. We teach them patriotism: love for the Motherland and for socialist labour. We instil in them the ideals of our revolutionary heroes. They must not only understand but be made to *feel* the deeply moral principles on which our society is founded.'

In the rare and noticeably reticent descriptions of juvenile colonies in the Soviet press, there is considerable praise for the inmates' humane treatment, which, it is stressed, rigidly excludes all hint of fear and corporal punishment. Do they protest too much? The conflicting evidence is in the sullen, strangled – and unmistakably hungry – look of the boys at the colony I visited, and in the behaviour of a girl I met a week after her release from a colony in southern Russia. Incarcerated for prostitution at fifteen (she had fallen in with a group of Georgians, she said, who forced her to sleep with foreigners in exchange for articles of clothing they seized and sold), she was found work in a laundry after her 'rehabilitation'. Her hair prison-short, her body abnormally skinny, she devoured the unpalatable cream of cheap doughnuts as if it was ambrosia, but cringed in shame at being sick after a restaurant meal. She claimed she had been struck by some of her guards, and, altogether, she could only be called pathetic.

Why are girls tempted despite such deterrents? Curiosity and eagerness to be 'adult' play roughly the same role as in other countries, and probably there are a few nymphomaniacs. Beyond this, Soviet conditions – low wages and sombre work prospects – enhance the lure of a few extra rubles. But the hope of excitement is at least as important; above all, Russian women with a bent for glitter are profoundly bored. In the article on why she had gone astray, sixteen-year-old Marina Kovaleva was quoted as saying, 'You only live once, youth never returns – and I want something to remember in my old age.' Apprehensive as they are of the 101st kilometre, many young girls are more eager for adventure: for the defiant thrill that will transport them from evening Moscow's dreariness and the tedium of their 'depressed-area' lives. Furthermore, not a few pride themselves on their sideline. The peasant-looking potato-nosed girl whom I watched championing prostitution heatedly to friends, comparing it to her ordinary job in a carton factory, was strikingly reminiscent of Tolstoy's Katushka Maslova (the heroine of *Resurrection*), who 'not only wasn't ashamed of her position ... but seemed even happy with it, somehow, even proud of it'. In contrast to Soviet penal policy, the sentiments of ordinary citizens, especially those who make use of prostitutes, indicate a powerful continuity in Russian social attitudes. Brothels were called literally 'houses of toleration' in pre-revolutionary Russia: all manner of perversions were tolerated within. The unfortunate inmates, whose rights were not significantly greater than those of their serf mothers and grandmothers, had virtually no say in what they were required to perform. Bonded to the brothel-owner, in fear of their clients and masters as well as the police, they rested at the very bottom of society, and this encouraged some of the customers, principally muzhiks with a bit of money to inflate their bigoted arrogance, to torment and degrade them still further.

Prostitutes in modern Moscow, also in constant fear of the police and their clients, still tolerate a steady ration of venom and even brutality, for many of their customers are less interested in buying sex than in asserting their dominance over a defenceless woman. Among the great corps of ill-educated, often demoralized men (usually un- or semi-skilled labourers) who still constitute much of Moscow's population, it is a solemn tradition to drink to oblivion and then, for occasional diversion, to humiliate prostitutes,* if not engage in some drunken wife-beating. In youth, such men had shown off by torturing stray cats; as adults, they revert to women, the traditional scapegoats. In encounters with them, prostitutes consider themselves lucky to escape with no more than forced drinking beyond their limits, and a contemptuous 'Get to work, you,' as the woman is pushed into position, 'what do you think I'm paying you for?' They are not always so fortunate: 'They pay their fiver and order you to strip,' said a young woman who left

* Sharper and ruder to the Russian ear than 'whore' is to the English, slang terms for 'prostitute', as well as for girls who 'put out', reflect this attitude. The precise flavour of most terms is untranslatable, for they combine an extremely strong verb with the affectionate but slightly ironical 'ka' diminutive suffix. The closest translation of *baralka*, for example, might be 'good little fucker'.

the profession after several beatings. 'Then they laugh at you, make you crawl on all fours or something. They don't really want to make love; they want to show how powerful they are. Later they can take back the five rubles, plus anything else you were stupid enough to carry.'

But deep compassion for prostitutes exists alongside this vile rudeness; the one derives from the other, as the guilt and despair of pre-revolutionary intellectuals flowed from Russia's peasant backwardness. In Tsarist days, many Russians genuinely pitied 'unfortunate women' even more than convicts and exiles; in a country of hard times, they were regarded as having fallen upon especially great misfortune. And nowhere was the sorrow greater than among some of the intelligentsia. Although clients themselves, they were completely unlike the coarse, arrogant men who humiliated their subjects. Their compassion – extending, in a distinctly 'Russian' way, to the client himself – was expressed in a typically soul-searching, self-deprecating monologue, bemoaning the 'vileness' of all involved.

We all agree that prostitution is one of mankind's very greatest calamities, and also agree that the guilt for this evil lies not with women but with us men, since the demand gives birth to the offer. And so, if I drink one glass of wine too many and go to some prostitute all the same, despite my convictions, then I'm committing a triple odiousness: before the miserable, dumb woman whom I subject to the most humiliating form of slavery for my dirty ruble; before mankind because in 'renting' a communal woman for an hour or two to satisfy my repulsive lust I am supporting and even justifying prostitution; and, finally, it is an odious act before my own conscience and intellect. And before logic.*

This type is still well-represented in contemporary Moscow: damning his every meeting with a prostitute – yet succumbing again and again, perhaps less for sexual release than as an outlet for nagging remorse for mankind and his own conscience. Occa-

* Alexander Kuprin, *The Abyss*, 1913.

sionally, curious relationships are formed in the capital; that of Evgeny and Masha, for example. He is a Chekhovian intellectual, with steel-rimmed spectacles, delicate hands and a comfortable flat which is crammed from floor to ceiling with yellowing books. She is a large, jolly construction worker, living in a workers' hostel with two room-mates who, like her, are part-time prostitutes. Evgeny's contributions add significantly to Masha's sixty-five rubles a month as an unskilled labourer. He gives her more than the usual five rubles: an extra fiver after many visits, as well as food and presents. And he recruits new clients from among his friends – not in cynicism, but as an expression of his absorbing concern.

Prostitutes themselves are often relatively unconcerned about their own welfare, a state of mind reflected in their casual attitude towards venereal disease and birth control. Although some women give their clients condoms (nicknamed 'four-kopekers', or 'galoshes', which gives some idea of their grossness) and others equip themselves with 'bonnets' – diaphragms of domestic manufacture – many bother with neither, and in the absence of the pill, which is unavailable in Russia, rely on abortion. Free to working women and very inexpensive to others, prescribed virtually on demand, abortion is used by much of the general population as a substitute for contraception. The claim that this is the cruellest form of birth control is lent extra weight in Russia, where hurried, gruff staff perform dilation and curettage without anaesthetic, except in extraordinary circumstances. The 'back-street' doctors to whom many prostitutes turn (to avoid attracting attention to themselves at free state clinics) are often worse, and, as in other countries, women run the risk of serious infection and haemorrhage, loss of fertility and death.

By law, every person infected with a venereal disease must name all his sexual contacts. To avoid having to do this, many prostitutes have hypodermic syringes of their own at home; antibiotics are obtained from black-market contacts, diagnostic and remedial skills from experience. In this matter as so many others involving modern technology and service – repair of cars, maintenance of one's own plumbing – Soviet shortages have endowed some Russians with much 'Yankee' ingenuity. Cheerfully and resourcefully, they cope with all manner of emergencies.

Yet in the performance of sex itself, supposedly the purpose of the exercise, most are stolidly unimaginative. However accessible Russian girls, it is the 'standard' coital position which most expect to assume after their quick surrenders. Perhaps recent peasant background accounts for their tendency to consider other variants, let alone more experimental expression, 'perverted'.* Essentially the same considerations apply to prostitutes and their customers. Although some girls are willing to accommodate all tastes, nude frolics and unfamiliar methods are the exception to the rule of unembellished face-to-face intercourse, just as the rare copy of the *Kama Sutra* or Danish sex magazine smuggled in from abroad and the amateurish (although sometimes politically amusing) pornography by domestic cartoonists and photographers is the exception to the rule of the absence of public titillation.

The exception to *this* rule, however, is communal sex. Whether because of cramped living conditions, ideological training or national character, Russians are distinctly less individualistic than Westerners in their approach to social life: more inclined to share activities in small groups rather than separate couples. This tendency extends to being far less squeamish about taking sexual pleasure in view of others – indeed *with* others in the sense of several couples copulating in the same room (sometimes, but not necessarily, exchanging partners). Although elsewhere evenings spent in this way would qualify as orgies, in Moscow they usually seem to be spontaneous and relaxed – in a sense too innocent – for anything so formal-sounding. Prostitutes are often hired in two and threes for 'parties' of this sort, or one girl is asked to accommodate several men. Perpetually broke students are moved by more than good fellowship to favour group arrangement; and the same motive

* 'Because of the lack of appropriate sexual education,' a magazine pointed out in one of the rare public mentions of the subject, 'a crudely oversimplified attitude towards the content, function and forms of sexual love has become widespread.'

impels many prostitutes to agree. Two young girls who served six students recently in a temporarily free Moscow flat were quite pleased with their rewards: three rubles each, one from each student, in addition to their full evening of food and drink. 'Why not?' said the older girl, surprised at my question. 'It's all the same to me except the money's better – can't a man from the capitalist world see that?'

An entire category of customers, the foreigner, is relatively insignificant in size, but of greatly disproportionate importance to prostitutes' aspirations, rewards and anxieties. For the girls, the temptation is obvious: every visiting Westerner is a fabulously rich uncle who can pay in nylon tights or a bright mohair scarf from the hard-currency shop. But the dangers are equally obvious. Ironically, the authorities themselves are the only organized violators of the Soviet prohibition against exploiting sex. Although the notion that any Russian girl who sleeps with a Westerner is likely to be working for – or quickly impressed by – the K.G.B. is vastly exaggerated, police prostitution, almost as old as the profession itself, is used with rare persistence and faith by the directors of Soviet security, perhaps providing an insight into their mentality. In Intourist hotels, for example, surveillance is so intense that any Moskvichka who frequents a hard-currency bar, not to speak of foreigners' rooms, surely does so with the K.G.B.'s sanction – and in the knowledge that failure to co-operate would quickly deliver her to the 101st kilometre, exile in a distant village or a labour colony. Most of the unsolicited telephone calls which startle Westerners in their hotel rooms – gay young voices (although a few betray a pitiable nervousness) which apologize for reaching a wrong number but nevertheless seem eager to talk (in enchantingly broken English, French or German, as the situation requires) – are similarly planted. Trite as it sounds, a visit by such a girl to a foreigner's room and bed can easily be recorded in sound and film.

The K.G.B.'s recruitment 'pitch' is rather too obvious for the discriminating writer of modern spy stories. Recently a brash young girl who had had several brief affairs with Western businessmen and journalists was summoned to a meeting by an officer of the organization. Although not strictly speaking a prostitute, Natasha's contacts with half a dozen foreigners and acceptance of clothing and perfume had exposed her to damaging charges.

'Sit down, Natashinka,' the major offered pleasantly. 'There's no reason to make that face – no reason to fear us. You know our work in protecting the country from the wrong kind of visitors. What is there for you to be frightened of?' Strangely calm, Natasha already understood that she was lost.

'We know the activities you engage in with foreigners,' the officer continued. 'And we're not going to stop you. It's all up to you, Natashinka: we can have excellent relations with you.' (Harder.) 'But there are certain things you should tell us about your "generous" friends – things we have a right to know.' (Softer.) 'You understand what can happen if the police become interested in you. You *do* want to stay in Moscow, don't you? But there's no need for such talk with *you*; we know you're a patriotic girl. Of course you want to tell us about people hostile to our country.'

Few interviewees refuse to co-operate. After hesitating, to suggest serious thought, the cleverer girls agree that it is their duty to enter into an association with the K.G.B. whose intensity, length and distastefulness depend substantially on their wits and dramatic talent. Like many intellectuals and others in whom the secret police have a special interest, prostitutes eager to keep at their work meet with K.G.B. officers from time to time to transmit bits of irrelevant or innocuous information or report that there is nothing to report. To enhance her appearance of 'loyalty', as the Russians say, a cunning girl may even lodge an accusation about a foreigner who has permanently left the country – better game than someone still near because less likely to involve her in further investigation. Although it does not guarantee safety, observance of the cardinal rule for Russians trapped by the K.G.B. – to play obliging and dumb, revealing nothing that might lead to deeper entrapment – allows many to prolong their status until interest in them wanes.

The most prosperous prostitutes serving foreign clientele – in most cases, simultaneously the most successful in coping with the K.G.B. – enjoy relatively handsome rewards. The profession's *crème de la crème*,* they are adorned exclusively in Western gear from eyelashes to boots, hair-spray to underwear, and their rooms are cluttered with Japanese transistors and other prizes of the hard-currency shops. It is not only for their great value in rubles that girls prefer presents to cash, but also because they are marginally less incriminating if an arrest is made at the moment of transfer.

Like their less glamorous colleagues, prostitutes with foreign customers maintain steady jobs, often as interpreters, foreign-language teachers and high-calibre guides for foreign delegations. Educated beyond their knowledge of languages, they have left the Russian masses' naïve curiosity about the West well behind and, if their relations with the authorities seem secure, appear quite sure of themselves. Grooming far above the Moscow norm helps some of them seem striking and sophisticated although – perhaps too through their contact with Westerners – they are likely to be more mercenary than girls whose experience is limited to natives. Like Intourist officials convinced they have mastered capitalist ways and designers eager to be 'modern', Russians with limited Western contact often first choose the most grasping and garish characteristics to imitate and overdo.

One of the most successful courtesans to foreigners is a tall, blue-eyed blonde whose pride it is that she never wears 'a single crummy Soviet stitch'. A teacher at a well-known language institute, she tutored one of the early Soviet cosmonauts in English. Until her unusual beauty began to fade several years ago, she spurned even East Europeans, working exclusively with Western-ers, preferably businessmen – who helped outfit her in furs, from hats to boots. 'I have a hundred ways to meet them,' Lida explained. 'But all I really have to do is sit in a café with a *Morning Star*. The poor man at my table speaks no Russian and hasn't had a woman in

---

* Excluding only the women who are said to serve high military officers, Party officials and diplomats but about whose work almost nothing is known because it takes place in the villas of carefully fenced and guarded government preserves.

weeks. He looks at me and at the newspaper; squirms a bit and finally says something. "Oh, you're English?" I say, full of surprise. "How interesting. And" (this is with a 'Russian' accent and a tiny smile) "I'm *Russian*. I don't suppose that's any reason why we shouldn't meet." '

Dina is fifteen years younger, wears her hair in a boyish bob and trades on her teenage looks to pass as a student. (In fact, her cover is secretarial work in German at research institutes and export enterprises.) Her special method of soliciting is to ask a hotel switchboard for a room at random and, in charming German, English or French, beg the pardon of any man who answers. When she telephones again minutes later, the man may have resolved not to let a second opportunity pass to meet an enchanting-sounding Russian girl.

Dina is hypercautious: when foreign clients leave Moscow, she supplies them with self-addressed envelopes, care of poste restante, or pre-written cables which require the insertion of only the day and time of their return. She never gives a foreigner her telephone number or calls one from her flat, using only public boxes. In taxis, she addresses all her clients as 'Kolya', forbidding them to talk, and when she attends trade fairs and international exhibitions, it is always in the company of a Russian friend, to prevent detection by the closed-circuit television cameras which she is convinced keep watch for, among other things, Russian girls making up to foreign salesmen and representatives. But all this rings false to experienced Muscovites: although Dina may in fact try to conceal the extent of her soliciting, it is just as likely that her elaborate precautions are a device to deceive foreigners into trusting her. Contacts with foreigners on such a scale without the K.G.B.'s knowledge are virtually impossible for a Russian of any profession.

Despite the heavy surveillance of foreign trade fairs and industrial exhibitions – by K.G.B. officers in mufti, if not the suspected television cameras – Western businessmen at their stands are sometimes startled by a striking girl with expertly applied mascara showing deep interest in pipe-drilling equipment. Experienced girls can complete an acquaintance in minutes. Others occasionally stroll through the central peasant market, which in the Soviet context is the equivalent of a luxury mart; here the richest Soviet citizens and much of the Western colony shop for the capital's best and most expensive meat, fruit and vegetables. The old game is still played of hawking an extra ticket at a theatre entrance just before curtain time, especially at Bolshoi ballet performances, whose audiences are heavily weighted with resident and visiting foreigners. Explaining that 'mama has taken ill,' a girl tries to sell a ticket for the seat adjoining hers to a likely-looking man – or, conversely, to approach someone waiting to ask whether *he* might have a ticket to sell. In winter, the space between the double glass doors of the new Palace of Congresses provides a warm vantage point to survey the entering audience. In more hospitable weather, tourists manœuvring for the right perspective to photograph St Basil's Cathedral in Red Square may bump into a comely Russian girl seeking a similar snapshot. If her camera is Japanese, it is likely to have been given her by an earlier client.

So the profession survives, enjoys an occasional better-than-average season – usually in the intervals between noisy police campaigns – and its very tenacity and tenuous little triumphs over severe adversity speak of the continuity of Russian social attitudes.

'The history of Russian prostitution –' wrote Kuprin in 1913, 'oh what a tragic, pitiful, blood-stained, funny and stupid road it has travelled! Everything is mixed up in it: Russian religion, Russian happy-go-lucky recklessness and wide generosity, Russian despair and moral degradation, Russian primitiveness and naïveté, Russian tolerance, Russian shamelessness.' And Russian accommodation to circumstances, which is more conspicuous than ever.

6. Our Motherland

The farm is called 'Our Motherland': twenty-eight thousand of the Soviet Union's richest agricultural acres, which I am permitted to visit (a rare privilege, for over ninety per cent of Soviet farmland is ordinarily closed to Western journalists) for ten days. It is on the southernmost edge of Russia, some eight hundred miles south of Moscow; an oasis of sunshine and lush foliage in the vast land's otherwise far colder, harsher and poorer expanses.

Our Motherland's relative modernity and wealth flow directly from the region's natural blessings. This is the Kuban territory (watered by the Kuban River) known as 'the granary of Russia' and 'pearl of Russian agriculture'. Summers are long and hot, winters mild and often snowless, and the topsoil, heavy-smelling 'black earth' legendary for its fertility, runs six to nine feet deep. When the Wehrmacht occupied the region in 1942, they forced workers to shovel this precious loam into railroad cars for shipment to Germany. 'Shove a stick into the ground,' goes a local proverb, 'and tomorrow it will come up a tree.'

Kuban Cossacks once lived here (under Soviet rule, they no longer exist as a distinctive social unit) and in the nineteenth century, enterprising Germans migrated to the territory to make their fortunes from the soil, bringing with them a higher level of expertise and efficiency whose legacy is still visible. Now delegations from abroad are sent to visit the farm, a model for Soviet collectivized agriculture.

The office looks like that of a self-made, rich-but-Spartan cattle tycoon in America's Wild West. The telephone rings, and Chairman Cherkasov grips the receiver with a faint grimace of annoyance. It is his livestock chief, reporting on measures to prevent a foot-and-mouth epidemic from spreading to Our Motherland. Another ring a moment later: the chief agronomist reporting the tonnage of the morning's sugar-beet harvest. The next ring is from a young brigade leader whom Timofei Petrovich has recently reprimanded for delays in distributing fertilizer to the fields.

'This damn telephone,' he says hoarsely. 'Never lets you think. In the old days, at least, you could depend on it. I'd say, "Lovely one, get me Ivanovich" – every operator in the region knew my voice – and she'd find him fast, wherever he was. Now they've put in a dial system, and you can never get the man you need.'

Timofei Petrovich Cherkasov is Chairman of Our Motherland collective farm. Ten days as his guest are too few to acquire a perfect understanding of his place in the farm's management, or of his relationship to the territory's overlord, the First Secretary of the regional Communist Party branch who supervises a dozen farms from a neighbouring town. But it is immediately clear that Cherkasov is a figure of great importance in the Soviet power structure. His craggy good looks and personal charm apart, he is the prototype of the middle-level official who carries out the day-to-day 'operational' functions of Party and government. That he is the Chairman of a farm occasionally opened to foreigners speaks of his position as an especially trusted *cadrovik*.* Long years of 'front-line' supervision of regional and urban affairs through Party work preceded his selection as Chairman.

The telephone rings yet again, and Cherkasov answers in a tone of faint world-weariness. He is a man accustomed to power, and he wears it, like his dusty old suit, effortlessly and well. His immense authority on the farm derives not only from his prerogatives as Chairman ('We've had chairmen before whom we've spat on,' older farm hands profess) but also from an innate charisma. One imagines a man of such natural ascendency commanding an army or building an empire, and wonders what has brought him to this relatively prosaic position. It turns out that he has indeed been an empire builder – a high Party official – but he resigned, as he says, 'to return to the land'. The move brought a fifty per cent salary cut and put an end to his promising political career.

* A key member of the professional Party cadre. Cherkasov's brother is in a similar position as Party Secretary of a factory in the city of Khabarovsk. A second brother was killed in the Second World War.

'I asked myself, what am I really good for in this world? and I knew I didn't belong in Party or government work, no matter how high I got. Our collective farms suffered terribly from poor leadership in those days; there was the place a man could really test his own worth. I wanted to get my hands dirty, to see whether I could actually *produce* something for our society, instead of talking about it. People said I was crazy. But a man has to work where he feels the challenge, where he can drive for all he's worth.'

He is proud of the decision. 'That was in 1954. When I was elected Chairman, we didn't have a proper building so the general meeting took place in the street. Well, not so many years have passed, and we've doubled our wheat crop, increased milk production by five times and meat production by *twenty*. We've electrified and mechanized and organized the farm, and we've made our villages decent places to live instead of sorry slums. I only regret that I'm getting too old to see all our magnificent plans through to the end.'

Timofei Petrovich was born sixty-three years ago in a Siberian village. In those pre-revolutionary days, Siberian settlers could take all the land they could work; his family, therefore, was not poor – 'not the way peasants in other parts of Russia were poor at that time. My first boots were hand-me-downs from my grandfather, but they were leather, not bast like the poor devils in Russia wore.'

A certain woman in the village always knew all the news first. One day she ran to the Cherkasov farm, shouting that the Tsar had been overthrown. 'We couldn't believe it. In a ragged Siberian village, who could believe there was no more Tsar? But we soon saw for ourselves. By 1918, Soviet rule was established in our village. Then came Kolchak's counter-revolutionary army. Later, the Reds fought back again; it was bitter, bloody, and chaotic.

'I was only eight at the time, but there was one episode I'll never forget. It was when Kolchak's forces held the village and found out about a boy who was leading the Red partisan resistance. Either he surrenders, they announce, or they burn the village to the ground. So he gave himself up. To save the village. He walked towards the White officers – to his death, of course; nobody thought twice about mercy in those days – singing a revolutionary song about one's last days on earth. That brave, beautiful lad. I watched him. It was my first important memory.

'I envy that lad whenever I think of him: the way he died, and what he died for. This wasn't kamikaze fanaticism. The rationality of it made it *genuine* bravery, an act of pure humanity. It was giving your life for things bigger and better than you – for the village and the socialist future. The way that boy died!

'That episode burned in my mind. When I hear patriotic songs today, I remember his song. Maybe this sounds simple, but I'm a simple man. When things are tough with me, I remember his courage, try to live up to his example. Of course, that's not why I'm a Communist; I'm a Communist because I believe in it, because only Communism will give everyone leather boots – and a sense of human dignity. But years before I could understand anything like that, I was hooked by that splendid, shining hero of a boy. He was the beginning of my education.'

In the sense that it was more practical and political than formally academic, Cherkasov's education was to follow this pattern. In 1929, at the age of eighteen, he failed the entrance examination of a polytechnic institute in the Siberian city of Tomsk. Rather than take up the dreary alternative of returning to his village, the impatient young man, already a Young Communist activist, volunteered for gold prospecting in the wastes of extreme northern Siberia. His revolutionary enthusiasm and capacity for work and leadership asserted themselves quickly in that harsh environment; he was elected Secretary of his brigade's Young Communist organization and nominated for Party membership. In background, aptitude and dedication he was a near-perfect candidate.

The Party accepted him in 1933 – more evidence of his sterling political potential – placing him in a special training school for full-time workers in the *apparat*. Before he had quite finished the two-year course, he was assigned to the Party headquarters of a small far-eastern city, his first job in a typical career as a trusted Party official. Throughout the Stalinist 1930s, he rose steadily in the Party hierarchy in a series of jobs – Secretary of a District Bureau, Chief of the Department of Agitation and Propaganda in a Regional Bureau, First Secretary of a Regional Bureau – in a series of Russian cities and territories. ('I followed the old saying without question: "Wherever the Party sends you, that's where you go." ')

He spent the Second World War as a political commissar of a garrison on the Manchurian border, preparing for possible Japanese attack. ('I fought thirteen days in all in 1945, so I'm no military hero. But it wasn't easy to keep the troops at battle-readiness for seven years, especially for a political commissar.') Demobilized with the Order of the Red Star, he returned to civilian Party work. In 1949, he was selected for a two-year course in a Higher Party School, where Party officials with outstanding political talents and tested loyalty are trained for greater responsibilities. With an excellent record in the school, he continued up the Party hierarchy until resigning to come to Our Motherland. But as a prominent member of the Party bureaux of the farm, district and region, his ties to the Party are still intimate.

'I'm a Party man through and through. I work for the Party, take orders from the Party, live for the Party. My first loyalty is always to the Party, above anything else in the world. Does that frighten you?'

The telephone rings for the tenth time in half an hour; it is an official with instructions from district Party headquarters. Farm administrators rush into the office for instant consultations. At noon there is a brief meeting of heads of departments to outline Monday's work. Alone again, Timofei Petrovich surveys a sheaf of documents, grimaces again – he 'abhors' paperwork – and returns to the question of whether I will be permitted to stay my ten days as his guest.

At first, he is hardly eager to have me. 'What do you want here, poking around in our affairs? Our job is to increase production, not pose for journalists ... And while I'm thinking of it, where do you stand on your country's filthy business in Vietnam?' Eyeing me carefully while I answer, he seems to make up his mind. 'All right, get your things – you can move into the hostel.' Of course, the visit has been arranged through official channels over a period of months; a foreigner does not simply turn up at random at a collective farm. But one has the impression that even if Cherkasov is not empowered to turn me away, he could raise a serious protest with the regional Party overseers.

Having decided to welcome me, however, Timofei Petrovich switches quickly to 'tu' terms, and suggests I come with him as he hurries from the office and the hated paperwork for a tour of the farm. He surveys Our Motherland's 28,000 acres from the front seat of a car (one of two ordinary automobiles owned by the farm) driven by a young worker who beams with the honour of his job. Signalling where to stop by nodding his head, the Chairman investigates the day's trouble spots, visits new constructions, instructs, gossips, jokes with, and occasionally chides, workers and foremen. ('Konstantin Konstantinovich, there are reports the cows aren't eating your yeast. I want you to make it so delicious that even gorged cows will gobble it up.') Tractor drivers wave and shout greetings as he passes. Three young milkmaids offer him a glass of milk, giggling girlishly as their hero drinks it in two gulps. Farm hands grin at his approach and hang their heads when he finds fault with their work. Whatever they think of their lives and of collectivized agriculture in general, their admiration for him is unquestionable.

This is *his* farm, although he owns no part of it; the force of his experience and personality commands as much authority as sole ownership of a Texas ranch. Its success depends on his ability to manage, to plan, and, most important, to inspire the members to work harder; and in this Timofei Petrovich is a master. Our Motherland's workers bless their good fortune.

'I remember this farm', says an old herdsman, 'when the Chairman used to steal everything he could lay his hands on. People were actually swollen from hunger, but the boss cared only about swilling his vodka and squeezing his girls. We had another Chairman, also a Communist – and a Hero of Socialist Labour on top of it – who ran things so badly that everybody spat on the interests of the farm and just tried to stay alive. Timofei Petrovich is one in a

thousand. I don't care whether he's a Communist or not – he's a
real man. You can take your personal problems to him too, because
he *cares* about people. He's the most respected person for miles
around.'

Our Motherland is slightly smaller than the average Soviet collective farm, of which there are some thirty-two thousand. Apart
from a minute scattering of private farmsteads in inaccessible
areas, the remainder of Soviet agricultural land is divided among
some sixteen thousand state farms – a 'higher form' of socialist
property because, like factories, they are owned by the Soviet
people as a whole. In theory, collective farms belong to the farmer-
members themselves, who share the produce and (after taxes and
obligatory sales to the state) the profits.*

The plight of Soviet agriculture under collectivization – the
unworkable controls, horrendous mismanagement, lack of incentives, shortage of investment and, above all, indifference of farm
workers – is too well known to require documentation here. A
half-hour tour of Moscow food shops and markets is enough to
establish the general fact of limping performance: crowds besiege
counters offering stunted produce at astonishing prices (a kilo of
cucumbers in winter costs three days' wages of a skilled worker),
and among the thrusting women are many provincials who have
made the trip to the capital because their own shops, even in major
cities, can be bare of meat and fruit for months. Despite the grandiose schemes, huge sacrifices in the name of future production and
considerable capital investment, the production of many essential
crops in Russia is only fractionally higher than in the period before
the First World War.

Whether the immense failure is due to Soviet determination to
keep farming politically 'pure' – that is, at the higher Marxian
level represented by collectives – or to the legacy of the ruthless-
ness with which the collectives were originally founded is a matter

* Though not the land, which is nationalized in the Soviet Union, and which the
farms use by right of a governmental charter.

for speculation. What is beyond dispute is the staggering waste of the present system, even discounting the celebrated grain crop failures, huge purchases abroad and shortages of bread and meat in recent years. Despite far greater mechanization, the average Soviet collective farmer has a lower standard of living than the backward peasant in Poland, where most farms are private.

In Moscow, the stories about poverty in average collective farms are shocking, even in a country where material hardship is taken for granted. One hears of eighty-year-old grandmothers forced to return to work because they cannot survive on their pensions of eight rubles a month (the price of two kilos of good beef); of farmers who have seen no potatoes in years; of fifty-mile trips for bologna, many families' only source of meat. Muscovites return appalled from visits to relatives in the countryside. 'We had forgotten how bad things are,' they whisper. 'And they are getting worse.' No one can say how representative these personal plaints are, but national statistics speak for themselves about the continuing fiasco of collectivization. In 1972, almost one-third of all Soviet agricultural output (thirty-eight per cent of the milk, forty per cent of the vegetables, sixty per cent of the eggs, sixty-five per cent of the potatoes) came from the meagre herds and tiny private plots, representing *two per cent* of the country's farmland, which collective farmers are permitted to maintain, supposedly for use of their own families – in other words, from the vestiges of private enterprise.*

When I visited Our Motherland, the Soviet press was full of its usual exhortations to improve agricultural standards and, by implication, irritation over the seemingly chronic shortcomings. The extent of the problem is perhaps most clearly demonstrated by the practice in most Soviet areas of holding farm workers to the

---

* In Our Motherland, each household is allowed a half-acre plot, one cow, two sows and up to forty-five hens, ducks or geese for its own use or sale in peasant markets. Even senior farm officials spend much of their spare time working their own soil and minding their own animals for individual profit. In more northern areas, retired farmers have found that they can do better from their tiny vegetable patches than they did as full-time workers in the collective, with all its machinery, bureaucracy and production campaigns.

land (rather like serfs) by denying them the necessary papers to move
to a city. This practice also underlines the lush Kuban region's
untypicality, for here the problem is to keep out unhappy families
from poorer areas considered overpopulated. Since many of the
general conditions of Soviet agriculture obviously do not apply to
Our Motherland, it seems better to abandon any idea of using it as a
model for general conditions, take this 'millionaire' farm for what it
is and see what can be learned from that. If the ambitious Soviet
agricultural plans succeed at last, the average collective farm may
reach Our Motherland's present standards of methods, mechanization and wealth within a generation.

'Welcome to Our Motherland!'

'Welcome to the Kuban!'

'Try our Kuban milk!'

'Taste this Kuban borscht! There is borscht and borscht, but
nothing compares to our Kuban borscht.'

'Just smell it – what could be better than Kuban air? I'm not sure
of much, but one thing I know: I couldn't live anywhere else on
earth but on the Kuban.'

Such are the greetings during my first days – but how to
respond? Men who never travelled farther than Kiev *know* that
the Kuban is the best place on earth.

Everywhere in Russia, love-thy-land patriotism is whipped up
so calculatedly, often through methods repugnant to a Westerner,
that one is almost surprised by the genuine article: the peasant's
deep, mystical attachment to the soil which sustains him. To an
outsider, the Kuban countryside is pleasant but undistinguished:
flat, faintly monotonous plains reminiscent of the American Mid-
West, dotted with villages similar to those seen in the Ukraine
(which are richer and better kept than Russian villages). But Our
Motherland's people, with their elemental patriotism and insu-
larity, love it fiercely, simply because it gave birth to them.

Twenty-five thousand of Our Motherland's twenty-eight
thousand acres are cultivated. Wheat, corn, sugar-beets and sun-

flower seeds are the principal crops; cattle (1,800 head), pigs (10,000), sheep and hens the chief livestock. The work is accomplished by ninety-eight tractors, forty-one combines, fifty lorries and several herds of work horses, supplemented by two jeeps, several buses for transport and the two ordinary cars. The farm also owns a flour mill, yeast plant, brick factory, creamery and antibiotic laboratory.

Our Motherland's four thousand souls live in seven adjoining villages, of which Sokolovsky, the administrative centre, is the central and largest. Like most Russian settlements, it is strung out along the main road, a dusty, pitted artery badly in need of repaving. An office building festooned with propaganda posters and slogans, a cafeteria with rooms for transients, a general store under construction, the Palace of Culture ... the village has an unsettled, unfinished appearance, as if it had been put up hurriedly to decay as fast as it grows. A convoy of olive-drab lorries feels its way along the road, each one losing part of its load at each bump. Simple people and endless earth, partial mechanization and raw construction – a scene from a Russian film about the Second World War.

One building on Sokolovsky's main road is so unlike the others that it demands immediate exploration. The Palace of Culture, a two-storey structure in neo-Russian classical style, stands like the Royal Albert Hall in the middle of a village on the moors. It is the centre of the farm's social, cultural and mass-political activities: the setting for weekend films (in a five-hundred-seat auditorium), ideological lectures and performances by travelling theatre groups. There are smaller rooms for political instruction, meetings of the photography club, choir practice, band practice, fencing ... the Palace of Culture is the community centre in a settlement where all activities which would be run by church, state and private individuals in other countries are here financed and supervised by a single authority. As in all public buildings of this sort, the corridors are covered in wall newspapers, political slogans, photographs of national economic progress and busts of Lenin. Our Motherland's palace was built in 1958 at great expense to the members, and still fills them with visible pride. Faced by columns and crowned by a red star, it is bigger, grander, more solemn and more pompous than anything in sight. How Russian – how Soviet!

A French village, as we have learned at the cinema, is run by its mayor, priest and schoolteacher (and richest landowner, when he happens not to be the mayor), who meet in the café to co-ordinate their authority in the best interests of a rational order, the villagers and, incidentally, themselves. The intricate, somewhat obscure pattern of Soviet local government, with its layers of seemingly overlapping authority, makes the roles of Our Motherland's elders more difficult to categorize.

The Chairman of the village soviet (the rough equivalent of the mayor) seems to have little power. Although he is the local representative of Soviet government, his office is open but a few hours a day and most of his functions appear to be purely bureaucratic, such as the recording of official statistics and distribution of decrees and regulations from Moscow ministries.

The Chairman of the farm, by contrast, is lord of the manor. Production – *the harvest* – is the criterion of criteria in Soviet social life and, as the man responsible for this stretch of land, Timofei Petrovich Cherkasov has the overriding authority, in which his personal charisma and Party standing also help.

A more inscrutable role is played by Semyon Mikhailovich Kandobarev, the Party 'commissar' – more precisely, Secretary of the farm's Communist Party organization.

Although 'Partorg' (Party organizer) is Orwellian, Kandobarev's resemblance to the Party *apparatchiks* suggested by Orwell and others is otherwise faint. A staid, soft-spoken man with a shy smile, he is the picture of a modest schoolteacher – which, in fact, was his profession before taking up full-time Party work: he taught biology for sixteen years in the Sokolovsky school. In all things he is moderate, the model middle-class husband.

Kandobarev was born and raised on the farm, and his horizons have not spread much farther. An average student, an average Young Communist, a not-very-ambitious-worker (he is only now, at forty-three, completing his teaching degree by correspondence courses), an active but not outstanding Communist – why, then, was he chosen Party Secretary? Perhaps because he is known and trusted in the villages; even a poor and disgruntled farmhand, who complained bitterly about his poverty compared to the 'bosses'' riches, was full of praise for Semyon Mikhailovich's kindness towards ordinary workers. Perhaps because this type too – the solid citizen ... does well low in the Party. He is a dedicated Communist, but Communism in Russia now often means Being Upstanding; this man could not be farther removed from revolution, class struggle, all things radical. He is ninety-five parts conservatism and convention, five parts reform, no part revolution.

His job defies description to anyone unfamiliar with the role of the Communist Party in contemporary life. (While I am on the farm, his job is to escort me everywhere, whispering, introducing, arranging interviews, making sure that the people I am to visit are prepared to give the proper impression and that things I should not see are kept from view.) The Party is everywhere, leading, lecturing, exhorting, nagging, planning every aspect of Soviet life, and Semyon Mikhailovich, as its agent, does for the farm what Partorg Viktor Savitsky does for the Hotel Rossiya.* Increased production, better education, more study of Marxism-Leninism, enriched cultural life, domestic happiness: he leads the campaigns and conducts the propaganda and agitation for all approved social goals. The Party is party to every decision at every meeting. Kandobarev is also a counsellor-confessor-fixer; when personality clashes break out on the job or at home, when a worker wants a favour or a change of work, Semyon Mikhailovich is always ready to intercede.

One of his primary functions is to organize 'mass-cultural' work: all social and communal activities – sports, amateur evenings, hobby clubs, choir and band practice – fall under his jurisdiction. This involves him in activities one would have thought strange for a Party overseer: he organizes political lectures and study groups, of course, but also buys rock 'n' roll records for teenage dances. And helps bring Marilyn Monroe as well as Marx and Lenin to the masses: this week's film at the Palace of Culture is

* See p. 114.

'Some Like It Hot'.

'The Party organization', Kandobarev explains, 'stands politically higher than the management of the farm as such. Personally, my main function is upbringing and education. I am responsible for instilling Communist ideals everywhere on the farm.'

Shaving me every other morning with his treasured, pre-war German razor, the village barber talks about the events of the day. In the 1930s, he was chairman of a small collective farm, but war wounds left him unfit for such strenuous activity and he acquired a simpler trade. He came to Our Motherland because his children work here and 'an old man must be near his family'.

'What about the church?' I ask. 'Does anyone still attend?'

'Only a few old women. Hardly anybody these days.'

'What about you?'

'Why bother? It's impossible to believe.'

'And you've got no worries on that score?'

'Can't tell yet; I'll have to wait till I die.'

'How about going to church occasionally just for insurance?'

'Maybe I should, but it's a terrible bore. The church was all right in the old days when there was nothing to do around here. Now we have movies, television, amateur evenings at the Palace of Culture. Everything else is much more *fun*.'

Twenty broad-backed women, a 'link' in a field cultivation brigade, bunched in the back of a truck (the bus has broken down again) and singing as they ride to the potato fields at 7.30 a.m. Hand labour such as weeding and harvesting is 'of course' women's work on the farm.

I ask the women if they would rather work together with men.

'Oh, there are plenty of men in the fields, drivers and mechanics and that. If it's a man you want you can always find one.'

'Who works harder here, men or women?'

'Who works harder everywhere? A man might sweat once or

twice during the day, but a woman's work is never done.'

Two days are enough to see that the farm's most impressive aspect is its facilities for children. There is a day-nursery for a hundred pre-school tots of working mothers – free, but as inviting as many on Fifth Avenue costing a thousand dollars a year – and a pleasant dormitory for a hundred and fifty older children who live far from the Sokolovsky school or whose parents are hard-pressed to mind their offspring during the week. A big bowl of meaty borscht here costs less than five cigarettes – or nothing, if the child's parents are in dire financial need. The elaborateness of these institutions is out of proportion to everything else (except the medical facilities) on the farm, but entirely in keeping with general Soviet conditions. As everywhere in the country, children get the best of everything, both within the family – even farm parents who go threadbare dress their children carefully – and in the distribution of community wealth. The nursery and dormitory governesses are farm wives who lavish on their charges the same unembarrassed warmth-cum-easy-discipline with which they have raised their own children. Serene yet bright, plump and gay, the children themselves are as appealing as any in the world.

The schoolhouse is new but, like most new buildings in Russia, already crumbling, and the curriculum is the standard one for all schools in the Russian Republic. Strong emphasis is placed on mathematics and science: chemistry, physics and biology are taught in handsomely equipped laboratories from the age of thirteen. And on vocational training related to the farm: courses in metalwork, woodwork, tractor-driving and mechanics are obligatory. And on patriotism: classrooms and common rooms, foyers and corridors abound with displays of revolutionary and war heros, slogans and banners, and portraits of Lenin, Lenin, Lenin. For along with the care and resources lavished on youth goes an incessant inescapable programme of political indoctrination in every aspect of their comprehensively planned activities – a kind of Marxist-Leninist catechization which is repeated throughout the day in one form or another and which concentrates, in tones of the worst yellow journalism, on the 'hostility', 'decadence' and 'massive poverty' of the 'bourgeois West'.

Class 9B has its weekly hour with its class teacher (or homeroom hour) on Tuesday afternoon. The teacher reads aloud a long clipping from *Komsomolskaya Pravda*, the newspaper of the Young Communist League; it is the story of two railway workers who sacrificed their lives to prevent a train crash in which hundreds would have died. This kind of inspirational message, standard in every newspaper every day, has surrounded the children from their earliest years. The fifteen-year-olds listen passively, and after some minutes their attention wanders; but far from reducing the moralistic-patriotic-revolutionary-ideological teaching, the farm school is constantly planning ways to increase it.

'Our main problem', explains the school's director, 'is making our message to the children real, rather than mere words. For example, we teach them that the fight to increase labour productivity is essential for building Communism. A child may memorize this and get "A's" in his exams – but then go on to be a poor worker. That is an impermissible rupture between practice and theory. We must make every child a *conscious* and *active* participant in the struggles of our society. Our main task, in other words, is not merely to teach but to instil Communist habits in every pupil.'

Every child over eight is a member of the Pioneers, and wears his white blouse and red kerchief on school and national holidays. The Pioneer meeting-room on the ground floor is crammed with patriotic slogans and portraits of national and revolutionary heroes. A group of ten-year-old girls are discussing the river outings and educational activities they had arranged for younger children during the previous summer. Hands over a plaster bust of Lenin, the Pioneers pledge allegiance.

Solemn Promise of a Young Pioneer of the Soviet Union

'I, a Young Pioneer of the Soviet Union, do solemnly promise before my comrades: to deeply love my Soviet Motherland, to live, study and fight as the great Lenin directed in his

testament, and as the Communist Party teaches us.'
FOR THE STRUGGLE, FOR THE CAUSE OF THE COMMUNIST
PARTY – BE PREPARED, ALWAYS PREPARED.

Natasha is a barefoot girl of seventeen whose milkmaid's body
strains at a calico dress. She blushes at a query about a boy-friend
and giggles painfully when asked if she has been kissed – but
experience and interest, rather than innocence, twinkle from her
eyes.

It is difficult to ask members of the farm about sex, but I am
lucky to meet a wry, middle-aged lorry driver from Kharkov
whose information seems reliable. Pre- and extra-marital relations,
he says, are pursued in the tradition of the Russian village: willing
participation, usually starting at the age of fifteen or sixteen for the
girls, but with a persistent taboo against any talk about the act. A
young girl may have a casual lover or two, but any talk would fly
through the village, disgracing her permanently. A young man
who brags of a conquest might well be beaten severely for his
cheap breach of honour. A young couple might meet regularly in
a hayloft or corn field, but if on Saturday evening in the palace of
culture he asks her to dance in the presence of her girl-friends, she
will turn crimson. This is not Soviet puritanism, for relations
between teenagers are not, in fact, puritan, and farm officials do
not campaign to make them so. But an ancient peasant modesty
(reflected in Russian literature long before the Revolution) requires
that intimate pleasure be taken in total secrecy.

I seek out the village storyteller for clues to the local history,
heroes and yarns, expecting that there will be much reminiscing in
a village which has experienced Russia's twentieth-century tem-
pests of revolution, civil war, collectivization and invasion. As time
passes on the farm, I realize that it is precisely these reminiscences
which are so regrettably missing: the outpouring of production
statistics, Party slogans and love-thy-tractor messages accentuates
the absence of local lore and a certain hollowness of atmosphere.

The 'historylessness' imparts a lack of wholeness, as if this, like some string of American highway motels organized into a town for administrative convenience, were a community without a heart.

To some extent, the farmland itself is at fault. Our Motherland's tracts are relentlessly partitioned into immense 250- or 500-acre rectangles: convenient to farm and depressing to view. Cosy fields in age-old quilted patterns have no more place here than the stone walls that once bordered them. Russia too is making its contribution to the Americanization of the world, for these blueprinted fields have all the economic advantages – and the stark impersonality – of a giant supermarket. Still, the absence of a sense of organic community comes from more than the lie of the land. For all its careful organization as an economic unit, Our Motherland seems to have no social personality of its own. I become more and more certain that I cannot perceive its inner 'feel' until I absorb something about its roots.

But there is no local storyteller. Or if he does exist, I am not allowed to meet him; nor can farm officials quite understand why I want to: hasn't the Partorg fully explained the farm's purpose, plans and spirit? Eventually I come to sense that the Revolution and Soviet rule, together with their traumatic aftermath, have boiled away all sense of the past; no one shows any interest in the old days or the traditions of the villages as villages. In the absence of normal nostalgia, continuity and attachment to roots, Our Motherland seems less a genuine farm than a depersonalized agricultural factory. In this place of high-priority 'socialist construction' one is reminded of the concern about alienation which sparked the social investigations of Karl Marx.

Some of the reasons for the death of genuine local lore are suggested by the history of the Kuban. The area was solidly anti-Bolshevik during the Civil War: a single detachment of the famous Kuban Cossacks fought with the Red Army; all others joined the Whites, fleeing towards the Black Sea after their defeat. Decades later, Cossack life was glamorized on film, but almost all remnants of it except gay costumes and songs had already been exterminated in the uniformity of Soviet rule. A second mass exodus took place some dozen years later, during the collectivization of agriculture. Together with much of the intelligentsia, virtually all prosperous farmers – and the rich Kuban soil had made many such 'class enemies' – were dispossessed and exiled thousands of miles to naked steppes. Thus the natural preservers of local lore were skimmed away, and the poor farmers who remained, together with the cadres sent in to supervise collectivization, mentioned the great upheavals in text-book terms if at all. Only the hardships of the German invasion are talked about freely, since here local sentiment and official history roughly match. But the overriding impression is that this area, like so many in Russia, is virtually traditionless, with only a thin veneer of political mythology designed to glorify the recent Soviet past.

The bits and pieces of recent history which I do learn are principally neutral facts. Sokolovsky is named after a rich cattle rancher whose estate occupied most of the neighbouring land until the Revolution. When this probably genuine class enemy fled, his land was divided among joyful peasants who worked it privately for ten years. In 1927, a young political activist who had fought in the Red Army during the Civil War arrived to organize a co-operative – the first step in the often brutal process of collectivization. By tempting and terrorizing the fiercely independent local farmers, Our Motherland was established as a proper collective farm in 1930, immediately receiving a tractor from the state. The original farm was composed of but thirty peasant families, but resistance was soon crushed and all others in the area forced to join. In 1950, the six collective farms which had formed around neighbouring villages (Lenin's Legacies, Red Plougher, Land of the Soviets, etc.) were merged and the present giant called Our Motherland was born. But it was only in 1956, after Khrushchev increased the prices paid for obligatory state deliveries, that Our Motherland began to prosper. Wages in cash were paid from 1959.

Many were the lean years during Our Motherland's slow development, but there is vague, circumspect talk of the 'terrible three'. 'Three times in my life', said one old man blandly, 'my tongue was hanging out to stay alive – and it was a close thing.'

Nineteen twenty-one is remembered for chaos and hunger caused by economic disruptions following the Civil War. Nineteen thirty-three was a year of starvation and agony caused by famine and the effects of the enforced collectivization several years before, when unwilling peasants slaughtered almost half of Russia's livestock in protest. 'There was a good harvest here that year, but people were actually starving to death by the millions everywhere else in the country. So government men came down here and took everything we had. *Everything.* "How much wheat did you harvest?" they'd ask. "Fifteen poods." "Then hand over fifteen poods." They left us to starve too.'

And 1947 was 'the worst of all', a year of misery caused by drought and the destruction of the Second World War. 'It was fearful; the crops simply didn't grow. People came in droves from the north, near dead, but things were just as terrible here. You lived on plain bread then, and there was never enough even of that. We swelled up from hunger. The queue would form at dawn one morning for a half-loaf to be handed out the next day. But plenty of people on other farms ate *grass*.'

Even in this most blessed region of Russia, the old enemy of starvation has visited often since 1917. Without an understanding of past hardships and the lingering fear of them, no one can quite comprehend why most Russians greatly prefer security to freedom, or why (even without Soviet propaganda) the 'open opportunity' of a free-market system usually provokes a fear of what will be lost rather than a hankering for what might be gained.

Perhaps it is past hardship, too, that accounts for the astonishingly low economic ambitions of the Russian people and, as in the case of Our Motherland, the exultant crowing over recent progress. 'Look what *we've* done, see what *we've* built, isn't it amazing?' – as if no other community on earth were building and improving; as if they themselves do not quite believe their own accomplishments. They are erecting commendable schools – but less impressive than those on rich land elsewhere. They have accomplished much since the starvation under Stalin – but even an untrained eye sees the lag behind progressive European farmers working with far less

favourable soil and climate. Their successes would be so common-
place in the West that it would be considered embarrassing to talk
about them. But they are not yet normal in this land of misfortune;
hence the occasionally inspiring, usually irritating, ever-clacking
pride. But does satisfaction in collective achievement also play a
role? Do these cries of self-congratulation also resound in a primitive kibbutz?

The hardest effect of the war can still be seen by the same untrained
eye: the farm's population is lopsided with fifty- and sixty-year-
old widows. One day, I come across seven women of this age
awaiting transport to another field. Each is kerchiefed and bent: the
picture of the Russian grandmother wearied by a life of hard work,
suffering and deficient nourishment. But all gossip gaily and joke
about their 'girlish charms' until I make the mistake of asking one
about her husband. He was killed in Stalingrad in 1942. Another
died in Leningrad, a third near Berlin. Of seven husbands, only
one survived the war – having lost both legs. Without money,
machinery or their men, the struggle to stay alive in the hungry
post-war years left the women middle-aged at thirty.

'Tell your people we don't want war. We've had too much of
it – *oi*, too much trouble.'

'The men go to war and don't come back. We're not cowards
but we want our children to live. We were young and strong, and
our men didn't come back.'

'The war took away everything we had. We're old now, but
tell your countrymen that our young people need peace.'

The fighting in the Kuban itself was fierce: Wehrmacht armies
thrust towards the Caucasus, and Russian defenders were initially
forced into retreat after retreat. However, the Germans are remembered more for their occupation than for the bloodletting on
the front. The Wehrmacht ruled the Kuban for six months in
1942 and 1943, ravaging and killing. It was here, the villagers say,
that the Germans developed a new, portable gas chamber on
wheels to speed the extermination of undesirable elements as they

drove from village to village. 'They packed people in at one village, and when they arrived at the next, unloaded the corpses.'

'It wasn't just the killing – we'd seen death before – but the way they did it. The way they did everything. They'd open up their cans of meat and taunt us because they liked to torture starving people. That's how they're made.'

When the Wehrmacht withdrew, they stole what they could and destroyed what they were unable to transport. 'Cows, grain, barns, even plates – they smashed everything that wasn't hidden. We had to dress our sons as girls because they were stealing boys, too.' (A bridge across the neighbouring Kuban River which was demolished by the Germans in early 1943 remains unreplaced to this day; trucks and passengers are transported from one muddy bank to the other by an ancient ferry which uses the current for power.)

'Sometimes agricultural delegations come here from East Germany, and everything's supposed to be Peace and Friendship with them. East Germany is supposed to have changed, supposed to have a new socialist spirit, full of humanity, fraternity, inter-nationalist proletarianism and all that. But nobody here can stomach them. Germans are Germans – inhuman.'

Medical facilities: a new clinic, a fifty-bed hospital, a maternity home; five doctors (four of them women), a dentist and twenty-two nurses and assistants ... extraordinary. The chief doctor per-forms all but the most complicated surgery in a well-equipped operating room. (His private car, one of two owned by the farm's four thousand members, was subsidized by the state and equipped with hand controls. In 1942, when the doctor was thirteen, he stepped on a mine while guiding a Red Army reconnaissance patrol through nearby woods, and his left leg was blown off.)

'Preventive medicine through regular check-ups is the least glamorous but most important aspect of our work. We've beaten typhus completely in the past few years, tuberculosis is almost eliminated, and dysentery is now rare. I opened this hospital in

1961; since then we've cut some infectious diseases by ten times and child mortality by four.'

Childbirth is by the natural method, which is standard and obligatory throughout the Soviet Union. Prospective mothers attend a course of lectures and have two months' leave from work before and another two after birth. 'For thousands of years, religion taught women that they had to give birth in pain. Soviet medicine has freed them from that, and from their awful fear. Childbirth is a *natural* phenomenon, and if *properly* prepared for rarely brings pain. Our maternity home was once known as "the scream-house", but in my six years here there hasn't been more than the grunts that accompany any heavy physical labour.'

Newborn infants are swaddled in the traditional Russian *kosinka*, but 'there's nothing symbolic about that. It's just that the *kosinka* is convenient and an excellent protection against draughts.' About birth control, he said, 'If a mother doesn't want more children, she consults us and we explain about contraceptives, which are available at a chemist's. This is done on an individual basis only; there are no public lectures on this subject.' The doctor does not add that the contraceptives – condoms only – are extremely crude, and hardly anyone bothers with them; or that abortion is the principal means of birth control, and that it is by this method that the average farm family limits itself to three children.

Predictably, the village poor are the old, the unskilled and the unambitious. I cannot tell how many or how poor they are, for I am kept well clear of their homes, and with my escorts never more than two minutes away, there is no opportunity to investigate. Soon after I arrived, an old rag of a woman husking corn wailed bitterly to me that she never got enough to eat. 'She's lying,' cackled her partner. 'She's got twenty geese and everything but a maid.' It can only be said that a poor person here is far better off than elsewhere in rural Russia.

One morning, I strike up a conversation with a gnarled old

blacksmith who looks thirty years older than his age of sixty-two. 'This is paradise compared to the old days. In the old days, you worked till you dropped and schemed all day just to stay alive. Now we've got food and clothes – *everything*. If we told the people who died in the war how we live now, they wouldn't believe us.' He is immensely proud that his children are university students, although he has forgotten which universities they attend.

Later that morning I meet a gaunt fieldhand who must remain unidentified, although he made a deeper impression on me than anyone except Chairman Cherkasov. A shy man, he tenderly stroked a stray kitten in his hand while pleading for understanding. He spoke in a whisper and peered over his shoulder frequently to see that we were not observed. 'If you mention my name, it'll be the end of me. They'll kick me out of here within an hour – or punish me worse. Please understand why I'm talking to you, I just want you to know the truth. We knew you'd be shown the cream and kept from meeting any ordinary workers.

'This is how it really is here: I earn fifty rubles (£20) a month, and in winter it can go down to thirty. How can you live on fifty rubles? You don't live; you exist. On bread, potatoes and tea; I haven't had meat in months. Look at these rags I'm in: I can't even afford to patch them right. I wish you could see the hovel I live in and how I have to dress my daughter. And the big shots on this farm are building garages for their private cars. This isn't socialism, it's exploitation like it always was – only they ruin your life forever if you open your mouth. Somehow, I hope that you won't be fooled, but *please* don't say who I am.'

Although journalism of this sort inevitably contaminates its environment by provoking reactions to the observer, the disturbance caused by an American in a Soviet village is unusually severe and the chances to observe the pristine village correspondingly rare. 'Oh, you're the foreign journalist! We heard you'd be coming to look us over.'

Every effort is made to conceal the efforts to impress me, doub-
ling the agitation. One evening, a senior farm official swallows
enough vodka (and sees to it that I swallow plenty too) to confess.
'Oh, we want to please you, very much. We want you to like us.
Will you criticize us? Please try not to. Maybe you won't like
everything you see here, but you must understand how much
progress we've made and what we're trying to do. It is terribly
important for everyone here that you approve.'

The next day, however, this man has sobered up, and again I'm
guided towards the farm's best and hurried past what cannot be
shown with pride. But what is best to the farm officials – the
clusters of new three-room houses and, above all, machinery – is
the most familiar to the visitor, and therefore the dullest. A proud
old water-bearer delivers fresh well water by horse and cart to
members' houses and to workers in the fields; he allows his grand-
son to drive his team from his lap and jokes with women weeders –
a colourful and delightful old man. But officials do not want me to
photograph him, or the old whitewashed cottages with thatched
roofs, one of the few sights with charm. 'Why are you so interested
in horses, elderly people and old houses? Why don't you describe
our combines?'

I am not shown the home of an ordinary labourer, and in the
homes to which I am invited – the schoolteacher's, medallist tractor
driver's, Chairman's, Chief Engineer's – each host prepares a
huge banquet of food and drink. Day after day, evening after
evening, feast after feast, I spend endless hours toasting, eating and
drinking to stupefaction – doing my duty as a guest in a Russian
home. Are these orgies of ingestion intended to divert me from
exploring the village's daily routine?

Of course, they are also an expression of Russian hospitality,
which on the Kuban is as overwhelming as legend has it. Hospitality
in Russian cities is also lavish, but Our Motherland's emphasis on
eating and drinking exceeds anything I've previously seen. A
Soviet journalist passing through the farm says that even he can't
explore here without observing the rituals of hospitality. 'If I came
to this village for an interview with a tractor driver and didn't

have my long talk first in the office, the managers would be gravely insulted. It's the custom in these villages to get to work only after you've first made friends. Personally, I love the food and drink, but it just about kills your work as a journalist. It takes a day to get a ten-minute story – and how can you criticize somebody who plies you with a bottle and makes you his buddy?'

Thus it is impossible to distinguish between hospitality and the urge to impress. The whispers that precede me everywhere – are they to ensure that I do not find things in 'working disorder', as the Partorg puts it, or simply that I am hospitably received? Everywhere, too, greetings and flowers are presented to the foreigner by people apparently not whispered to. The villagers' dual role as hosts and subjects confuses them; they would be more comfortable if I wrote nothing and behaved solely as their guest.

All through my first week on the farm runs the undercurrent of Chairman Cherkasov's presence, like a favourite headmaster in an otherwise faintly alien school. It is him one yearns to talk with; all his lieutenants are lack-lustre by comparison. But since he is too busy to attend my daily banquets, all I can manage from him is snatches of explanation and banter. 'Let's see how you work, young lad. If we like the looks of you, we'll invite you back for six months.'

At last he has some free hours after his customary Saturday afternoon inspection of the farm. With visible relish, he prepares for his cherished weekly ritual – a visit to the traditional Russian bath-house. This one is a ramshackle cabin behind Sokolovsky's main street, its steam rooms heated by a log fire. Timofei Petrovich wraps birch branches into a stout but flexible besom, and in the tiny, torrid steam room – his endurance of the heat is known to be greater than anyone else's on the farm – slaps himself slowly with it until his skin is a fierce pink. In the showers, he takes his turn scrubbing workers' backs. 'In Siberia, we used to dive straight from the steam into the snow – maybe that's why Siberians are healthy. Anyway, I've never been sick a day in my life.'

Afterwards, he cools off on a sagging bench near the bath-

house where two grizzled workers, surrounded by a circle of
kibbitzers, are playing chess. 'Pipe down, Timofei Petrovich,' says
the losing player. 'You may know something about labour
productivity but your chess is a disaster.'

At twilight, Cherkasov walks home at a relaxed pace. Saturday
evening is the time for family and family friends.

Family life on the farm has the kind of country 'togetherness' that
American women's magazines futilely propagandized in the 1950s.
The unselfconscious physical contact of family members – they
are constantly holding and hugging each other – symbolizes the
intimacy of emotional relationships. Children are squeezed,
pampered and talked about with unashamed sentimentality.
Grandparents live with their children and grandchildren, and social
life is primarily family life because most people spend most of their
free time with relatives. The attachment to family has a simplicity
and earthiness that have disappeared in more developed societies.
Here married men still go fishing with their elderly fathers and
deliver the catch to mother to prepare in the old family way.

Of course intense family relationships are a product of hundreds
of years of Russian culture; but modern (middle-class) Communism
is determined to preserve them. 'If a family's having trouble,' the
Party Secretary volunteers, 'I speak to them. As the Partorg, the
person responsible for the farm's moral tone. Suppose a wife comes
to me to complain about her husband: he's a bad father, a bad
husband, drinks too much or spends his free time with persons
unknown. I investigate and get him to mend his ways – that's my
job.'

What if the husband doesn't heed the Party's advice? 'Oh, there
are ways to influence him, even if he tells me – this is very rare –
that it's none of my business. We can write about him in the local
press, see that his case is taken up by his deputy to the local soviet.
Or we can raise the issue with the husband's fellow workers: they
don't like one of their own to mistreat his family. A rational man
will reform; nobody likes to face a meeting of his fellow workers a

second time. But usually a talk with me is enough.'

Aren't farm workers reluctant to discuss their family affairs before outsiders? 'But we're not "outsiders", that's just it. Every family's affairs concern all of us directly. Communism's changed the old Russian saying that "someone else's family is a mystery". Now every family is everyone's concern. Family happiness is a communal affair, a village affair, even a national affair. Don't forget the Moral Code of the Builder of Communism includes a commandment about "Mutual Respect in the Family and Concern for the Upbringing of Children".

'It's my obligation as Partorg and the responsibility of the entire community to ensure that every family enjoys domestic peace. This farm is one big collective working towards one common goal, and strife, unhappiness or bad behaviour anywhere impedes our production and other progress.'

As time passes, it appears that the Partorg's potentially sinister interpretation of his obligations and powers to control private behaviour is largely rhetoric: another statement of what the Party would like to establish rather than what actually exists. Family privacy is indeed curtailed on the farm, but it is traditional in Russia that the community concerns itself with matters considered personal in the West. Despite the Party's campaign for wholesomeness, rectitude and domestic bliss, Our Motherland is hardly a Quaker settlement. Time and money permitting, the normal Russian urges to drink and dally are satisfied – but discreetly, so that the Party's less-than-vigilant eye is not attracted. The machinery of community intervention in family affairs is activated only when misbehaviour is flagrant or disturbs the good order of the village. A young lorry driver put it pithily: 'Swig your bottle, take your roll in the hay – only watch you don't offend anybody. The Party preaching is rubbish, but they can knock you over the head with it if they're out to get you for something else.'

The farm's Management Board meets in a small auditorium of the Palace of Culture decorated with busts of Lenin, reproductions of revolutionary battle scenes and political and production slogans. Ten board members, heads of departments and chief technicians sit at a table, flanking Chairman Cherkasov. The auditorium's front rows are occupied by second-level specialists and a dozen interested bystanders: the farm's most ambitious and responsible workers. For this is where most major decisions – where, when and what to plant, how many men and machines to use – are taken.

Cherkasov taps his water glass and the meeting begins. Interrupted occasionally by questions and comments from Cherkasov and others, the chief agronomist reports on the past ten days' progress in fulfilling the harvest plans of various crops in various parts of the farm. Next, the assistant livestock manager (the chief is on summer holiday!) reports the figures for each barn's meat and milk production, and the litres achieved by the leading milkmaids in the 'socialist competition'. Criticism, discussion and debate follow each report. Where should the combines be employed now? What's holding up the manure? Why aren't the tractors *still* properly lubricated? The discussion is conducted roughly according to universal rules of order; the person who has the floor, seemingly, is the one with most to say. Cherkasov comments freely but interrupts only when the discussion wanders or it is time to reach a decision. The meeting is informal yet businesslike, serious but unstrained – as effective as any town-meeting committee I have seen.

Here is the hope of Russian democracy. Nothing less resembles the rubber-stamp, unanimous-vote Supreme Soviet Session than this open exchange of opinion in search of collective decision. Spectators as well as board members speak their minds quietly and confidently, without deference to rank. The criticism, self-criticism and arguments are uninhibited, and Cherkasov himself is not above reproach. Russians, it seems, have a natural talent for making this kind of communal corporate body work for decision-making at the lowest level; the traditions of the *mir* (a form of collective self-government in which much of Russia's peasantry made its daily decisions from the sixteenth to the nineteenth century) are very much alive.

A heated dispute breaks out between a woman in the audience and a man at the board table. The controversy concerns the poor production figures of dairy barn number six, of which she is manager; he, the chief of the fourth brigade, is her direct superior. *Whose* idea was it to send the herd to that pasture? *Who* is responsible for slow deliveries of feed? Flushed with anger, the woman defends her personal and professional pride. Finally her boss mollifies her by taking some of the blame on himself, and she subsides.

The next dispute concerns hay deliveries. 'I think the will of the meeting is to fine you five rubles', Cherkasov informs the chief of the fifth brigade, 'for not fulfilling your plan ... A fiver, O.K.? Any comments? Any objections?' But as the discussion is about to move on, an argument erupts about who in fact held up the hay deliveries, and since the fault is unclear Cherkasov rescinds the fine and orders an investigation.

'Look, Anatolii Petrovich' – Cherkasov is now addressing the man in charge of hay storage – 'your work discipline is plain lousy. We discuss everything here. Take decisions, make great plans and it all seems marvellous – but the work doesn't get done. *Do* it, Anatolii Petrovich, will you? I think we'll give you two days. Is two days enough? Then for God's sake, get it *done*!

'And all of you – go to it, will you, comrades? We must buckle down and *work* if we're going to fulfil our plans. We've got to work at maximum effectiveness – make every man and machine do its best, and then find ways to do it *better*. What about getting those combines working full-time at last? It's still the old story of repairs. And believe me, comrades, it's up to us whether we sink or swim – only us. I'm appealing to your consciences. It's your business if you take time off to watch the football game; but you've got to get the work done. Cheaper, better, with more profit every day. Sometimes I feel I'm batting my head against a wall. Don't slow down, will you, fellows? Let's give it everything we've got.'

Cherkasov takes a sip of water, comments on his penchant for sermons, and offers his audience a new joke.

When the agenda of general business has been completed the board takes up personal requests from farm members. The first is from a prospective member, a haggard young man who, accompanied by his wife with their baby in her arms, asks to join Our Motherland. Quick questions reveal that he is a metalworker second-class who left a neighbouring farm because of unsatisfactory housing; and that his wife is a tractor driver. ('Do you know that every able-bodied person of working age must have a job on the farm?' Cherkasov challenges. 'We believe in equal rights between men and women here. Housewives don't interest us, we need people eager to *work*.') Their willingness to work satisfactorily established, the couple are told that they can start on the following day.

By contrast, several members have asked to leave the farm, although only two are present, the others evidently having reconsidered. The woman who has come offers a sick mother in a distant city as her reason for wanting to withdraw. 'Oh, you're always changing your mind – quitting today, joining again tomorrow. Request granted, but this is the last time.' Greater efforts are made to persuade a middle-aged man to stay. 'Do you know you won't get cheap food in the city? Why do you want to give up a good thing?' Finally Cherkasov asks for a consensus, and on the strength of a voice from the audience – 'Let him go, he's got a high-paying job in the north' – he grants permission to leave.

Next, the board deals with the petitions of several families to be assigned the private plots to which they are entitled, and with the final request, from a dirty, scrawny and apparently feeble-minded young tractor driver, for a five-hundred-ruble loan to help him build a house. 'You've got a nerve,' Cherkasov snorts in mock anger. 'You've been in and out of the farm, in and out of trouble – we've fined you more than I can remember. No, we can't rely on you.' In vain, the young man whines, begs and almost cries. Cherkasov ignores him and, as the meeting is about to adjourn, tells stories about old days and hard times.

'I'm not babbling to hear myself talk. Because we've got to keep driving, Comrades. Got to keep pushing up that production, getting more *efficiency* out of the equipment. We want more tonnage out of that sugar-beet acreage. And that number six dairy – let's get things *moving* again. I don't care if you sing love songs to your cows, just push up the yields. Will you *please* understand the importance of your responsibilities?'

' ... rational use of equipment ... increased productivity of labour ... make every kilogram of fertilizer count ... not one metre of unused crop-land ... mechanization, automation, efficiency, PRODUCTION ... ' This kind of talk is perhaps to be expected at the management board meeting, but the office too buzzes with facts, figures, and overfulfil-the-plan declamations from dawn to dusk, as if it were the front office of a team striving for the world series or a cup final.

The administrators are fired by a sense of perpetual emergency: of a commitment to attack the ploughing of this field, the harvest of those sugar beets, the cutting of these last fields of corn in the spirit of do or die. Every day, every task is the subject of a *campaign*. The repair of tractors, the need to do it, how to do it, why it must be done quickly and well, is urgently discussed as if this is the first and not the thousandth time the problem has arisen; as if this were the crucial battle in the most desperate of production wars. Why the fierce campaigns here for attitudes and activities that in other countries are taken for granted?

Perhaps because of Russia's long agricultural backwardness, strongly sensed despite the Kuban's German settlers and comparatively advanced farming methods. Perhaps because Stalin's murderous agricultural policies destroyed peasant initiative and, therefore, efficiency. Decades of rigid planning (under which hungry peasants were forced to deliver crushing state quotas at merciless prices) inhibited the development of orderly working habits and the urge to maximize production and profits. In Our Motherland, nothing can be taken for granted or left to the workers' instincts.

But more efficient agronomy and machinery are rapidly dispelling the backwardness, and the stultifying central-planning controls are slowly – still very slowly – giving way to more economic autonomy for the farm. Roughly two-thirds of Our

Motherland's output must be delivered to the state, allowing outside Party officials and bureaucrats to meddle in its affairs; but less than before. Our Motherland is at last able to make significant profits, used for improving life on the farm in a hundred ways: in raising salaries and awarding bonuses, building new schools and laying mains for running water, providing loans for private houses and buying football uniforms and a new phonograph for the Palace of Culture. For decades, profit meant nothing to many farms too poor to provide their members with bare subsistence; but Our Motherland is rich and can become much richer,* and its managers respond to the new opportunities by maintaining a campaign spirit: if efficient working habits are neither inherent nor acquired naturally, then they must be instilled. Until then, the Russian countryside, like the Russian town, will be festooned with slogans – as is Our Motherland's every weatherworn barn: FURTHER INTENSIFY SOCIALIST COMPETITION FOR FULFILMENT OF THE FIVE-YEAR PLAN BEFORE SCHEDULE! WHEN HARVESTING WHEAT, REMEMBER: A LOST DAY CANNOT BE MADE UP IN A YEAR! THE DUTY OF EVERY AGRICULTURAL WORKER, DEPUTY TO THE SOVIET AND HOUSEWIFE, PIONEER AND SCHOOL CHILD: BAR THE WAY TO WEEDS ON ALL FIELDS! WE ARE APPROACHING THE VICTORY OF COMMUNIST LABOUR! GLORY TO LABOUR! LIQUIDATION OF THE DIFFERENCES IN SOCIAL, ECONOMIC, CULTURAL AND LIVING STANDARDS BETWEEN CITY AND COUNTRY IS ONE OF THE GREATEST ACHIEVEMENTS OF THE BUILDING OF COMMUNISM.

*

* This raises the question of what degree of 'socialism' can be achieved in a state so vast, so ponderously organized, with such wide variations in natural resources and personal drive, even given a strong ideological commitment. Great inequality in the wealth of farms has led some Russians to charge that 'millionaire' collectives are motivated by nothing more than a group reversion to the greed of the rich private farmers dispossessed during collectivization. As they grow richer, such collectives forge forward towards their own embourgeoisement, showing little interest in sharing their bounty with poorer northern farms. When Our Motherland has its swimming pool (already planned), collective farmers elsewhere will no doubt still be short of meat.

The farm work itself is organized in the usual Soviet system, with departments, brigades and platoons, each under a foreman, assigned specific tasks. Fields are ploughed by teams of tractors, each team representing a platoon of a brigade, in competition with teams on neighbouring fields for small job-by-job bonuses. Where the platoon goes, there go its individual workers.

The work week is forty-one hours, seven hours a day from Monday to Friday and six on Saturday, except for overtime during harvests. Payment is in cash wages, rather than the system of labour-days still employed on poorer collective farms. An ordinary field hand earns some sixty rubles* in a good month; a skilled tractor driver twice that plus up to thirty per cent in bonuses for overful-filling his plan. A trained agronomist can earn almost as much as an engineer and his living costs are lower because of cheaper food on the farm.

One of the young men I meet is an agronomist. A thirty-year-old graduate of a neighbouring agricultural institute, he is now high on the management staff and as enthusiastic for Our Motherland as any all-American college graduate for 'his' corporation. The farm's chief engineer, he earned an average of four hundred rubles a month last year, an excellent wage anywhere in the country, and more testimony to the black earth region's exceptional wealth.

For all his income, position and higher education, the young chief engineer is enrolled in correspondence courses at his old agricultural institute and regularly attends the farm's own classes in management for senior personnel. 'I must learn more,' he says fervidly, 'must study, study, study – especially the art of manage-ment, which is almost virgin land to us. For example, a simple study we ran proved that on our fields one make of tractor pays for itself in thirty months, while a bigger one, which everyone thought better, takes six years. That's what I mean by efficient

---

* Roughly £24 or $56, according to the exchange rate established by the Soviet government. However, these figures are meaningless as a guide to the standard of living, since Soviet consumer prices, on average, are significantly higher than in the West, whereas housing expenses are negligible. Sixty rubles is two pairs of shoes or twenty bottles of vodka.

management – and why I'm taking my correspondence courses in economics.'

Throughout Our Motherland, enthusiasm for adult education is on this level. Fifty members of the farm, principally recent high school graduates, are studying full time in agricultural institutes and technical colleges,* and 350 more men and women are enrolled in one or more courses, largely by correspondence. Even discounting the system which (as in most armed forces) ranks everyone according to his qualifications – mechanic third-, second- and first-class – and in which completed courses represent higher qualification and therefore more pay, the drive for 'more learning, for enriching our lives and running the farm skilfully' is remarkable. There is a naive faith not only in knowledge as such but, as in a more innocent American age, in standardized, officially-sponsored courses as the means to acquire it. When riches are at last secured, will youth here too substitute the ethos of drop-out for that of get-ahead?

A large white workshop stands on a rise above the village in the place where the church would have been before the Revolution. It is an apt location, for the workshop plays a key role in the religion of production. Equipped like a small factory, it not only services all the farm's trucks and tractors, but manufactures almost all spare parts. 'It's easier to do it ourselves than to order parts from the factory,' says a senior mechanic. 'You wait six months and still the damn brake linings never arrive.' Although one high official under Chairman Cherkasov heads a special department for obtaining spare parts, the Soviet economy's chronic shortages and confusion – no local service depots here of major firms – have bred an instinctive do-it-yourself autarky into managers and mechanics.

* Our Motherland pays them stipends – fifteen per cent higher than the corresponding state grants – so that they will return directly from their institutes to management positions in the farm. Students on state stipends – the vast majority – are at the disposal of the 'distribution' system which, directly upon graduation, obliges them to repay their grants by serving three years at jobs assigned anywhere in the country. Thus a young man from Our Motherland on a state grant might be sent to fill a vacancy in the Urals.

Repair of machinery, therefore, is one of Our Motherland's most pressing preoccupations. When a platoon of tractors plough a field it is taken for granted that they will be plagued by mechanical failures, and a repair lorry always stands by, an integral part of the team, to service them. The number of breakdowns really is astonishing: every fourth driver on road and field has dismounted to mend his motor. Experts estimate that a fifth of all Soviet agricultural equipment must be written off every year – a scale of depreciation that would quickly bankrupt any Western farm. Although Our Motherland tries very hard, its maintenance efforts are clearly unequal to the well-known capriciousness of Soviet machinery.

Of all the crews of tractor drivers, I'm taken to interview one who can only be called gorgeous: a blond, square-jawed young hero of a 1930s battle-for-farm-production film. As a teenager fifteen years ago, he volunteered to work on the Virgin Lands and won a Young Communist medal for his devotion. Last year, the Russian Republic's Supreme Soviet decorated him the best tractor driver in the Kuban. Now a deputy to the regional Soviet, his ambition is to enter the Communist Party.

'To join the ranks of Lenin's party is the greatest honour I can attain. But I'm not ready yet; a Communist must be an example in his cultural life, as well as in production ... I want to build Communism; that's what I am thinking about when I drive my tractor and volunteer for extra work. Plough that field, cut that corn – we're building a better life for Our Motherland, for Russia, for the world.' He plays with his huge hands, ill at ease parted from his tractor.

One would have thought that such men, such language, existed only in the coinage of hack propagandists. But the ambitions of the tractor driver's wife, a book-keeper in the farm office, are closer to home and correspondingly more believable. 'Maybe this place seems shabby to you, but it's paradise compared to ten years ago when my husband brought me here. I'm a city girl; I took one look at Sokolovsky and wept because I wanted to go back. It was a godforsaken hole: no lights in the houses, no radio, nothing but mud. It was a great event when we got radios – and now we're saving for a washing machine.'

On Saturday evening, Chairman Cherkasov is at home with his family and friends. He lives in a rambling frame house with a fruit and vegetable garden which he tends before and after work, at dawn and dusk. ('My apples are the smallest in the village because I'm a lousy farmer – isn't that justice?') Although it is the largest house in the village, its atmosphere – in pleasant contrast to the houseproud prissiness of some young technicians' standard new bungalows – is of comfortable disorder.

Cherkasov's guests are two couples who are old friends; both husbands are relatively minor workers in the farm office. His family – those members living on the farm – consists of a wife, son, daughter, daughter-in-law and four grandchildren. To someone unacquainted with a Russian family of this kind, it is impossible to describe their easy but profound intimacy, springing from a sentimental yet unselfconscious need to be close. Timofei Petrovich's grandchildren crawl over him and his eyes mist as he strokes their hair and slips chocolates into their hands. ('My little ones, my hope, my flesh and blood ... ') Despite his own assertion, his loyalty is not only to the Party.

The evening is a celebration of food, toasts, singing, reminiscing, story-telling, hugging, joking – the only spontaneous and joyful feast I have attended on the farm. Timofei Petrovich supervised the preparation of his favourite Siberian meat dumplings and now spears them with a fork or pushes dozens on to the plates of his guests. He drinks in the Russian manner, switching from vodka to cognac and back to vodka, and downing his series of four-ounce glasses in a single gulp. 'I'm not an ascetic, I like a good drink with friends. What the hell, you can even write that I don't object to a binge once in a while. When my wife can't find me in at the office, she likes to say I'm at the bottle. Well, maybe – but she's not an ascetic in that way either, you know.'

His wife is a former Party official, and their courtship might be the basis for a patriotic short story. They met in 1933 on a volunteer outing from Party School to help dig potatoes, and married on the anniversary of the October Revolution. A middle-aged woman who has aged less handsomely than Cherkasov, she is easy-going, gregarious and utterly unaffected. Whatever she was as a Party official, she now likes to eat, laugh and gossip about the romances of the village's good-looking girls.

Timofei Petrovich drinks, sees that his guests drink, blesses the fortune that found him a wife and gave him a family, removes his shirt and seems to forget that a foreign reporter is present. Then he bares his soul, a curious mixture of Party battle cries, Russian chauvinism and Cherkasov intuition. By this time it is no surprise that this captivating man, a born leader whom even the village poor admire, is a Stalinist by inclination. Although it is hard to imagine him approving the purges and terror, he yearns for those good old days when the country was ruled by an iron hand – the days of his adventurous youth, when he was rising rapidly in the Party hierarchy which was carrying out those ruthless measures. Solzhenitsyn is right: Stalinists are still deeply entrenched in the operational 'command posts' of Soviet institutions, from which they exercise vast influence and tight control of the daily running of Soviet life. But Cherkasov's Stalinism must be taken in the context of his urge for accomplishment and preference for clear goals and simple solutions. By mid-evening, he is inclined to speechify, but his words are unslurred.

On his goals: 'For years I asked the Party to free me from staff work so I could plough the land. I always wanted to be a farmer. I came from the land, after all, and want to pass on the land to my children and grandchildren in better condition than I found it ... This sounds like newspaper propaganda, so you can believe it or not: my goal in life is to make things better for ordinary people. I dream of every family having running water in their houses and reading books, of freeing women from heavy field work. I want to help my people move towards Communism, when each person's life will be rich in every sense. And, as Lenin said, life can only be rich for everyone when everyone thinks first of the common good.

'I'm not talking May Day slogans about saving civilization or world revolution. I'm talking about what I know about and what is possible: improving life for *these* people on *this* farm. Making it possible for every member of *this* collective to achieve his own human potential. That's *my* Communism.

'If there hadn't been a Revolution, I'd probably be a private farmer, like my father. I'd probably be rich by now, like an Iowan farmer. If you live under capitalism, it's only natural to strive for personal wealth. But under socialism I've been brought up to seek satisfaction in working for the common good. If someone offered me a prosperous American farm today, I'd turn it down; I'd feel cheap working for just my private benefit – and so would ninety per cent of our collective farmers.

'My goal is working to the limits of my energy and talents for the people of this farm. My joy is hearing people talk about how much their life has improved. I tingle when I pass the new schools and houses I helped build – the Palace of Culture. Westerners can't understand that because they get their tingles building things for themselves. Ask a Westerner to contribute to the common good and he'll laugh in your face.'

On Vietnam: 'When I was a boy my father was a soldier in the First World War, and I remember the terrible waiting for him. Was he alive? Would we ever see him again? My kids probably waited for me like that during the second war. Even children, far from the killing and mangling, are damaged by war in one way or another.

'War is misery; nothing *ever* justifies it except when you're actually attacked. But this war in Vietnam is one of the most barbaric of all time. A rich and powerful nation bombing peasants to oblivion – it's sickening. Nothing can make me understand the reasons. If I thought you approved, I would want you off this farm. We're supposed to be civilized in this twentieth century ... You ask about the Soviet Army and its role in Eastern Europe?' He is surprised and angered by the impudence of my question. 'What rubbish – you're not a baby any longer, how dare you compare the two? The Soviet army helps *liberate* oppressed nations, and sometimes helps the people repulse counter-revolution.'

On his agricultural training: 'I was never trained as a farmer, and it worries me. Of course, I read all the technical material I can' (he himself has published two manuals on collective farm organization) 'but I know all about my big scientific gaps.

'A few years ago, I applied to enter a local agricultural institute. An old fogey of fifty, cramming for the entrance exams day and night, memorizing physics formulas up to the last minute. (I wrote my Russian composition exam in the simplest possible sentences – Russian's complicated, you know; even educated people make mistakes.) I wasn't above begging the examiners for mercy because of my age. Then I sweated out the results like a teenager. A ridiculous old man cheering when he sees his name on the "pass" list.

'But the courses themselves were too much, I couldn't keep up with both study and work. So I ended my career a common dropout: just what we lecture the kids not to be.'

On literature: 'I don't read enough outside of agricultural literature, but when I retire, I'm going to bury myself in the world's classics. My favourite Western authors are Mark Twain and H. G. Wells. Wells's *Russia in the Shadows* – I love that book. He was one of the few Westerners with enough courage to write honestly about us.

'Gorky and Mayakovsky are my favourite Russians – the proletarian writers. Mayakovsky's poem about Lenin is one of the most magnificent things in the world. Every word is a revolutionary bullet. The final test of a poet is to write well about Lenin.'

On the future of collectivized agriculture: 'I know the Western notion about the inherent unworkability of collectivized agriculture. I know that the Soviet Union has been forced to buy wheat abroad recently. But if I'm convinced of anything, it's that collectivized agriculture will overtake capitalist in the not too distant future. In five or ten years, the Kuban will overtake Iowa in total production – not yet labour productivity, but that will come later. Soviet agriculture will win, it's historically inevitable.

'Western experts say that collectivized agriculture will never work because personal interest and initiative are missing where peasants don't own their own land. But how can you explain Our

Motherland's rushing progress in the last ten years? We're still far behind; we've still got much to learn, especially in cost accounting and organization of labour, which are infant disciplines here. The average American farmer produces much more than the average Russian. But we're catching up. The foundation – investment, mechanization and proper organization – has just been laid – and *Western* text-books show that socialism provides greater opportunities for higher production. So it's not just propaganda, but a question of time.'

On Stalin: 'I was in love with that man, and I still am. I love him like I can never love another. The day he died, I wept like a baby. I own his collected works, and I read them again and again for my inspiration. His *Short Course** is the most brilliant and humane analysis I've ever seen.

'I love him for his mind, his logic, his manliness – above all, his courage. He was the one person great enough to hold the Soviet Union together and make us a great power after Lenin died. True, when he was old, he made some serious mistakes; democracy suffered and innocent people died. But only he kept *everything* from being lost. Only he could have saved socialism from the Trotskys and Bukharins, and later from the Nazis. It was for him, only him, we all worked and sacrificed and died. Stalin was the genius of his time. Maybe my first daughter's name – we called her Stalina – will tell you how I feel ... ' (Timofei Petrovich breaks into a song unheard officially in Russia for ten years: a Second World War march entitled 'For Stalin and the Motherland'.)

On Khrushchev: 'He was a genial man with a good heart and fine intentions – but that's not enough for the leader of a great country. Nikita Sergeevich had too much wild enthusiasm and not enough brains, which resulted in silly schemes and massive economic waste.

* *A Short Course of the History of the Communist Party of the Soviet Union*, published under Stalin's name, is a particularly crude simplification of Marxism-Leninism in which all-encompassing explanations of history, philosophy, sociology and psychology are reduced to a scheme in which the Party's commanding role is glorified. For many Stalinist years it was quoted in every article, whether scholarly or popular, and treated as the fount of wisdom: a kind of Soviet Bible in a community of fanatic political fundamentalists.

'Khrushchev's trouble was that he meddled in absolutely everything – telling farmers where to plant what, for example – on the basis of his personal whims instead of scientific data. No man can know everything, but he thought his instincts were infallible.

'It's not true that experts didn't criticize his schemes. Some protested loudly, but Khrushchev simply ignored them. Yes, he could be simple-minded, and he made some colossal blunders. But I always wondered how I'd have done in his shoes. Probably much worse.'

On travel: 'I've never been abroad, but always dreamed of visiting Italy and India. Italy because the Italians are wonderful: they live for love, music and wine. India because … I'm not sure why. Their music has always haunted me, maybe because it represents something mysterious and exotic I've missed in life.'

On the Russian character: 'Russians are marvellous, generous, open, honest, *human*. I know this, although I've never travelled to compare. A Russian will give you the shirt off his back, or treat you to a bottle with literally his last ruble.

'But Russians also have an inherent lack of self-discipline; anarchy is in their bones. They simply don't share Westerners' sense of duty and organization. Never developed an inbred working discipline – which is why it's so difficult to manage affairs properly here. Russians will drink and talk all night even if they know they've got an important job in the morning. Somehow, the job gets forgotten. But' (he downs another tumbler of vodka) 'that's what makes life worth living.'

On his relationship with farm workers: 'If you think I have dictatorial powers here, you're wide of the mark. When matters are up for decision, everyone has his say; everyone speaks with an equal voice, and I can be outvoted – and voted out of my job. Ordinary farm hands aren't afraid to criticize me. It's a person's opinions that count, not his rank. We have real democracy, not some bourgeois sham. Once a matter is decided, of course, everyone must abide by the decision. As in any well run enterprise, my orders must be obeyed.

'As for punishment, we have a system for that, going all the way to expulsion from the farm. But this is rare. Punishment can't be the foundation for working relationships here any more than in a family. I'm sometimes criticized for being too soft: for giving a man too many "one more" chances. Then he comes to work drunk yet again. But I'm a sucker for a sad story.

'The ordinary farm worker avoids me only when he's drunk during the working day. And I avoid that kind too. I like to drink, as you might notice, but never with a man who lets it interfere with his job.'

The village is fast asleep when Timofei Petrovich walks his guests to his gate. After such an evening he is as sentimental as any muzhik, and his deep sigh seems to express the characteristic Russian soul-searching about life's meaning. 'I wonder whether you can understand what we're trying to do here, trying to build for our people under socialism. Our plans are made, all we need now is modern equipment. And time. It doesn't matter that I personally have too little left.'

He picks up a fallen leaf and holds it to the moon, studying its configuration. 'But sometimes I wonder. We're trying to build a new society, nobility on earth – but no achievement of man, not even Communism, can be as beautiful as this dying leaf.'

In the following days, Cherkasov's spell grows. Like the captain of my old destroyer, he is a politically narrow and perhaps potentially dangerous man, yet his skill and iron purpose somehow lift him above politics to communion with universal aspirations, as my skipper was somehow in contact with the ocean. Timofei Petrovich rises at 5 a.m. and lifts eighty-pound weights 'to keep this creaky body going a bit longer'. In the afternoon, he takes a break from an unpleasant task* to watch a convoy of lorries because 'the sight of those lads in the cabs, our own Russian proletariat, fills a person with strength'. He quotes Lenin all day on the principles

---

* Our Motherland is building a kind of general store on Sokolovsky's main street, but the construction firm engaged made errors in the foundation, and the matter may go to court.

underlying his every decision, and in the evening, one eye on his television set, peruses agricultural journals. Cherkasov's wife, too, is more likable, because more artless, at every meeting. More than any achievement of her own life or of socialism, this former Party official seems prouder of all her grandchildren having been born here on the farm. 'Wherever they were, my children all came back to me to give birth. Came back to their old mama.'

Then why are the children themselves so unimpressive? Tamara, their daughter (home on vacation from her studies in an agricultural institute) was married at eighteen, bore a son soon afterwards and was divorced soon after that. She has a demure charm. The son, Igor, must be a more obvious disappointment to his parents. The picture of a callow youth, he has all of Cherkasov's 'vices' – and some of his authority – without a hint of his strengths. He races his prized new motorcycle along Sokolovsky's main street, throwing dust into the faces of passers-by. He runs errands for his father and for Partorg Kandobarev (for he is the head of the farm's Young Communist Organization), but his attempts to talk of socialism and Leninism ring wholly false and only intensify the suspicion of nepotism. Neither working class nor intellectual, lacking a sense of himself as well as all leadership qualities, he seems to be the familiar figure of the weak son of a commanding father. And although he drinks less than Cherkasov, it affects him far less pleasantly even before he vomits. This happens as Igor is returning from his father's Saturday evening gathering; and while he is being loudly sick behind the little square with the statue of Lenin, his wife, a sexy bleached blonde, snickers in contempt. Her own drinking apparently having aroused rather than sickened her, she hungrily kisses the mouth of a young man who had also been at our party that evening. 'I want a real *man* tonight,' she says. 'Don't worry, he's too far gone to hear anything or care.'

On Thursday afternoon, a league football game between Our Motherland and a neighbouring collective farm. Farm work slows down noticeably as tractors and lorries detour to the field for a glimpse of the play. Cherkasov's wife is among the starry-eyed schoolgirls on the sidelines, cheering for the home team heroes.

On Saturday evening, a dance in the Palace of Culture. Boys bunch in one corner with boys, girls – some in stiletto heels and beehive coiffures, caricatured 'city clothes' of profound bad taste – with girls. The Young Communist dance committee works hard to ease the embarrassment with folk songs, games of skill and party dances. (Igor Cherkasov wins the prize for lighting a cigarette while sitting cross-legged on a beer bottle.) A village dance like almost all village dances.

On Sunday afternoon, a 'civil ceremony' at the Palace of Culture – something quite different. Once a month (to economize on the farm's working time, the ceremonies are combined) Our Motherland's new babies are greeted by the Soviet people and state, through the village soviet as the local agency of government. Entitled 'Ceremonial Registration of Newborns,' the ritual is conducted according to an instructional booklet printed in Moscow.

On the auditorium stage, under the inevitable crimson banners (MAY THE NEW CITIZENS OF THE SOVIET STATE HAVE A GOOD JOURNEY! WELCOME INTO THE WORLD OF INSPIRED LABOUR AND HAPPINESS!) sit half a dozen shy young parents with their swaddled infants. A band plays wobblingly from behind the stage, red-kerchiefed pioneers await the signal to present their bunches of flowers, an almost-full auditorium watches impassively, settling in for the Sunday afternoon film that follows. Reading from his instructional booklet, the Chairman of the village soviet produces what is known as a 'newspaper' speech: ' ... a new Soviet citizen is born ... a gift from his mother to the Motherland ... the joy of being born into Soviet society ... the comfort and glory assured by the Socialist Motherland ... the highest fulfilment ahead: of becoming an honest, hardworking son of the land of Lenin ... '

Losing his place in the text, the Chairman falters, the trumpeter choosing this moment to sound a shrill wrong note. Even an atheist, perhaps especially an atheist, winces at this ersatz baptismal service; never has the liturgy of the Orthodox Church, with its haunting chants, incantations and ancient solemnity, had so much dignity as in comparison with this. When eventually the Soviet authorities acknowledged the importance of ritual (especially to Russians), they designed what was intended to be an impressive civil marriage ceremony in new palaces of marriage. A replacement for baptism is more important still, since even thoroughly 'Soviet' parents who never attend church want to sanctify their children 'as insurance'. But this crude state service, replacing worship of God with that of Lenin and the Motherland, only emphasizes Our Motherland's historical hollowness, its role as an agricultural factory, lacking traditions and roots.

The awkward ceremony is mercifully brief. Cherkasov provides needed relief by presenting toys to the newborn, gifts from the farm, and offering a toast of wine 'in the Russian manner'. Son Igor is meant to greet them in the name of the Young Communist League, but he is glassy-eyed drunk in mid-afternoon and does not attempt to rise from his seat in the audience. Later, he offers me a swig of 'real fine' home-brew, subject of incessant press campaigns and criminal prosecutions.

By the eighth day, time seems to drag for my hosts. Although still laying on gargantuan meals, they are running short, understandably, of toasts. My hope of spending an unchaperoned day with workers in the fields is clearly not going to be realized, and I must satisfy myself with more random observations. The decal on the dashboard of a jeep: a leggy pin-up in a one-piece bathing costume that screams 'World War Two' and reinforces the impression everywhere on the farm of having been whooshed back thirty years by a time machine. Seven old women husking corn by hand near a sagging shed: kerchiefed, toothless and bent, existing principally on old-age pensions of nineteen rubles a month (the price of the cheapest pair of shoes), they earn about a ruble a day in pocket money from this volunteer husking – but pity for them might be misplaced, for in their own scheme of expectations, they consider themselves well-provided-for and lucky.

On my last full day, I overhear a conversation reflecting the attitude towards authority and discipline on the farm. A young brigade leader is reprimanding a tractor driver twice his age for failure to service his tractor on time.

'For God's sake do it tomorrow, will you?'

'Right you are, Pavel Ivanovich. Tomorrow without fail.'

'Who else in the platoon hasn't serviced yet?'

'So far, nobody. Not yet.'

'For crying out loud, do I have to stand over you like children?'

'Tomorrow, Pavel Ivanovich. I promise: tomorrow.'

If this exchange is typical, working relations on the farm are in the pattern of most throughout Russia: in overcoming the workman's proverbial procrastination, those in authority resort far more to nagging, cajoling and blustering than to disciplinary measures.

A final supper, many final toasts, bear-hugs, kisses, poignant goodbyes. 'Farewell! Good health! Good journey! Write to us, please remember to write.' Fumbling for last-minute mementoes, Cherkasov and I exchange neckties. 'Come back whenever you want, son. Write what you want about us, but one thing: don't forget to tell *the truth*.' His arm around my shoulders, we might be comrades in the struggle for a better mankind.

The truth? Our Motherland is a microcosm of a successful segment of Soviet society, with most of the advantages of public ownership of property and none of the benefits of private. A foreigner is most impressed by the energy, good fellowship and determination to build a better future. As everywhere in the Soviet Union, great attention is given to investment in heavy equipment and in medical and educational facilities. What disappoints a foreigner most is that the countryside as well as the land has been nationalized; that amidst the thrust to build and work in accordance with national goals, the community's need to rest and relax – and, at times, be left in peace with its past – is ignored. For all Sokolovsky's new construction of public projects and private houses, none will supply what it lacks most: a touch of rural charm. Every Yugoslav village half the size and fractionally as rich has a café with an unofficial, spontaneous social life that helps bridge the distance between field and civilization, farmer and citizen. Our Motherland cries out for a bar where men can be men after the Saturday afternoon *banya*. But sipping a drink in public is not 'Soviet' enough to merit a café, and even when built, it will be a state institution like the Palace of Culture.

Still, Our Motherland is hardly a place of rural isolation. It has leapt forward in the last decade, after the relaxation of the cruel squeeze on collective farms, and, with the rapid penetration of agricultural expertise and general education, is certain to sustain its progress.

AFTERWORD

Excerpts from my report on Our Motherland appeared in a prominent English magazine. There was no reference to the brutality of collectivization, to Cherkasov's son Igor or to the destruction of the Cossacks as a social organization – to anything that might offend Soviet sensibilities. Without deliberately distorting my general impression of the farm (my article did include references to disgruntled workers' complaints and to Cherkasov's fondness for Stalin) I excluded almost all 'sensitive' matters for the sake of future visas. The abridged article led to accusations in the Western press that I had glorified collectivized agriculture, and to charges by a disgusted émigré friend that I was the first Western journalist to make an *apparatchik* (Cherkasov) seem alive, let alone likeable. This disturbed me less than omissions I had made in other articles: the Kuban, after all, *is* a lush region and Our Motherland one of its best farms, and, on the whole, my stay there had been enjoyable.

On the strength of the English article, publishers there and in America asked me to return to the farm for additional material for a book, one of a series on villages around the world (reports on village life in Cuba, England, Germany, the United States, China, France and other countries have already appeared). I felt that I needed several weeks to gain the additional material, and that my article, of which I had sent many copies to Novosti and Cherkasov, would surely guarantee my quick return. Indeed, in Novosti's judgment nothing ought to prevent me spending more time on Our Motherland and writing my book.

The disappointments which followed Novosti's initial encouragement were too many, too repetitive, trivial, tedious and, in the long run, too familiar, to bear a detailed recounting. Letter after letter from me (some answered, most ignored), telephone calls from London to Moscow (often informing me, after many wasted hours and pounds, merely that no one in the Novosti office could guess where the man I wanted was and when he might return to his desk), trips to Moscow tentatively agreed upon and invariably cancelled, pre-paid telegrams unanswered, visits to Soviet Embassies unrewarded ... anyone who has encountered Soviet officials in a similar pursuit has sufficient knowledge of their bureaucratic impermeability; those innocent of the experience will be justifiably sceptical of any recounting of its frustrations.

The rudeness grew in inverse proportion to my chances. Having called Moscow from abroad week after week and been promised ('this time I *promise*, old boy') a return call with a final answer within two days, my next call a week later would produce a chorus of 'we'll have to find out' – and another promise. The breaking of the last one was no deterrent to the formulation of the next; nor was there any suggestion of an apology or excuse. Often a man who had sworn upon his Russian soul to produce an answer the following day would be absent from his office for a week, without, of course, leaving any message. More expensive in terms of time, nerves and money were travel arrangements I was too late to cancel because no one in Novosti had thought to inform me of yet another 'postponement'. Meanwhile, not only money but opportunities for other assignments were lost, and for several summers I was without work in the months planned for Our Motherland.

Although no final refusal ever came, a series of reasons were adduced for the postponements. A freakishly severe winter on the Kuban required the replanting of several crops, and (as I was informed) I would not want to write about an 'untypical harvest'. Next, a 'rare' outbreak of foot-and-mouth disease closed the area to all outsiders. When nature had apparently returned to normal, the 'events in Czechoslovakia', as the Soviet euphemism had it, were said to make the times 'inappropriate' for a sensitive project such as mine. After 'normalization' in this sphere too, Novosti officials told me that the obstacle resided in the Kuban authorities, who had grown tired of foreigners and refused to allow an American to 'poke into their affairs' again. According to this explanation, high officials of the Ministry of Agriculture in Moscow had approved my visit in principle (more precisely, the Vice-Minister who had dealt with the case had no objection), but final sanction had to come from the local authorities – whose opposition only hardened as time passed.

Novosti assured me that they had worked long and hard to persuade the Kuban Party officials, but that the latter saw no reason to extend themselves for me. ('You must understand', said one high Novosti man sadly, 'that a visit by you creates much extra work for them, and they are busy with their own concerns.') To what extent the explanation was the deciding one is a matter for speculation, but it is not uncommon for provincial officials, often of an orthodox or Stalinist cast, to be more rigid than their superiors in Moscow. That Novosti actually did make efforts on my behalf seemed proved by an incident in its offices during one of my visits to Moscow for other articles. (In addition to letters, cables and telephone calls, I used every trip to Moscow to pursue my campaign in person.) To substantiate a point about the Ministry of Agriculture's approval, an official turned to the file on my 'case', a blue folder stuffed with papers, presumably about me and Our Motherland. Eager to see even one of the interdepartmental letters or memoranda for what it might reveal about the workings of Soviet institutions, my curiosity soared when the Novosti man found the wanted document among the thick pile, presumably the one considered innocent enough for my eyes. But having glanced at it, he returned the paper to its companions and closed the folder. 'It's not really very important,' he faltered, giving me to surmise that not even the one among the hundred should be seen by me.

In Moscow, the Novosti men I knew best were occasionally apologetic about my steady rebuffs in this ostensibly reasonable project, as well as about their apparent inability to influence Ministries and Party secretaries. In apparently sincere efforts to change my luck, several of them suggested turns of phrase likely to appeal to their own superiors or other officials. I penned a few letters based on their advice. During the 'jubilee year' celebrating the fiftieth anniversary of Soviet rule, virtually everything published in Russia was presented as a tribute to the historic event, and my appeals, too, were couched in terms of recording the progress of the collective farm system at the great watershed. This having failed, Novosti counselled that future letters establish a connection between my project and the next great Soviet celebratory campaign marking the hundredth anniversary of Lenin's birth. I found myself advocating the importance of describing 'V. I. Lenin's plan for co-operative agriculture' to the West, and 'how this plan has been developed ... how the Soviet people are now living and working under the Leninist plan'. I suggested that my book might be published in 1970, to join the thousands of Soviet volumes issued in 'the Leninist year'. This was my contribution to what a recent novel about Russia called 'mental gymnastics' and the 'astonishing renaissance of sophistry' essential to most aspects of official Soviet life.

Supplementing these communications, somewhat droll in retrospect, I continued to address plea after plea to every official I knew, stressing *their* frequent admonishments that the West must know more about the Soviet people for the sake of peace and friendship; and that an honest report about a rich farm – which I had obviously liked, and whose chairman was widely admired – was in their interests as well as mine. In time, the failure to receive even an acknowledgment to most of these letters disappointed me less and less, but I never understood the reaction of Cherkasov himself. For I had written him several times (as he had urged me so paternally) and received no reply to my fond and respectful letters. After our ten days of bantering affection and near-tearful parting, after his gruff-but-warm invitation to 'visit this old farm of ours any time you want' and challenges to work there for six months 'to show us what Americans are made of', he did not even answer my queries about the safe arrival of several sets of my articles posted from London.

A Novosti official visited the Kuban and, so he said, established that Cherkasov had been insulted by my reference to him as a drinking man. This seemed extraordinary in view of his generally heroic appearance in my article, but when a Russian friend suggested that he might indeed have been offended,* I wrote to him again to explain that his conduct as a host could only have charmed Western readers. For the last time, I asked to return to Our Motherland.

Perhaps Cherkasov himself decided not to respond to my letters because he disliked my article or felt that further involvement with a foreigner was unwise and unnecessary. Perhaps he was directed not to write by his regional Party organization or someone in Moscow. In either case, one's impression of him as the resolute captain in firm command of his own ship is inevitably altered. Or was he angered that 'the truth' for which he had pleaded appeared differently in my eyes than his?

Saddened, I abandoned my campaign to return to Our Motherland. But my reporter's curiosity is piqued: if this opposition was encountered with one of the best Soviet farms, what is the condition of the average one? Or of northern collectives on the opposite extremes of climate and wealth? Perhaps the country will be opened to journalists while I am of an age to make the journey. In this case, and if my expulsion is rescinded, I should like very much to return and to roam about. It is still a virgin land for reportage.

* My friend felt that I had violated an important Soviet bureaucratic rule by my failure to keep separate my roles as Cherkasov's guest and as a journalist. 'Cherkasov no doubt thinks like this: "That American is a two-timing rat. We invited him here. He was our guest. We offered him drink as a guest. Then he writes that we drink!" What you don't understand is that the Cherkasovs – Party officials in general – can swill vodka until they pass out in each others' arms. But in their own company and behind closed doors; not a word must be said about it anywhere. It's a small example of the hypocrisy of our bureaucracy.'

66593

FEIFER, GEORGE
   OUR MOTHERLAND.

DATE DUE